I0686838

Don Rodriguez
Chronicles of Shadow Valley

SPECIAL LARGE PRINT EDITION

with easy-to-read text

LORD DUNSANY

Serenity
Publishers, LLC

ROCKVILLE, MARYLAND
2013

ISBN: 978-1-61242-838-3

NOTE

Serenity Publishers can custom create classic texts in large print

We can create new titles with text/margins to your specifications

Add your notes and create the book as you want it

Combine different classic texts in one volume

Produce an edition with a special introduction or an afterword

Add your footnotes

Visit **www.SerenityPublishers.com** &
www.ArcManor.com

or email **chandi@serenitypublishers.com**

Published by Serenity Publishers
An Arc Manor Company
P. O. Box 10339
Rockville, MD 20849-0339
www.SerenityPublishers.com

Printed in the United States of America/United Kingdom

To

William Beebe

Chronology

After long and patient research I am still unable to give to the reader of these Chronicles the exact date of the times that they tell of. Were it merely a matter of history there could be no doubts about the period; but where magic is concerned, to however slight an extent, there must always be some element of mystery, arising partly out of ignorance and partly from the compulsion of those oaths by which magic protects its precincts from the tiptoe of curiosity.

Moreover, magic, even in small quantities, appears to affect time, much as acids affect some metals, curiously changing its substance, until dates seem to melt into a mercurial form that renders them elusive even to the eye of the most watchful historian.

It is the magic appearing in Chronicles III and IV that has gravely affected the date, so that all I can tell the reader with certainty of the period is that it fell in the later years of the Golden Age in Spain.

Contents

The First Chronicle

HOW HE MET AND SAID FAREWELL TO MINE HOST OF THE DRAGON AND KNIGHT

*B*eing convinced that his end was nearly come, and having lived long on earth (and all those years in Spain, in the golden time), the Lord of the Valleys of Arguento Harez, whose heights see not Valladolid, called for his eldest son. And so he addressed him when he was come to his chamber, dim with its strange red hangings and august with the splendour of Spain: "O eldest son of mine, your younger brother being dull and clever, on whom those traits that women love have not been bestowed by God; and know my eldest son that here on earth, and for ought I know Hereafter, but certainly here on earth, these women be the arbiters of all things; and how this be so God knoweth only, for they are vain and variable, yet it is surely so: your younger brother then not having been given those ways that women prize, and God knows why they prize them for they are vain ways that I have in my mind and that won me the Valleys of Arguento

Harez, from whose heights Angelico swore he saw Valladolid once, and that won me moreover also ... but that is long ago and is all gone now ... ah well, well ... what was I saying?" And being reminded of his discourse, the old lord continued, saying, "For himself he will win nothing, and therefore I will leave him these my valleys, for not unlikely it was for some sin of mine that his spirit was visited with dullness, as Holy Writ sets forth, the sins of the fathers being visited on the children; and thus I make him amends. But to you I leave my long, most flexible, ancient Castilian blade, which infidels dreaded if old songs be true. Merry and lithe it is, and its true temper singeth when it meets another blade as two friends sing when met after many years. It is most subtle, nimble and exultant; and what it will not win for you in the wars, that shall be won for you by your mandolin, for you have a way with it that goes well with the old airs of Spain. And choose, my son, rather a moonlight night when you sing under those curved balconies that I knew, ah me, so well; for there is much advantage in the moon. In the first place maidens see in the light of the moon, especially in the Spring, more romance than you might credit, for it adds for them a mystery to the darkness which the night has not when it is merely black. And if any statue should gleam on the grass near by, or if the magnolia be in blossom, or even the nightingale singing, or if anything be beautiful in the night, in any of these things also there is advantage; for a maiden will attribute to her lover all manner of things that are not his at all, but are only outpourings from the hand of God. There is this advantage also in the moon, that, if interrupters come, the moonlight is better suited to the play of a blade than the mere darkness of night; indeed but the merry play of my sword in the moonlight was often a joy to see, it so flashed, so danced, so sparkled. In the moonlight also one makes no unworthy stroke, but hath scope for those fair passes that Sevastiani taught, which were long ago the wonder of Madrid."

The old lord paused, and breathed for a little space, as it were gathering breath for his last words to his son. He breathed deliberately, then spoke again. "I leave you," he said, "well content that you have the two accomplishments, my son, that are most needful in a Christian man, skill with the sword and a way with the mandolin. There be other arts indeed among the heathen, for the world is wide and hath full many customs, but these two alone are needful." And then with that grand manner that they had at that time in Spain, although his strength was failing, he gave to his eldest son his Castilian sword. He lay back then in the huge, carved, canopied bed; his eyes closed, the red silk curtains rustled, and there was no sound of his breathing. But the old lord's spirit, whatever journey it purposed, lingered yet in its ancient habitation, and his voice came again, but feebly now and rambling; he muttered awhile of gardens, such gardens no doubt as the hidalgos guarded in that fertile region of sunshine in the proudest period of Spain; he would have known no others. So for awhile his memory seemed to stray, half blind among those perfumed earthly wonders; perhaps among these memories his spirit halted, and tarried those last few moments, mistaking those Spanish gardens, remembered by moonlight in Spring, for the other end of his journey, the glades of Paradise. However it be, it tarried. These rambling memories ceased and silence fell again, with scarcely the sound of breathing. Then gathering up his strength for the last time and looking at his son, "The sword to the wars," he said. "The mandolin to the balconies." With that he fell back dead.

Now there were no wars at that time so far as was known in Spain, but that old lord's eldest son, regarding those last words of his father as a commandment, determined then and there in that dim, vast chamber to gird his legacy to him and seek for the wars, wherever the wars might be, so soon as the obsequies of the sepulture were ended. And of those obsequies I tell not here, for they are fully told in the Black Books of Spain, and the deeds of that old lord's youth are told in the Golden Stories. The Book of Maidens mentions him, and again we read of him in Gardens of Spain. I take my leave of him, happy, I trust, in Paradise, for he had himself the accomplishments that he held needful in a Christian, skill with the sword and a way with the mandolin; and if there be some harder, better way to salvation than to follow that which we believe to be good, then are we all damned. So he was buried, and his eldest son fared forth with his legacy dangling from his girdle in its long, straight, lovely scabbard, blue velvet, with emeralds on it, fared forth on foot along a road of Spain. And though the road turned left and right and sometimes nearly ceased, as though to let the small wild flowers grow, out of sheer good will such as some roads never have; though it ran west and east and sometimes south, yet in the main it ran northward, though wandered is a better word than ran, and the Lord of the Valleys of Arguento Harez who owned no valleys, or anything but a sword, kept company with it looking for the wars. Upon his back he had slung his mandolin. Now the time of the year was Spring, not Spring as we know it in England, for it was but early March, but it was the time when Spring coming up out of Africa, or unknown lands to the south, first touches Spain, and multitudes of anemones come forth at her feet.

Thence she comes north to our islands, no less wonderful in our woods than in Andalusian valleys, fresh as a new song, fabulous as a rune, but a little pale through travel, so that our flowers do not quite flare forth with all the myriad blaze of the flowers of Spain.

And all the way as he went the young man looked at the flame of those southern flowers, flashing on either side of him all the way, as though the rainbow had been broken in Heaven and its fragments fallen on Spain. All the way as he went he gazed at those flowers, the first anemones of the year; and long after, whenever he sang to old airs of Spain, he thought of Spain as it appeared that day in all the wonder of Spring; the memory lent a beauty to his voice and a wistfulness to his eyes that accorded not ill with the theme of the songs he sang, and were more than once to melt proud hearts deemed cold. And so gazing he came to a town that stood on a hill, before he was yet tired, though he had done nigh twenty of those flowery miles of Spain; and since it was evening and the light was fading away, he went to an inn and drew his sword in the twilight and knocked with the hilt of it on the oaken door. The name of it was the Inn of the Dragon and Knight. A light was lit in one of the upper windows, the darkness seemed to deepen at that moment, a step was heard coming heavily down a stairway; and having named the inn to you, gentle reader, it is time for me to name the young man also, the landless lord of the Valleys of Arguento Harez, as the step comes slowly down the inner stairway, as the gloaming darkens over the first house in which he has ever sought shelter so far from his father's valleys, as he stands upon the threshold of romance. He was named Rodriguez Trinidad Fernandez, Concepcion Henrique Maria; but we shall briefly name him Rodriguez in this story; you and I, reader, will know whom we mean; there is no need therefore to give him his full names, unless I do it here and there to remind you.

The steps came thumping on down the inner stairway, different windows took the light of the candle, and none other shone in the house; it was clear that it was moving with the steps all down that echoing stairway. The sound of the steps ceased to reverberate upon the wood, and now they slowly moved over stone flags; Rodriguez now heard breathing, one breath with every step, and at length the sound of bolts and chains undone and the breathing now very close. The door was opened swiftly; a man with mean eyes, and expression devoted to evil, stood watching him for an instant; then the door slammed to again, the bolts were heard going back again to their places, the steps and the breathing moved away over the stone floor, and the inner stairway began again to echo.

"If the wars are here," said Rodriguez to himself and his sword, "good, and I sleep under the stars." And he listened in the street for the sound of war and, hearing none, continued his discourse. "But if I have not come as yet to the wars I sleep beneath a roof."

For the second time therefore he drew his sword, and began to strike methodically at the door, noting the grain in the wood and hitting where it was softest. Scarcely had he got a good strip of the oak to look like coming away, when the steps once more descended the wooden stair and came lumbering over the stones; both the steps and the breathing were quicker, for mine host of the Dragon and Knight was hurrying to save his door.

When he heard the sound of the bolts and chains again Rodriguez ceased to beat upon the door: once more it opened swiftly, and he saw mine host before him, eyeing him with those bad eyes; of too much girth, you might have said, to be nimble, yet somehow suggesting to the swift intuition of youth, as Rodriguez looked at him standing upon his door-step, the spirit and shape of a spider, who despite her ungainly build is agile enough in her way.

Mine host said nothing; and Rodriguez, who seldom concerned himself with the past, holding that the future is all we can order the scheme of (and maybe even here he was wrong), made no mention of bolts or door and merely demanded a bed for himself for the night.

Mine host rubbed his chin; he had neither beard nor moustache but wore hideous whiskers; he rubbed it thoughtfully and looked at Rodriguez. Yes, he said, he could have a bed for the night. No more words he said, but turned and led the way; while Rodriguez, who could sing to the mandolin, wasted none of his words on this discourteous object. They ascended the short oak stairway down which mine host had come, the great timbers of which were gnawed by a myriad rats, and they went by passages with the light of one candle into the interior of the inn, which went back farther from the street than the young man had supposed; indeed he perceived when they came to the great corridor at the end of which was his appointed chamber, that here was no ordinary inn, as it had appeared from outside, but that it penetrated into the fastness of some great family of former times which had fallen on evil days. The vast size of it, the noble design where the rats had spared the carving, what the moths had left of the tapestries, all testified to that; and, as for the evil days, they hung about the place, evident even by the light of one candle guttering with every draught that blew from the haunts of the rats, an inseparable heirloom for all who disturbed those corridors.

And so they came to the chamber.

Mine host entered, bowed without grace in the doorway, and extended his left hand, pointing into the room. The draughts that blew from the rat-holes in the wainscot, or the mere action of entering, beat down the flame of the squat, guttering candle so that the chamber remained dim for a moment, in spite of the candle, as would naturally be the case. Yet the impression made upon Rodriguez was as of some old darkness that had been long undisturbed and that yielded reluctantly to that candle's intrusion, a darkness that properly became the place and was a part of it and had long been so, in the face of which the candle appeared an ephemeral thing devoid of grace or dignity or tradition. And indeed there was room for darkness in that chamber, for the walls went up and up into such an altitude that you could scarcely see the ceiling, at which mine host's eyes glanced, and Rodriguez followed his look.

He accepted his accommodation with a nod; as indeed he would have accepted any room in that inn, for the young are swift judges of character, and one who had accepted such a host was unlikely to find fault with rats or the profusion of giant cobwebs, dark with the dust of years, that added so much to the dimness of that sinister inn. They turned now and went back, in the wake of that guttering candle, till they came again to the humbler part of the building. Here mine host, pushing open a door of blackened oak, indicated his dining-chamber. There a long table stood, and on it parts of the head and hams of a boar; and at the far end of the table a plump and sturdy man was seated in shirt-sleeves feasting himself on the boar's meat. He leaped up at once from his chair as soon as his master entered, for he was the servant at the Dragon and Knight; mine host may have said much to him with a flash of his eyes, but he said no more with his tongue than the one word, "Dog": he then bowed himself out, leaving Rodriguez to take the only chair and to be waited upon by its recent possessor. The boar's meat was cold and gnarled, another piece of meat stood on a plate on a shelf and a loaf of bread near by, but the rats had had most of the bread: Rodriguez demanded what the meat was. "Unicorn's tongue," said the servant, and Rodriguez bade him set the dish before him, and he set to well content, though I fear the unicorn's tongue was only horse: it was a credulous age, as all ages are. At the same time he pointed to a three-legged stool that he perceived in a corner of the room, then to the table, then to the boar's meat, and lastly at the servant, who perceived that he was permitted to return to his feast, to which he ran with alacrity. "Your name?" said Rodriguez as soon as both were eating. "Morano," replied the servant, though it must not be supposed that when answering Rodriguez he spoke as curtly as this; I merely give the reader the gist of his answer, for he added Spanish words that correspond in our depraved and decadent language of to-day to such words as "top dog," "nut" and "boss," so that his speech had a certain grace about it in that far-away time in Spain.

I have said that Rodriguez seldom concerned himself with the past, but considered chiefly the future: it was of the future that he was thinking now as he asked Morano this question:

"Why did my worthy and entirely excellent host shut his door in my face?"

"Did he so?" said Morano.

"He then bolted it and found it necessary to put the chains back, doubtless for some good reason."

"Yes," said Morano thoughtfully, and looking at Rodriguez, "and so he might. He must have liked you."

Verily Rodriguez was just the young man to send out with a sword and a mandolin into the wide world, for he had much shrewd sense. He never pressed a point, but when something had been said that might mean much he preferred to store it, as it were, in his mind and pass on to other things, somewhat as one might kill game and pass on and kill more and bring it all home, while a savage would cook the first kill where it fell and eat it on the spot. Pardon me, reader, but at Morano's remark you may perhaps have exclaimed, "That is not the way to treat one you like." Not so did Rodriguez. His attention passed on to notice Morano's rings which he wore in great profusion upon his little fingers; they were gold and of exquisite work and had once held precious stones, as large gaps testified; in these days they would have been price-less, but in an age when workers only worked at arts that they understood, and then worked for the joy of it, before the word artistic became ridiculous, exqui-site work went without saying; and as the rings were slender they were of little value. Rodriguez made no comment upon the rings; it was enough for him to have noticed them. He merely noted that they were not ladies' rings, for no lady's ring would have fitted on to any one of those fingers: the rings therefore of gallants: and not given to Morano by their owners, for whoever wore precious stone needed a ring to wear it in, and rings did not wear out like hose, which a gallant might give to a servant. Nor, thought he, had Morano stolen them, for whoever stole them would keep them whole, or part with them whole and get a better price. Besides Morano had an honest face, or a face at least that seemed honest in such an inn: and while these thoughts were passing through his mind Morano spoke again: "Good hams," said Morano. He had already eaten one and was starting upon the next. Perhaps he spoke out of gratitude for the hon-our and physical advantage of being permitted to sit there and eat those hams, perhaps tentatively, to find out whether he might consume the second, perhaps merely to start a conversation, being attracted by the honest looks of Rodriguez.

"You are hungry," said Rodriguez.

"Praise God I am always hungry," answered Morano. "If I were not hungry I should starve."

"Is it so?" said Rodriguez.

"You see," said Morano, "the manner of it is this: my master gives me no food, and it is only when I am hungry that I dare to rob him by breaking in, as you saw me, upon his viands; were I not hungry I should not dare to do so, and so ..." He made a sad and expressive movement with both his hands suggestive of autumn leaves blown hence to die.

"He gives you no food?" said Rodriguez.

"It is the way of many men with their dog," said Morano. "They give him no food," and then he rubbed his hands cheerfully, "and yet the dog does not die."

"And he gives you no wages?" said Rodriguez.

"Just these rings."

Now Rodriguez had himself a ring upon his finger (as a gallant should), a slender piece of gold with four tiny angels holding a sapphire, and for a moment he pictured the sapphire passing into the hands of mine host and the ring of gold and the four small angels being flung to Morano; the thought darkened his gaiety for no longer than one of those fleecy clouds in Spring shadows the fields of Spain.

Morano was also looking at the ring; he had followed the young man's glance.

"Master," he said, "do you draw your sword of a night?"

"And you?" said Rodriguez.

"I have no sword," said Morano. "I am but as dog's meat that needs no guarding, but you whose meat is rare like the flesh of the unicorn need a sword to guard your meat. The unicorn has his horn always, and even then he sometimes sleeps."

"It is bad, you think, to sleep," Rodriguez said.

"For some it is very bad, master. They say they never take the unicorn waking. For me I am but dog's meat: when I have eaten hams I curl up and sleep; but then you see, master, I know I shall wake in the morning."

"Ah," said Rodriguez, "the morning's a pleasant time," and he leaned back comfortably in his chair. Morano took one shrewd look at him, and was soon asleep upon his three-legged stool.

The door opened after a while and mine host appeared. "It is late," he said. Rodriguez smiled acquiescently and mine host withdrew, and presently leaving Morano whom his master's voice had waked, to curl up on the floor in a corner, Rodriguez took the candle that lit the room and passed once more through the passages of the inn and down the great corridor of the fastness of the family that had fallen on evil days, and so came to his chamber. I will not waste a multitude of words over that chamber; if you have no picture of it in your mind already, my reader, you are reading an unskilled writer, and if in that picture it appear a wholesome room, tidy and well kept up, if it appear a place in which a stranger might sleep without some faint foreboding of disaster, then I am wasting your time, and will waste no more of it with bits of "descriptive writing" about that dim, high room, whose blackness towered before Rodriguez in the night. He entered and shut the door, as many had done before him; but for all his youth he took some wiser precautions than had they, perhaps, who closed that door before. For first he drew his sword; then for some while he stood quite still near the door and listened to the rats; then he looked round the chamber and perceived only one door; then he looked at the heavy oak furniture, carved by some artist, gnawed by rats, and all blackened by time; then swiftly opened the door of the largest cupboard and thrust his sword in to see who might be inside, but the carved satyr's heads at the top of the cupboard eyed him silently and nothing moved. Then he noted that though there was no bolt on the door the furniture might be placed across to make what in the wars is called a barricado, but the wiser thought came at once that this was too easily done, and that if the danger that the dim room seemed gloomily to forebode were to come from a door so readily barricadoed, then those must have been simple gallants who parted so easily with the rings that adorned Morano's two little fingers. No, it was something more subtle than any attack through that door that brought his regular wages to Morano. Rodriguez looked at the window, which let in the light of a moon that was getting low, for the curtains had years ago been eaten up by the moths; but the window was barred with iron bars that were not yet rusted away, and looked out, thus guarded, over a sheer wall that even in the moonlight fell into blackness. Rodriguez then looked round for some hidden door, the sword all the while in his hand, and very soon he knew that room fairly well, but not its secret, nor why those unknown gallants had given up their rings.

It is much to know of an unknown danger that it really is unknown. Many have met their deaths through looking for danger from one particular direction, whereas had they perceived that they were ignorant of its direction they would have been wise in their ignorance. Rodriguez had the great discretion to understand clearly that he did not know the direction from which danger would come. He accepted this as his only discovery about that portentous room which seemed to beckon to him with every shadow and to sigh over him with every mournful draught, and to whisper to him unintelligible warnings with every rustle of tattered silk that hung about his bed. And as soon as he discovered that this was his only knowledge he began at once to make his preparations: he was a right young man for the wars. He divested himself of his shoes and doublet and the light cloak that hung from his shoulder and cast the clothes on a chair. Over the back of the chair he slung his girdle and the scabbard hanging therefrom and placed his plumed hat so that none could see that his Castilian blade was not in its resting-place. And when the sombre chamber had the appearance of one having undressed in it before retiring Rodriguez turned his attention to the bed, which he noticed to be of great depth and softness. That something not unlike blood had been spilt on the floor excited no wonder in Rodriguez; that vast chamber was evidently, as I have said, in the fortress of some great family, against one of whose walls the humble inn had once leaned for protection; the great family were gone: how they were gone Rodriguez did not know, but it excited no wonder in him to see blood on the boards: besides, two gallants may have disagreed; or one who loved not dumb animals might have been killing rats. Blood did not disturb him; but what amazed him, and would have surprised anyone who stood in that ruinous room, was that there were clean new sheets on the bed. Had you seen the state of the furniture and the floor, O my reader, and the vastness of the old cobwebs and the black dust that they held, the dead spiders and huge dead flies, and the living generation of spiders descending and ascending through the gloom, I say that you also would have been surprised at the sight of those nice clean sheets. Rodriguez noted the fact and continued his preparations. He took the bolster from underneath the pillow and laid it down the middle of the bed and put the sheets back over it; then he stood back and looked at it, much as a sculptor might stand back from his marble, then he returned to it and bent it a little in the middle, and after that he placed his mandolin on the pillow and nearly covered it with the sheet, but not quite, for a little of the curved dark-brown wood remained still to be seen. It looked wonderfully now like a sleeper in the bed, but Rodriguez was not satisfied with his work until he had placed his kerchief and one of his shoes where a shoulder ought to be; then he stood back once more and eyed it with satisfaction. Next he considered the light. He looked at the light of the moon and remembered his father's advice, as the young often do, but considered that this was not the occasion for it, and decided to leave the light of his candle instead, so that anyone who might be familiar with the moonlight in that shadowy chamber should find instead a less sinister light. He therefore dragged a table to the bedside, placed the candle upon it, and opened a treasured book that he bore in his doublet, and laid it on the bed near by, between the candle and his mandolin-headed sleeper; the name of the book was Notes in a Cathedral and dealt with the confessions of a young girl, which the author claimed to have jotted down, while concealed behind a pillow near the Confessional, every Sunday for the entire period of Lent. Lastly he pulled a sheet a little loose from the bed, until a corner of it lay on the floor; then he lay down on the boards, still keeping his sword in his hand, and by means of the sheet and some silk that hung from the bed, he concealed himself sufficient for his purpose, which was to see before he should be seen by any intruder that might enter that chamber.

And if Rodriguez appear to have been unduly suspicious, it should be borne in mind not only that those empty rings needed much explanation, but that every house suggests to the stranger something; and that whereas one house seems to promise a welcome in front of cosy fires, another good fare, another joyous wine, this inn seemed to promise murder; or so the young man's intuition said, and the young are wise to trust to their intuitions.

The reader will know, if he be one of us, who have been to the wars and slept in curious ways, that it is hard to sleep when sober upon a floor; it is not like the earth, or snow, or a feather bed; even rock can be more accommodating; it is hard, unyielding and level, all night unmistakable floor. Yet Rodriguez took no risk of falling asleep, so he said over to himself in his mind as much as he remembered of his treasured book, Notes in a Cathedral, which he always read to himself before going to rest and now so sadly missed. It told how a lady who had listened to a lover longer than her soul's safety could warrant, as he played languorous music in the moonlight and sang soft by her low balcony, and how she being truly penitent, had gathered many roses, the emblems of love (as surely, she said at confession, all the world knows), and when her lover came again by moonlight had cast them all from her from the balcony, showing that she had renounced love; and her lover had entirely misunderstood her. It told how she often tried to show him this again, and all the misunderstandings are sweetly set forth and with true Christian penitence. Sometimes some little matter escaped Rodriguez's memory and then he longed to rise up and look at his dear book, yet he lay still where he was: and all the while he listened to the rats, and the rats went on gnawing and running regularly, scared by nothing new; Rodriguez trusted as much to their myriad ears as to his own two. The great spiders descended out of such heights that you could not see whence they came, and ascended again into blackness; it was a chamber of prodigious height. Sometimes the shadow of a descending spider that had come close to the candle assumed a frightening size, but Rodriguez gave little thought to it; it was of murder he was thinking, not of shadows; still, in its way it was ominous, and reminded Rodriguez horribly of his host; but what of an omen, again, in a chamber full of omens. The place itself was ominous; spiders could scarce make it more so. The spider itself was big enough, he thought, to be impaled on his Castilian blade; indeed, he would have done it but that he thought it wiser to stay where he was and watch. And then the spider found the candle too hot and climbed in a hurry all the way to the ceiling, and his horrible shadow grew less and dwindled away.

It was not that the rats were frightened: whatever it was that happened happened too quietly for that, but the volume of the sound of their running had suddenly increased: it was not like fear among them, for the running was no swifter, and it did not fade away; it was as though the sound of rats running, which had not been heard before, was suddenly heard now. Rodriguez looked at the door, the door was shut. A young Englishman would long ago have been afraid that he was making a fuss over nothing and would have gone to sleep in the bed, and not seen what Rodriguez saw. He might have thought that hearing more rats all at once was merely a fancy, and that everything was all right. Rodriguez saw a rope coming slowly down from the ceiling, he quickly determined whether it was a rope or only the shadow of some huge spider's thread, and then he watched it and saw it come down right over his bed and stop within a few feet of it. Rodriguez looked up cautiously to see who had sent him that strange addition to the portents that troubled the chamber, but the ceiling was too high and dim for him to perceive anything but the rope coming down out of the darkness. Yet he surmised that the ceiling must have softly opened, without any sound at all, at the moment that he heard the greater number of rats. He waited then to see what the rope would do; and at first it hung as still as the great festoons dead spiders had made in the corners; then as he watched it it began to sway. He looked up into the dimness then to see who was swaying the rope; and for a long time, as it seemed to him lying gripping his Castilian sword on the floor he saw nothing clearly. And then he saw mine host coming down the rope, hand over hand quite nimbly, as though he lived by this business. In his right hand he held a poniard of exceptional length, yet he managed to clutch the rope and hold the poniard all the time with the same hand.

If there had been something hideous about the shadow of the spider that came down from that height the shadow of mine host was indeed demoniac. He too was like a spider, with his body at no time slender all bunched up on the rope, and his shadow was six times his size: you could turn from the spider's shadow to the spider and see that it was for the most part a fancy of the candle half crazed by the draughts, but to turn from mine host's shadow to himself and to see his wicked eyes was to say that the candle's wildest fears were true. So he climbed down his rope holding his poniard upward. But when he came within perhaps ten feet of the bed he pointed it downward and began to sway about. It will be readily seen that by swaying his rope at a height mine host could drop on any part of the bed. Rodriguez as he watched him saw him scrutinise closely and continue to sway on his rope. He feared that mine host was ill satisfied with the look of the mandolin and that he would climb away again, well warned of his guest's astuteness, into the heights of the ceiling to devise some fearfuller scheme; but he was only looking for the shoulder. And then mine host dropped; poniard first, he went down with all his weight behind it and drove it through the bolster below where the shoulder should be, just where we slant our arms across our bodies, when we lie asleep on our sides, leaving the ribs exposed: and the soft bed received him. And the moment that mine host let go of his rope Rodriguez leaped to his feet. He saw Rodriguez, indeed their eyes met as he dropped through the air, but what could mine host do? He was already committed to his stroke, and his poniard was already deep in the mattress when the good Castilian blade passed through his ribs.

The Second Chronicle

HOW HE HIRED A MEMORABLE SERVANT

When Rodriguez woke, the birds were singing gloriously. The sun was up and the air was sparkling over Spain. The gloom had left his high chamber, and much of the menace had gone from it that overnight had seemed to bode in the corners. It had not become suddenly tidy; it was still more suitable for spiders than men, it still mourned and brooded over the great family that it had nursed and that evil days had so obviously overtaken; but it no longer had the air of finger to lips, no longer seemed to share a secret with you, and that secret Murder. The rats still ran round the wainscot, but the song of the birds and the jolly, dazzling sunshine were so much larger than the sombre room that the young man's thoughts escaped from it and ran free to the fields. It may have been only his fancy but the world seemed somehow brighter for the demise of mine host of the Dragon and Knight, whose body still lay hunched up on the foot of his bed. Rodriguez jumped up and went to the high, barred window and looked out of it at the morning: far below him a little town with red roofs lay; the smoke came up from the chimneys toward him slowly, and spread out flat and did not reach so high. Between him and the roofs swallows were sailing.

He found water for washing in a cracked pitcher of earthenware and as he dressed he looked up at the ceiling and admired mine host's device, for there was an open hole that had come noiselessly, without any sounds of bolts or lifting of trap-doors, but seemed to have opened out all round on perfectly oiled groves, to fit that well-to-do body, and down from the middle of it from some higher beam hung the rope down which mine host had made his last journey.

Before taking leave of his host Rodriguez looked at his poniard, which was a good two feet in length, not counting the hilt, and was surprised to find it an excellent blade. It bore a design on the steel representing a town, which Rodriguez recognised for the towers of Toledo; and had held moreover a jewel at the end of the hilt, but the little gold socket was empty. Rodriguez therefore perceived that the poniard was that of a gallant, and surmised that mine host had begun his trade with a butcher's knife, but having come by the poniard had found it to be handier for his business. Rodriguez being now fully dressed, girt his own blade about him, and putting the poniard under his cloak, for he thought to find a use for it at the wars, set his plumed hat upon him and jauntily stepped from the chamber. By the light of day he saw clearly at what point the passages of the inn had dared to make their intrusion on the corridors of the fortress, for he walked for four paces between walls of huge grey rocks which had never been plastered and were clearly a breach in the fortress, though whether the breach were made by one of the evil days that had come upon the family in their fastness, and whether men had poured through it with torches and swords, or whether the gap had been cut in later years for mine host of the Dragon and Knight, and he had gone quietly through it rubbing his hands, nothing remained to show Rodriguez now.

When he came to the dining-chamber he found Morano astir. Morano looked up from his overwhelming task of tidying the Inn of the Dragon and Knight and then went on with his pretended work, for he felt a little ashamed of the knowledge he had concerning the ways of that inn, which was more than an honest man should know about such a place.

"Good morning, Morano," said Rodriguez blithely.

"Good morning," answered the servant of the Dragon and Knight.

"I am looking for the wars. Would you like a new master, Morano?"

"Indeed," said Morano, "a good master is better to some men's minds than a bad one. Yet, you see senor, my bad master has me bound never to leave him, by oaths that I do not properly understand the meaning of, and that might blast me in any world were I to forswear them. He hath bound me by San Sathanas, with many others. I do not like the sound of that San Sathanas. And so you see, senor, my bad master suits me better than perhaps to be whithered in this world by a levin-stroke, and in the next world who knows?"

"Morano," said Rodriguez, "there is a dead spider on my bed."

"A dead spider, master?" said Morano, with as much concern in his voice as though no spider had ever sullied that chamber before.

"Yes," said Rodriguez, "I shall require you to keep my bed tidy on our way to the wars."

"Master," said Morano, "no spider shall come near it, living or dead."

And so our company of one going northward through Spain looking for romance became a company of two.

"Master," said Morano, "as I do not see him whom I serve, and his ways are early ways, I fear some evil has overtaken him, whereby we shall be suspect, for none other dwells here: and he is under special protection of the Garda Civil; it would be well therefore to start for the wars right early."

"The guard protect mine host then." Rodriguez said with as much surprise in his tones as he ever permitted himself.

"Master," Morano said, "it could not be otherwise. For so many gallants have entered the door of this inn and supped in this chamber and never been seen again, and so many suspicious things have been found here, such as blood, that it became necessary for him to pay the guard well, and so they protect him." And Morano hastily slung over his shoulder by leather straps an iron pot and a frying-pan and took his broad felt hat from a peg on the wall.

Rodriguez' eyes looked so curiously at the great cooking utensils dangling there from the straps that Morano perceived his young master did not fully understand these preparations: he therefore instructed him thus: "Master, there be two things necessary in the wars, strategy and cooking. Now the first of these comes in use when the captains speak of their achievements and the historians write of the wars. Strategy is a learned thing, master, and the wars may not be told of without it, but while the war rageth and men be camped upon the foughten field then is the time for cooking; for many a man that fights the wars, if he hath not his food, were well content to let the enemy live, but feed him and at once he becometh proud at heart and cannot a-bear the sight of the enemy walking among his tents but must needs slay him outright. Aye, master, the cooking for the wars; and when the wars are over you who are learned shall study strategy."

And Rodriguez perceived that there was wisdom in the world that was not taught in the College of San Josephus, near to his father's valleys, where he had learned in his youth the ways of books.

"Morano," he said, "let us now leave mine host to entertain la Garda."

And at the mention of the guard hurry came on Morano, he closed his lips upon his store of wisdom, and together they left the Inn of the Dragon and Knight. And when Rodriguez saw shut behind him that dark door of oak that he had so persistently entered, and through which he had come again to the light of the sun by many precautions and some luck, he felt gratitude to Morano. For had it not been for Morano's sinister hints, and above all his remark that mine host would have driven him thence because he liked him, the evil look of the sombre chamber alone might not have been enough to persuade him to the precautions that cut short the dreadful business of that inn. And with his gratitude was a feeling not unlike remorse, for he felt that he had deprived this poor man of a part of his regular wages, which would have been his own gold ring and the setting that held the sapphire, had all gone well with the business. So he slipped the ring from his finger and gave it to Morano, sapphire and all.

Morano's expressions of gratitude were in keeping with that flowery period in Spain, and might appear ridiculous were I to expose them to the eyes of an age in which one in Morano's place on such an occasion would have merely said, "Damned good of you old nut, not half," and let the matter drop.

I merely record therefore that Morano was grateful and so expressed himself; while Rodriguez, in addition to the pleasant glow in the mind that comes from a generous action, had another feeling that gives all of us pleasure, or comfort at least (until it grows monotonous), a feeling of increased safety; for while he had the ring upon his finger and Morano went unpaid the thought could not help occurring, even to a generous mind, that one of these windy nights Morano might come for his wages.

"Master," said Morano looking at the sapphire now on his own little finger near the top joint, the only stone amongst his row of rings, "you must surely have great wealth."

"Yes," said Rodriguez slapping the scabbard that held his Castilian blade. And when he saw that Morano's eyes were staring at the little emeralds that were dotted along the velvet of the scabbard he explained that it was the sword that was his wealth:

"For in the wars," he said, "are all things to be won, and nothing is unobtainable to the sword. For parchment and custom govern all the possessions of man, as they taught me in the College of San Josephus. Yet the sword is at first the founder and discoverer of all possessions; and this my father told me before he gave me this sword, which hath already acquired in the old time fair castles with many a tower."

"And those that dwelt in the castles, master, before the sword came?" said Morano.

"They died and went dismally to Hell," said Rodriguez, "as the old songs say."

They walked on then in silence. Morano, with his low forehead and greater girth of body than of brain to the superficial observer, was not incapable of thought. However slow his thoughts may have come, Morano was pondering surely. Suddenly the puckers on his little forehead cleared and he brightly looked at Rodriguez as they went on side by side.

"Master," Morano said, "when you choose a castle in the wars, let it above all things be one of those that is easy to be defended; for castles are easily got, as the old songs tell, and in the heat of combat positions are quickly stormed, and no more ado; but, when wars are over, then is the time for ease and languorous days and the imperilling of the soul, though not beyond the point where our good fathers may save it."

"Nay, Morano," Rodriguez said, "no man, as they taught me well in the College of San Josephus, should ever imperil his soul."

"But, master," Morano said, "a man imperils his body in the wars yet hopes by dexterity and his sword to draw it safely thence: so a man of courage and high heart may surely imperil his soul and still hope to bring it at the last to salvation."

"Not so," said Rodriguez, and gave his mind to pondering upon the exact teaching he had received on this very point, but could not clearly remember.

So they walked in silence, Rodriguez thinking still of this spiritual problem, Morano turning, though with infinite slowness, to another thought upon a lower plane.

And after a while Rodriguez' eyes turned again to the flowers, and he felt his meditation, as youth will, and looking abroad he saw the wonder of Spring calling forth the beauty of Spain, and he lifted up his head and his heart rejoiced with the anemones, as hearts at his age do: but Morano clung to his thought.

It was long before Rodriguez' fanciful thoughts came back from among the flowers, for among those delicate earliest blooms of Spring his youthful visions felt they were with familiars; so they tarried, neglecting the dusty road and poor gross Morano. But when his fancies left the flowers at last and looked again at Morano, Rodriguez perceived that his servant was all troubled with thought: so he left Morano in silence for his thought to come to maturity, for he had formed a liking already for the judgments of Morano's simple mind.

They walked in silence for the space of an hour, and at last Morano spoke. It was then noon. "Master," he said, "at this hour it is the custom of la Garda to enter the Inn of the Dragon and to dine at the expense of mine host."

"A merry custom," said Rodriguez.

"Master," said Morano, "if they find him in less than his usual health they will get their dinners for themselves in the larder and dine and afterwards sleep. But after that; master, after that, should anything inauspicious have befallen mine host, they will seek out and ask many questions concerning all travellers, too many for our liking."

"We are many good miles from the Inn of the Dragon and Knight," said Rodriguez.

"Master, when they have eaten and slept and asked questions they will follow on horses," said Morano.

"We can hide," said Rodriguez, and he looked round over the plain, very full of flowers, but empty and bare under the blue sky of any place in which a man might hide to escape from pursuers on horse back. He perceived then that he had no plan.

"Master," said Morano, "there is no hiding like disguises."

Once more Rodriguez looked round him over the plain, seeing no houses, no men; and his opinion of Morano's judgment sank when he said disguises. But then Morano unfolded to him that plan which up to that day had never been tried before, so far as records tell, in all the straits in which fugitive men have been; and which seems from my researches in verse and prose never to have been attempted since.

The plan was this, astute as Morano, and simple as his naive mind. The clothing for which Rodriguez searched the plain vainly was ready to hand. No disguise was effective against la Garda, they had too many suspicions, their skill was to discover disguises. But in the moment of la Garda's triumph, when they had found out the disguise, when success had lulled the suspicions for which they were infamous, then was the time to trick la Garda. Rodriguez wondered; but the slow mind of Morano was sure, and now he came to the point, the fruit of his hour's thinking. Rodriguez should disguise himself as Morano. When la Garda discovered that he was not the man he appeared to be, a study to which they devoted their lives, their suspicions would rest and there would be an end of it. And Morano should disguise himself as Rodriguez.

It was a new idea. Had Rodriguez been twice his age he would have discarded it at once; for age is guided by precedent which, when pursued, is a dangerous guide indeed. Even as it was he was critical, for the novelty of the thing coming thus from his gross servant surprised him as much as though Morano had uttered poetry of his own when he sang, as he sometimes did, certain merry lascivious songs of Spain that any one of the last few centuries knew as well as any of the others.

And would not la Garda find out that he was himself, Rodriguez asked, as quickly as they found out he was not Morano.

"That," said Morano, "is not the way of la Garda. For once let la Garda come by a suspicion, such as that you, master, are but Morano, and they will cling to it even to the last, and not abandon it until they needs must, and then throw it away as it were in disgust and ride hence at once, for they like not tarrying long near one who has seen them mistaken."

"They will soon then come by another suspicion," said Rodriguez.

"Not so, master," answered Morano, "for those that are as suspicious as la Garda change their suspicions but slowly. A suspicion is an old song to them."

"Then," said Rodriguez, "I shall be hard set ever to show that I am not you if they ever suspect I am."

"It will be hard, master," Morano answered; "but we shall do it, for we shall have truth upon our side."

"How shall we disguise ourselves?" said Rodriguez.

"Master," said Morano, "when you came to our town none knew you and all marked your clothes. As for me my fat body is better known than my clothes, yet am I not too well known by la Garda, for, being an honest man, whenever la Garda came I used to hide."

"You did well," said Rodriguez.

"Certainly I did well," said Morano, "for had they seen me they might, on account of certain matters, have taken me to prison, and prison is no place for an honest man."

"Let us disguise ourselves," said Rodriguez.

"Master," answered Morano, "the brain is greater than the stomach, and now more than at any time we need the counsel of the brain; let us therefore appease the clamours of the stomach that it be silent."

And he drew out from amongst his clothing a piece of sacking in which was a mass of bacon and some lard, and unslung his huge frying-pan. Rodriguez had entirely forgotten the need of food, but now the memory of it had rushed upon him like a flood over a barrier, as soon as he saw the bacon. And when they had collected enough of tiny inflammable things, for it was a treeless plain, and Morano had made a fire, and the odour of the bacon became perceptible, this memory was hugely intensified.

"Let us eat while they eat, master," said Morano, "and plan while they sleep, and disguise ourselves while they pursue."

And this they did: for after they had eaten they dug up earth and gathered leaves with which to fill the gaps in Morano's garments when they should hang on Rodriguez, they plucked a geranium with whose dye they deepened Rodriguez' complexion, and with the sap from the stalk of a weed Morano toned to a pallor the ruddy brown of his tough cheeks. Then they changed clothes altogether, which made Morano gasp: and after that nothing remained but to cut off the delicate black moustachios of Rodriguez and to stick them to the face of Morano with the juice of another flower that he knew where to find. Rodriguez sighed when he saw them go. He had pictured ecstatic glances cast some day at those moustachios, glances from under long eyelashes twinkling at evening from balconies; and looking at them where they were now, he felt that this was impossible.

For one moment Morano raised his head with an air, as it were preening himself, when the new moustachios had stuck; but as soon as he saw, or felt, his master's sorrow at their loss he immediately hung his head, showing nothing but shame for the loss he had caused his master, or for the impropriety of those delicate growths that so ill become his jowl. And now they took the road again, Rodriguez with the great frying-pan and cooking-pot; no longer together, but not too far apart for la Garda to take them both at once, and to make the doubly false charge that should so confound their errand. And Morano wore that old triumphant sword, and carried the mandolin that was ever young.

They had not gone far when it was as Morano had said; for, looking back, as they often did, to the spot where their road touched the sky-line, they saw la Garda spurring, seven of them in their unmistakable looped hats, very clear against the sky which a moment ago seemed so fair.

When the seven saw the two they did not spare the dust; and first they came to Morano.

"You," they said, "are Rodriguez Trinidad Fernandez, Concepcion Henrique Maria, a Lord of the Valleys of Arguento Harez."

"No, masters," said Morano.

Oh but denials were lost upon la Garda.

Denials inflamed their suspicions as no other evidence could. Many a man had they seen with his throat in the hands of the public garrotter; and all had begun with denials who ended thus. They looked at the mandolin, at the gay cloak, at the emeralds in the scabbard, for wherever emeralds go there is evidence to identify them, until the nature of man changes or the price of emeralds. They spoke hastily among themselves.

"Without doubt," said one of them, "you are whom we said." And they arrested Morano.

Then they spurred on to Rodriguez. "You are, they said, "as no man doubts, one Morano, servant at the

Inn of the Dragon and Knight, whose good master is, as we allege, dead."

"Masters," answered Rodriguez, "I am but a poor traveller, and no servant at any inn."

Now la Garda, as I have indicated, will hear all things except denials; and thus to receive two within the space of two moments infuriated them so fiercely that they were incapable of forming any other theory that day except the one they held.

There are many men like this; they can form a plausible theory and grasp its logical points, but take it away from them and destroy it utterly before their eyes, and they will not so easily lash their tired brains at once to build another theory in place of the one that is ruined.

"As the saints live," they said, "you are Morano." And they arrested Rodriguez too.

Now when they began to turn back by the way they had come Rodriguez began to fear overmuch identification, so he assured la Garda that in the next village ahead of them were those who would answer all questions concerning him, as well as being the possessors of the finest vintage of wine in the kingdom of Spain.

Now it may be that the mention of this wine soothed the anger caused in the men of la Garda by two denials, or it may be that curiosity guided them, at any rate they took the road that led away from last night's sinister shelter, Rodriguez and five of la Garda. Two of them stayed behind with Morano, undecided as yet which way to take, though looking wistfully the way that that wine was said to be; and Rodriguez left Morano to his own devices, in which he trusted profoundly.

Now Rodriguez knew not the name of the next village that they would come to nor the names of any of the dwellers in it.

Yet he had a plan. As he went by the side of one of the horses he questioned the rider.

"Can Morano write?" he said. La Garda laughed.

"Can Morano talk Latin?" he said. La Garda crossed themselves, all five men. And after some while of riding, and hard walking for Rodriguez, to whom they allowed a hand on a stirrup leather, there came in sight the tops of the brown roofs of a village over a fold of the plain. "Is this your village?" said one of his captors.

"Surely," answered Rodriguez.

"What is its name?" said one.

"It has many names," said Rodriguez.

And then another one of them recognised it from the shape of its roofs. "It is Saint Judas-not-Iscariot," he said.

"Aye, so strangers call it," said Rodriguez.

And where the road turned round that fold of the plain, lolling a little to its left in the idle Spanish air, they came upon the village all in view. I do not know how to describe this village to you, my reader, for the words that mean to you what it was are all the wrong words to use. "Antique," "old-world," "quaint," seem words with which to tell of it. Yet it had no antiquity denied to the other villages; it had been brought to birth like them by the passing of time, and was nursed like them in the lap of plains or valleys of Spain. Nor was it quainter than any of its neighbours, though it was like itself alone, as they had their characters also; and, though no village in the world was like it, it differed only from the next as sister differs from sister. To those that dwelt in it, it was wholly apart from all the world of man.

Most of its tall white houses with green doors were gathered about the market-place, in which were pigeons and smells and declining sunlight, as Rodriguez and his escort came towards it, and from round a corner at the back of it the short, repeated song of one who would sell a commodity went up piercingly.

This was all very long ago. Time has wrecked that village now. Centuries have flowed over it, some stormily, some smoothly, but so many that, of the village Rodriguez saw, there can be now no more than wreckage. For all I know a village of that name may stand on that same plain, but the Saint Judas-not-Iscariot that Rodriguez knew is gone like youth.

Queerly tiled, sheltered by small dense trees, and standing a little apart, Rodriguez recognised the house of the Priest. He recognised it by a certain air it had. Thither he pointed and la Garda rode. Again he spoke to them. "Can Morano speak Latin?" he said.

"God forbid!" said la Garda.

They dismounted and opened a gate that was gilded all over, in a low wall of round boulders. They went up a narrow path between thick ilices and came to the green door. They pulled a bell whose handle was a symbol carved in copper, one of the Priest's mysteries. The bell boomed through the house, a tiny musical boom, and the Priest opened the door; and Rodriguez addressed him in Latin. And the Priest answered him.

At first la Garda had not realised what had happened. And then the Priest beckoned and they all entered his house, for Rodriguez had asked him for ink. Into a room they came where a silver ink-pot was, and the grey plume of the goose. Picture no such ink-pot, my reader, as they sell to-day in shops, the silver no thicker than paper, and perhaps a pattern all over it guaranteed artistic. It was molten silver well wrought, and hollowed for ink. And in the hollow there was the magical fluid, the stuff that rules the world and hinders time; that in which flows the will of a king, to establish his laws for ever; that which gives valleys unto new possessors; that whereby towers are held by their lawful owners; that which, used grimly by the King's judge, is death; that which, when poets play, is mirth for ever and ever.

No wonder la Garda looked at it in awe, no wonder they crossed themselves again: and then Rodriguez wrote. In the silence that followed the jaws of la Garda dropped, while the old Priest slightly smiled, for he somewhat divined the situation already; and, being the people's friend, he loved not la Garda more than he was bound by the rules of his duty to man.

Then one of la Garda spoke, bringing back his confidence with a bluster. "Morano has sold his soul to Satan," he said, "in exchange for Satan's aid, and Satan has taught his tongue Latin and guides his fingers in the affairs of the pen." And so said all la Garda, rejoicing at finding an explanation where a moment ago there was none, as all men at such times do: little it matters what the explanation be: does a man in Sahara, who finds water suddenly, in quire with precision what its qualities are?

And then the Priest said a word and made a sign, against which Satan himself can only prevail with difficulty, and in presence of which his spells can never endure. And after this Rodriguez wrote again. Then were la Garda silent.

And at length the leader said, and he called on them all to testify, that he had made no charge whatever against this traveller; moreover, they had escorted him on his way out of respect for him, because the roads were dangerous, and must now depart because they had higher duties. So la Garda departed, looking before them with stern, preoccupied faces and urging their horses on, as men who go on an errand of great urgency. And Rodriguez, having thanked them for their protection upon the road, turned back into the house and the two sat down together, and Rodriguez told his rescuer the story of the hospitality of the Inn of the Dragon and Knight.

Not as confession he told it, but as a pleasant tale, for he looked on the swift demise of la Garda's friend, in the night, in the spidery room, as a fair blessing for Spain, a thing most suited to the sweet days of Spring. The spiritual man rejoiced to hear such a tale, as do all men of peace to hear talk of violent deeds in which they may not share. And when the tale was ended he reproved Rodriguez exceedingly, explaining to him the nature of the sin of blood, and telling him that absolution could be come by now, though hardly, but how on some future occasion there might be none to be had. And Rodriguez listened with all the gravity of expression that youth knows well how to wear while its thoughts are nimbly dancing far away in fair fields of adventure or love.

And darkness came down and lamps were carried in: and the reverend father asked Rodriguez in what other affairs of violence his sword had unhappily been. And Rodriguez knew well the history of that sword, having gathered all that concerned it out of spoken legend or song. And although the reverend man frowned minatorily whenever he heard of its passings through the ribs of the faithful, and nodded as though his head gave benediction when he heard of the destruction of God's most vile enemy the infidel, and though he gasped a little through his lips when he heard of certain tarryings of that sword, in scented gardens, while Christian knights should sleep and their swords hang on the wall, though sometimes even a little he raised his hands, yet he leaned forward always, listening well, and picturing clearly as though his gleaming eyes could see them, each doleful tale of violence or sin. And so night came, and began to wear away, and neither knew how late the hour was. And then as Rodriguez spoke of an evening in a garden, of which some old song told well, a night in early summer under the evening star, and that sword there as always; as he told of his grandfather as poets had loved to tell, going among the scents of the huge flowers, familiar with the dark garden as the moths that drifted by him; as he spoke of a sigh heard faintly, as he spoke of danger near, whether to body or soul; as the reverend father was about to raise both his hands; there came a thunder of knockings upon the locked green door.

The Third Chronicle

HOW HE CAME TO THE HOUSE OF WONDER

It was the gross Morano. Here he had tracked Rodriguez, for where la Garda goes is always known, and rumour of it remains long behind them, like the scent of a fox. He told no tale of his escape more than a dog does who comes home some hours late; a dog comes back to his master, that is all, panting a little perhaps; someone perhaps had caught him and he escaped and came home, a thing too natural to attempt to speak of by any of the signs that a dog knows.

Part of Morano's method seems to have resembled Rodriguez', for just as Rodriguez spoke Latin, so Morano fell back upon his own natural speech, that he as it were unbridled and allowed to run free, the coarseness of which had at first astounded, and then delighted, la Garda.

"And did they not suspect that you were yourself?" said Rodriguez.

"No, master," Morano answered, "for I said that I was the brother of the King of Aragon."

"The King of Aragon!" Rodriguez said, going to the length of showing surprise. "Yes, indeed, master." said Morano, "and they recognised me."

"Recognised you!" exclaimed the Priest.

"Indeed so," said Morano, "for they said that they were themselves the Kings of Aragon; and so, father, they recognised me for their brother."

"That you should not have said," the Priest told Morano.

"Reverend father," replied Morano, "as Heaven shines, I believed that what I said was true." And Morano sighed deeply. "And now," he said, "I know it is true no more."

Whether he sighed for the loss of his belief in that exalted relationship, or whether for the loss of that state of mind in which such beliefs come easily, there was nothing in his sigh to show. They questioned him further, but he said no more: he was here, there was no more to say: he was here and la Garda was gone.

And then the reverend man brought for them a great supper, even at that late hour, for many an hour had slipped softly by as he heard the sins of the sword; and wine he set out, too, of a certain golden vintage, long lost—I fear—my reader: but this he gave not to Morano lest he should be once more, what the reverend father feared to entertain, that dread hidalgo, the King of Aragon's brother. And after that, the stars having then gone far on their ways, the old Priest rose and offered a bed to Rodriguez; and even as he eyed Morano, wondering where to put him, and was about to speak, for he had no other bed, Morano went to a corner of the room and curled up and lay down. And by the time his host had walked over to him and spoken, asking anxiously if he needed nothing more, he was almost already asleep, and muttered in answer, after having been spoken to twice, no more than "Straw, reverend father, straw."

An armful of this the good man brought him, and then showed Rodriguez to his room; and they can scarcely have reached it before Morano was back in Aragon again, walking on golden shoes (which were sometimes wings), proud among lesser princes.

As precaution for the night Rodriguez took one more glance at his host's kind face; and then, with sword out of reach and an unlocked door, he slept till the songs of birds out of the deeps of the ilices made sleep any longer impossible.

The third morning of Rodriguez' wandering blazed over Spain like brass; flowers and grass and sky were twinkling all together.

When Rodriguez greeted his host Morano was long astir, having awakened with dawn, for the simpler and humbler the creature the nearer it is akin to the earth and the sun. The forces that woke the birds and opened the flowers stirred the gross lump of Morano, ending his sleep as they ended the nightingale's song.

They breakfasted hurriedly and Rodriguez rose to depart, feeling that he had taken hospitality that had not been offered. But against his departure was the barrier of all the politeness of Spain. The house was his, said his host, and even the small grove of ilices.

If I told you half of the things that the reverend man said, you would say: "This writer is affected. I do not like all this flowery mush." I think it safer, my reader, not to tell you any of it. Let us suppose that he merely said, "Quite all right," and that when Rodriguez thanked him on one knee he answered, "Not at all;" and that so Rodriguez and Morano left. If here it miss some flash of the fair form of Truth it is the fault of the age I write for.

The road again, dust again, birds and the blaze of leaves, these were the background of my wanderers, until the eye had gone as far as the eye can roam, and there were the tips of some far pale-blue mountains that now came into view.

They were still in each other's clothes; but the village was not behind them very far when Morano explained, for he knew the ways of la Garda, that having arrested two men upon this road, they would now arrest two men each on all the other roads, in order to show the impartiality of the Law, which constantly needs to be exhibited; and that therefore all men were safe on the road they were on for a long while to come.

Now there seemed to Rodriguez to be much good sense in what Morano had said; and so indeed there was for they had good laws in Spain, and they differed little, though so long ago, from our own excellent system. Therefore they changed once more, giving back to each other everything but, alas, those delicate black moustachios; and these to Rodriguez seemed gone for ever, for the growth of new ones seemed so far ahead to the long days of youth that his hopes could scarce reach to them.

When Morano found himself once more in those clothes that had been with him night and day for so many years he seemed to expand; I mean no metaphor here; he grew visibly fatter.

"Ah," said Morano after a huge breath, "last night I dreamed, in your illustrious clothes, that I was in lofty station. And now, master, I am comfortable."

"Which were best, think you," said Rodriguez, "if you could have but one, a lofty place or comfort?" Even in those days such a question was trite, but Rodriguez uttered it only thinking to dip in the store of Morano's simple wisdom, as one may throw a mere worm to catch a worthy fish. But in this he was disappointed; for Morano made no neat comparison nor even gave an opinion, saying only, "Master, while I have comfort how shall I judge the case of any who have not?" And no more would he say. His new found comfort, lost for a day and night, seemed so to have soothed his body that it closed the gates of the mind, as too much luxury may, even with poets.

And now Rodriguez thought of his quest again, and the two of them pushed on briskly to find the wars.

For an hour they walked in silence an empty road. And then they came upon a row of donkeys; piled high with the bark of the cork- tree, that men were bringing slowly from far woods. Some of the men were singing as they went. They passed slow in the sunshine.

"Oh, master," said Morano when they were gone, "I like not that lascivious loitering."

"Why, Morano?" said Rodriguez. "It was not God that made hurry."

"Master," answered Morano, "I know well who made hurry. And may he not overtake my soul at the last. Yet it is bad for our fortunes that these men should loiter thus. You want your castle, master; and I, I want not always to wander roads, with la Garda perhaps behind and no certain place to curl up and sleep in front. I look for a heap of straw in the cellar of your great castle."

"Yes, yes, you shall have it," his master said, "but how do these folks hinder you?" For Morano was scowling at them over his shoulder in a way that was somehow spoiling the gladness of Spring.

"The air is full of their singing," Morano said. "It is as though their souls were already flying to Hell, and cawing hoarse with sin all the way as they go. And they loiter, and they linger..." Oh, but Morano was angry.

"But," said Rodriguez, "how does their lingering harm you?"

"Where are the wars, master? Where are the wars?" blurted Morano, his round face turning redder. "The donkeys would be dead, the men would be running, there would be shouts, cries, and confusion, if the wars were anywhere near. There would be all things but this."

The men strolled on singing and so passed slow into distance. Morano was right, though I know not how he knew.

And now the men and the donkeys were nearly out of sight, but had not yet at all emerged from the wrath of Morano. "Lascivious knaves," muttered that disappointed man. And whenever he faintly heard dim snatches of their far song that a breeze here, and another there, brought over the plain as it ran on the errands of Spring, he cursed their sins under his breath. Though it seemed not so much their sins that moved his wrath as the leisure they had for committing them.

"Peace, peace, Morano," said Rodriguez.

"It is that," said Morano, "that is troubling me."

"What?"

"This same peace."

"Morano," said Rodriguez, "I had when young to study the affairs of men; and this is put into books, and so they make history. Now I learned that there is no thing in which men have taken delight, that is ever put away from them; for it seems that time, which altereth every custom, hath altered none of our likings: and in every chapter they taught me there were these wars to be found."

"Master, the times are altered," said Morano sadly. "It is not now as in old days."

And this was not the wisdom of Morano, for anger had clouded his judgment. And a faint song came yet from the donkey-drivers, wavering over the flowers.

"Master," Morano said, "there are men like those vile sin-mongers, who have taken delight in peace. It may be that peace has been brought upon the world by one of these lousy likings."

"The delight of peace," said Rodriguez, "is in its contrast to war. If war were banished this delight were gone. And man lost none of his delights in any chapter I read."

The word and the meaning of CONTRAST were such as is understood by reflective minds, the product of education. Morano felt rather than reflected; and the word CONTRAST meant nothing to him. This ended their conversation. And the songs of the donkey-drivers, light though they were, being too heavy to be carried farther by the idle air of Spring, Morano ceased cursing their sins.

And now the mountains rose up taller, seeming to stretch themselves and raise their heads. In a while they seemed to be peering over the plain. They that were as pale ghosts, far off, dim like Fate, in the early part of the morning, now appeared darker, more furrowed, more sinister, more careworn; more immediately concerned with the affairs of Earth, and so more menacing to earthly things.

Still they went on and still the mountains grew. And noon came, when Spain sleeps.

And now the plain was altering, as though cool winds from the mountains brought other growths to birth, so that they met with bushes straggling wild; free, careless and mysterious, as they do, where there is none to teach great Nature how to be tidy.

The wanderers chose a clump of these that were gathered near the way, like gypsies camped awhile midway on a wonderful journey, who at dawn will rise and go, leaving but a bare trace of their resting and no guess of their destiny; so fairy-like, so free, so phantasmal those dark shrubs seemed.

Morano lay down on the very edge of the shade of one, and Rodriguez lay fair in the midst of the shade of another, whereby anyone passing that way would have known which was the older traveller. Morano, according to his custom, was asleep almost immediately; but Rodriguez, with wonder and speculation each toying with novelty and pulling it different ways between them, stayed awhile wakeful. Then he too slept, and a bird thought it safe to return to an azalea of its own; which it lately fled from troubled by the arrival of these two.

And Rodriguez the last to sleep was the first awake, for the shade of the shrub left him, and he awoke in the blaze of the sun to see Morano still sheltered, well in the middle now of the shadow he chose. The gross sleep of Morano I will not describe to you, reader. I have chosen a pleasant tale for you in a happy land, in the fairest time of year, in a golden age: I have youth to show you and an ancient sword, birds, flowers and

sunlight, in a plain unharmed by any dream of commerce: why should I show you the sleep of that inel-
egant man whose bulk lay cumbering the earth like a
low, unseemly mountain?

Rodriguez overtook the shade he had lost and lay
there resting until Morano awoke, driven all at once
from sleep by a dream or by mere choking. Then
from the intricacies of his clothing, which to him
after those two days was what home is to some far
wanderer, Morano drew out once more a lump of bacon. Then came the fry-pan and then a fire: it was the
Wanderers' Mess. That mess-room has stood in many
lands and has only one roof. We are proud of that roof,
all we who belong to that Mess. We boast of it when
we show it to our friends when it is all set out at night.
It has Aldebaran in it, the Bear and Orion, and at the
other end the Southern Cross. Yes we are proud of our
roof when it is at its best.

What am I saying? I should be talking of bacon.
Yes, but there is a way of cooking it in our Mess that
I want to tell you and cannot. I've tasted bacon there
that isn't the same as what you get at the Ritz. And
I want to tell you how that bacon tastes; and I can't
so I talk about stars. But perhaps you are one of us,
reader, and then you will understand. Only why the
hell don't we get back there again where the Evening
Star swings low on the wall of the Mess?

When they rose from table, when they got up from
the earth, and the frying-pan was slung on Morano's
back, adding grease to the mere surface of his coat

whose texture could hold no more, they pushed on briskly for they saw no sign of houses, unless what Rodriguez saw now dimly above a ravine were indeed a house in the mountains.

They had walked from eight till noon without any loitering. They must have done fifteen miles since the mountains were pale blue. And now, every mile they went, on the most awful of the dark ridges the object Rodriguez saw seemed more and more like a house. Yet neither then, nor as they drew still nearer, nor when they saw it close, nor looking back on it after years, did it somehow seem quite right. And Morano sometimes crossed himself as he looked at it, and said nothing.

Rodriguez, as they walked ceaselessly through the afternoon, seeing his servant show some sign of weariness, which comes not to youth, pointed out the house looking nearer than it really was on the mountain, and told him that he should find there straw, and they would sup and stay the night. Afterwards, when the strange appearance of the house, varying with different angles, filled him with curious forebodings, Rodriguez would make no admission to his servant, but held to the plan he had announced, and so approached the queer roofs, neglecting the friendly stars.

Through the afternoon the two travellers pushed on mostly in silence, for the glances that house seemed to give him from the edge of its perilous ridge, had driven the mirth from Rodriguez and had even checked the garrulity on the lips of the tougher Morano, if garrulity can be ascribed to him whose words seldom welled up unless some simple philosophy troubled his deeps. The house seemed indeed to glance at him, for as their road wound on, the house showed different aspects, different walls and edges of walls, and different curious roofs; all these walls seemed to peer at him. One after another they peered, new ones glided imperceptibly into sight as though to say, We see too.

The mountains were not before them but a little to the right of their path, until new ones appeared ahead of them like giants arising from sleep, and then their path seemed blocked as though by a mighty wall against which its feeble wanderings went in vain. In the end it turned a bit to its right and went straight for a dark mountain, where a wild track seemed to come down out of the rocks to meet it, and upon this track looked down that sinister house. Had you been there, my reader, you would have said, any of us had said, Why not choose some other house? There were no other houses. He who dwelt on the edge of the ravine that ran into that dark mountain was wholly without neighbours.

And evening came, and still they were far from the mountain.

The sun set on their left. But it was in the eastern sky that the greater splendour was; for the low rays streaming across lit up some stormy clouds that were brooding behind the mountain and turned their gloomy forms to an astounding purple.

And after this their road began to rise toward the ridges. The mountains darkened and the sinister house was about to emerge with their shadows, when he who dwelt there lit candles.

The act astonished the wayfarers. All through half the day they had seen the house, until it seemed part of the mountains; evil it seemed like their ridges, that were black and bleak and forbidding, and strange it seemed with a strangeness that moved no fears they could name, yet it seemed inactive as night.

Now lights appeared showing that someone moved. Window after window showed to the bare dark mountain its gleaming yellow glare; there in the night the house forsook the dark rocks that seemed kin to it, by glowing as they could never glow, by doing what the beasts that haunted them could not do: this was the lair of man. Here was the light of flame but the rocks remained dark and cold as the wind of night that went over them, he who dwelt now with the lights had forsaken the rocks, his neighbours.

And, when all were lit, one light high in a tower shone green. These lights appearing out of the mountain thus seemed to speak to Rodriguez and to tell him nothing. And Morano wondered, as he seldom troubled to do.

They pushed on up the steepening path.

"Like you the looks of it?" said Rodriguez once.

"Aye, master," answered Morano, "so there be straw."

"You see nothing strange there, then?" Rodriguez said.

"Master," Morano said, "there be saints for all requirements."

Any fears he had felt about that house before, now as he neared it were gone; it was time to put away fears and face the event; thus worked Morano's philosophy. And he turned his thoughts to the achievements upon earth of a certain Saint who met Satan, and showed to the sovereign of Hell a discourtesy alien to the ways of the Church.

It was dark now, and the yellow lights got larger as they drew nearer the windows, till they saw large shadows obscurely passing from room to room. The ascent was steep now and the pathway stopped. No track of any kind approached the house. It stood on a precipice-edge as though one of the rocks of the mountain: they climbed over rocks to reach it. The windows flickered and blinked at them.

Nothing invited them there in the look of that house, but they were now in such a forbidding waste that shelter had to be found; they were all among edges of rock as black as the night and hard as the material of which Cosmos was formed, at first upon Chaos' brink. The sound of their climbing ran noisily up the mountain but no sound came from the house: only the shadows moved more swiftly across a room, passed into other rooms and came hurrying back. Sometimes the shadows stayed and seemed to peer; and when the travellers stood and watched to see what they were they would disappear and there were no shadows at all, and the rooms were filled instead with their wondering speculation. Then they pushed on over rocks that seemed never trodden by man, so sharp were they and slanting, all piled together: it seemed the last waste, to which all shapeless rocks had been thrown.

Morano and these black rocks seemed shaped by a different scheme; indeed the rocks had never been shaped at all, they were just raw pieces of Chaos. Morano climbed over their edges with moans and discomfort. Rodriguez heard him behind him and knew by his moans when he came to the top of each sharp rock.

The rocks became savager, huger, even more sharp and more angular. They were there in the dark in multitudes. Over these Rodriguez staggered, and Morano clambered and tumbled; and so they came, breathing hard, to the lonely house.

In the wall that their hands had reached there was no door, so they felt along it till they came to the corner, and beyond the corner was the front wall of the house. In it was the front door. But so nearly did this door open upon the abyss that the bats that fled from their coming, from where they hung above the door of oak, had little more to do than fall from their crannies, slanting ever so slightly, to find themselves safe from man in the velvet darkness, that lay between cliffs so lonely they were almost strangers to Echo. And here they floated upon errands far from our knowledge; while the travellers coming along the rocky ledge between destruction and shelter, knocked on the oaken door.

The sound of their knocking boomed huge and slow through the house as though they had struck the door of the very mountain. And no one came. And then Rodriguez saw dimly in the darkness the great handle of a bell, carved like a dragon running down the wall: he pulled it and a cry of pain arose from the basement of the house.

Even Morano wondered. It was like a terrible spirit in distress. It was long before Rodriguez dare touch the handle again. Could it have been the bell? He felt the iron handle and the iron chain that went up from it. How could it have been the bell! The bell had not sounded: he had not pulled hard enough: that scream was fortuitous. The night on that rocky ledge had jangled his nerves. He pulled again and more firmly. The answering scream was more terrible. Rodriguez could doubt no longer, as he sprang back from the bell-handle, that with the chain he had pulled he in- flicted some unknown agony.

The scream had awakened slow steps that now came towards the travellers, down corridors, as it sounded, of stone. And then chains fell on stone and the door of oak was opened by some one older than what man hopes to come to, with small, peaked lips as those of some woodland thing.

"Senores," the old one said, "the Professor wel- comes you."

They stood and stared at his age, and Morano blurted uncouthly what both of them felt. "You are old, grandfather," he said.

"Ah, Senores," the old man sighed, "the Professor does not allow me to be young. I have been here years and years but he never allowed it. I have served him well but it is still the same. I say to him, 'Master, I have served you long ...' but he interrupts me for he will have none of youth. Young servants go among the villages, he says. And so, and so ..."

"You do not think your master can give you youth!" said Rodriguez.

The old man knew that he had talked too much, voicing that grievance again of which even the rocks were weary. "Yes," he said briefly, and bowed and led the way into the house. In one of the corridors running out of the hall down which he was leading silently, Rodriguez overtook that old man and questioned him to his face.

"Who is this professor?" he said.

By the light of a torch that spluttered in an iron clamp on the wall Rodriguez questioned him with these words, and Morano with his wondering, wistful eyes. The old man halted and turned half round, and lifted his head and answered. "In the University of Saragossa," he said with pride, "he holds the Chair of Magic."

Even the names of Oxford or Cambridge, Harvard or Yale or Princeton, move some respect, and even yet in these unlearned days. What wonder then that the name of Saragossa heard on that lonely mountain awoke in Rodriguez some emotion of reverence and even awed Morano. As for the Chair of Magic, it was of all the royal endowments of that illustrious University the most honoured and dreaded.

"At Saragossa!" Rodriguez muttered.

"At Saragossa," the old man affirmed.

Between that ancient citadel of learning and this most savage mountain appeared a gulf scarce to be bridged by thought.

"The Professor rests in his mountain," the old man said, "because of a conjunction of the stars unfavourable to study, and his class have gone to their homes for many weeks." He bowed again and led on along that corridor of dismal stone. The others followed, and still as Rodriguez went that famous name Saragossa echoed within his mind.

And then they came to a door set deep in the stone, and their guide opened it and they went in; and there was the Professor in a mystical hat and a robe of dim purple, seated with his back to them at a table, studying the ways of the stars. "Welcome, Don Rodriguez," said the Professor before he turned round; and then he rose, and with small steps backwards and sideways and many bows, he displayed all those formulae of politeness that Saragossa knew in the golden age and which her professors loved to execute. In later years they became more elaborate still, and afterwards were lost.

Rodriguez replied rather by instinct than knowledge; he came of a house whose bows had never missed graceful ease and which had in some generations been a joy to the Court of Spain. Morano followed behind him; but his servile presence intruded upon that elaborate ceremony, and the Professor held up his hand,

and Morano was held in mid stride as though the air had gripped him. There he stood motionless, having never felt magic before. And when the Professor had welcomed Rodriguez in a manner worthy of the dignity of the Chair that he held at Saragossa, he made an easy gesture and Morano was free again.

"Master," said Morano to the Professor, as soon as he found he could move, "master, it looks like magic." Picture to yourself some yokel shown into the library of a professor of Greek at Oxford, taking down from a shelf one of the books of the Odyssey, and saying to the Professor, "It looks like Greek"!

Rodriguez felt grieved by Morano's boorish ignorance. Neither he nor his host answered him.

The Professor explained that he followed the mysteries dimly, owing to a certain aspect of Orion, and that therefore his class were gone to their homes and were hunting; and so he studied alone under unfavourable auspices. And once more he welcomed Rodriguez to his roof, and would command straw to be laid down for the man that Rodriguez had brought from the Inn of the Dragon and Knight; for he, the Professor, saw all things, though certain stars would hide everything.

And when Rodriguez had appropriately uttered his thanks, he added with all humility and delicate choice of phrase a petition that he might be shown some mere rudiment of the studies for which that illustrious chair in Saragossa was famous. The Professor bowed again and, in accepting the well-rounded compliments that Rodriguez paid to the honoured post he occupied, he introduced himself by name. He had been once, he said, the Count of the Mountain, but when his astral studies had made him eminent and he had mastered the ways of the planet nearest the sun he took the title Magister Mercurii, and by this had long been known; but had now forsaken this title, great as it was, for a more glorious nomenclature, and was called in the Arabic language the Slave of Orion. When Rodriguez heard this he bowed very low.

And now the Professor asked Rodriguez in which of the activities of life his interest lay; for the Chair of Magic at Saragossa, he said, was concerned with them all.

"In war," said Rodriguez.

And Morano unostentatiously rubbed his hands; for here was one, he thought, who would soon put his master on the right way, and matters would come to a head and they would find the wars. But far from concerning himself with the wars of that age, the Slave of Orion explained that as events came nearer they became grosser or more material, and that their grossness did not leave them until they were some while passed away; so that to one whose studies were with aetherial things, near events were opaque and dim. He had a window, he explained, through which Rodriguez should see clearly the ancient wars, while another window beside it looked on all wars of the future except those which were planned already or were coming soon to earth, and which were either invisible or seen dim as through mist.

Rodriguez said that to be privileged to see so classical an example of magic would be to him both a delight and honour. Yet, as is the way of youth, he more desired to have a sight of the wars than he cared for all the learning of the Professor.

And to him who held the Chair of Magic at Saragossa it was a precious thing that his windows could be made to show these marvels, while the guest to whom he was about to display these two gems of his learning was thinking of little but what he should see through the windows, and not at all of what spells, what midnight oil, what incantations, what witchcrafts, what lonely hours among bats, had gone to the gratification of his young curiosity. It is usually thus.

The Professor rose: his cloak floated out from him as he left the chamber, and Rodriguez following where he guided saw, by the torchlight in the corridors, upon the dim purple border signs that, to his untutored ignorance of magic, were no more than hints of the affairs of the Zodiac. And if these signs were obscure it were better they were obscurer, for they dealt with powers that man needs not to possess, who has the whole earth to regulate and control; why then should he seek to govern the course of any star?

And Morano followed behind them, hoping to be allowed to get a sight of the wars.

They came to a room where two round windows were; each of them larger than the very largest plate, and of very thick glass indeed, and of a wonderful blue. The blue was like the blue of the Mediterranean at evening, when lights are in it both of ships and of sunset, and lights of harbours being lit one by one, and the light of Venus perhaps and about two other stars, so deeply did it stare and so twinkled, near its edges, with lights that were strange to that room, and so triumphed with its clear beauty over the night outside. No, it was more magical than the Mediterranean at evening, even though the peaks of the Esterels be purple and their bases melting in gold and the blue sea lying below them smiling at early stars: these windows were more mysterious than that; it was a more triumphant blue; it was like the Mediterranean seen with the eyes of Shelley, on a happy day in his youth, or like the sea round Western islands of fable seen by the fancy of Keats. They were no windows for any need of ours, unless our dreams be needs, unless our cries for the moon be urged by the same Necessity as makes us cry for bread. They were clearly concerned only with magic or poetry; though the Professor claimed that poetry was but a branch of his subject; and it was so regarded at Saragossa, where it was taught by the name of theoretical magic, while by the name of practical magic they taught dooms, brews, hauntings, and spells.

The Professor stood before the left-hand window and pointed to its deep-blue centre. "Through this," he said, "we see the wars that were."

Rodriguez looked into the deep-blue centre where the great bulge of the glass came out towards him; it was near to the edges where the glass seemed thinner that the little strange lights were dancing; Morano dared to tiptoe a little nearer. Rodriguez looked and saw no night outside. Just below and near to the window was white mist, and the dim lines and smoke of what may have been recent wars; but farther away on a plain of strangely vast dimensions he saw old wars that were. War after war he saw. Battles that long ago had passed into history and had been for many ages skilled, glorious and pleasant encounters he saw even now tumbling before him in their savage confusion and dirt. He saw a leader, long glorious in histories he had read, looking round puzzled, to see what was happening, and in a very famous fight that he had planned very well. He saw retreats that History called routs, and routs that he had seen History calling retreats. He saw men winning victories without knowing they had won. Never had man pried before so shamelessly upon History, or found her such a liar. With his eyes on the great blue glass Rodriguez forgot the room, forgot time, forgot his host and poor excited Morano, as he watched those famous fights.

And now my reader wishes to know what he saw and how it was that he was able to see it.

As regards the second, my reader will readily understand that the secrets of magic are very carefully guarded, and any smatterings of it that I may ever have come by I possess, for what they are worth, subjects to oaths and penalties at which even bad men shudder. My reader will be satisfied that even those intimate bonds between reader and writer are of no use to him here. I say him as though I had only male readers, but if my reader be a lady I leave the situation confidently to her intuition. As for the things he saw, of all of these I am at full liberty to write, and yet, my reader, they would differ from History's version: never a battle that Rodriguez saw on all the plain that swept away from that circular window, but History wrote differently. And now, my reader, the situation is this: who am I? History was a goddess among the Greeks, or is at least a distinguished personage, perhaps with a well-earned knighthood, and certainly with widespread recognition amongst the Right Kind of People. I have none of these things. Whom, then, would you believe?

Yet I would lay my story confidently before you, my reader, trusting in the justice of my case and in your judicial discernment, but for one other thing. What will the Goddess Clio say, or the well-deserving knight, if I offend History? She has stated her case, Sir Bartimeus has written it, and then so late in the day I come with a different story, a truer but different story. What will they do? Reader, the future is dark, uncertain and long; I dare not trust myself to it if I offend History. Clio and Sir Bartimeus will make hay of my reputation; an innuendo here, a foolish fact there, they know how to do it, and not a soul will suspect the goddess of personal malice or the great historian of pique. Rodriguez gazed then through the deep blue window, forgetful of all around, on battles that had not all the elegance or neatness of which our histories so tidily tell. And as he gazed upon a merry encounter between two men on the fringe of an ancient fight he felt a touch on his shoulder and then almost a tug, and turning round beheld the room he was in. How long he had been absent from it in thought he did not know, but the Professor was still standing with folded arms where he had left him, probably well satisfied with the wonder that his most secret art had awakened in his guest. It was Morano who touched his shoulder, unable to hold back any longer his impatience to see the wars; his eyes as Rodriguez turned round were gazing at his master with dog- like wistfulness.

The absurd eagerness of Morano, his uncouth touch on his shoulder, seemed only pathetic to Rodriguez. He looked at the Professor's face, the nose like a hawk's beak, the small eyes deep down beside it, dark of hue and dreadfully bright, the silent lips. He stood there uttering no actual prohibition, concerning which Rodriguez's eyes had sought; so, stepping aside from his window, Rodriguez beckoned Morano, who at once ran forward delighted to see those ancient wars.

A slight look of scorn showed faint upon the Professor's face such as you may see anywhere when a master-craftsman perceives the gaze of the ignorant turned towards his particular subject. But he said no word, and soon speech would have been difficult, for the loud clamour of Morano filled the room: he had seen the wars and his ecstasies were ungoverned. As soon as he saw those fights he looked for the Infidels, for his religious mind most loved to see the Infidel slain. And if my reader discern or suppose some gulf between religion and the recent business of the Inn of the Dragon and Knight, Morano, if driven to admit any connection between murder and his daily bread, would have said, "All the more need then for God's mercy through the intercession of His most blessed Saints." But these words had never passed Morano's lips, for shrewd as he was in enquiry into any matter that he desired to know, his shrewdness was no less in avoiding enquiry where there might be something that he desired not to know, such as the origin of his wages as servant of the Inn of the Dragon and Knight, those delicate gold rings with settings empty of jewels.

Morano soon recognized the Infidel by his dress, and after that no other wars concerned him. He slapped his thigh, he shouted encouragement, he howled vile words of abuse, partly because he believed that this foul abuse was rightly the due of the Infidel, and partly because he believed it delighted God.

Rodriguez stood and watched, pleased at the huge joy of the simple man. The Slave of Orion stood watching in silence too, but who knows if he felt pleasure or any other emotion? Perhaps his mind was simply like ours; perhaps, as has been claimed by learned men of the best-informed period, that mind had some control upon the comet, even when farthest out from the paths we know. Morano turned round for a moment to Rodriguez:

"Good wars, master, good wars," he said with a vast zest, and at once his head was back again at that calm blue window. In that flash of the head Rodriguez had seen his eyes, blue, round and bulging; the round man was like a boy who in some shop window has seen, unexpected, huge forbidden sweets. Clearly, in the war he watched things were going well for the Cross, for such cries came from Morano as "A pretty stroke," "There now, the dirty Infidel," "Now see God's power shown," "Spare him not, good knight; spare him not," and many more, till, uttered faster and faster, they merged into mere clamorous rejoicing.

But the battles beyond the blue window seemed to move fast, and now a change was passing across Morano's rejoicings. It was not that he swore more for the cause of the Cross, but brief, impatient, meaningless oaths slipped from him now; he was becoming irritable; a puzzled look, so far as Rodriguez could see, was settling down on his features. For a while he was silent except for the little, meaningless oaths. Then he turned round from the glass, his hands stretched out, his face full of urgent appeal.

"Masters," he said, "God's enemy wins!"

In answer to Morano's pitiful look Rodriguez' hand went to his sword-hilt; the Slave of Orion merely smiled with his lips; Morano stood there with his hands still stretched out, his face still all appeal, and something more for there was reproach in his eyes that men could tarry while the Cross was in danger and the Infidel lived. He did not know that it was all finished and over hundreds of years ago, a page of history upon which many pages were turned, and which lay as unalterable as the fate of some warm swift creature of early Eocene days over whose fossil today the strata lie long and silent.

"But can nothing be done, master?" he said when Rodriguez told him this. And when Rodriguez failed him here, he turned away from the window. To him the Infidel were game, but to see them defeating Christian knights violated the deeps of his feelings.

Morano sulky excited little more notice from his host and his master who had watched his rejoicings, and they seem to have forgotten this humble champion of Christendom. The Professor slightly bowed to Rodriguez and extended a graceful hand. He pointed to the other window.

Reader, your friend shows you his collection of stamps, his fossils, his poems, or his luggage labels. One of them interests you, you look at it awhile, you are ready to go away: then your friend shows you another. This also must be seen; for your friend's collection is a precious thing; it is that point upon huge Earth on which his spirit has lit, on which it rests, on which it shelters even (who knows from what storms?). To slight it were to weaken such hold as his spirit has, in its allotted time, upon this sphere. It were like breaking the twig of a plant upon which a butterfly rests, and on some stormy day and late in the year.

Rodriguez felt all this dimly, but no less surely; and went to the other window.

Below the window were those wars that were soon coming to Spain, hooded in mist and invisible. In the centre of the window swam as profound a blue, dwindling to paler splendour at the edge, the wandering lights were as lovely, as in the other window just to the left; but in the view from the right-hand window how sombre a difference. A bare yard separated the two. Through the window to the left was colour, courtesy, splendour; there was Death as least disguising himself, well cloaked, taking mincing steps, bowing, wearing a plume in his hat and a decent mask. In the right-hand window all the colours were fading, war after war they grew dimmer; and as the colours paled Death's sole purpose showed clearer. Through the beautiful left-hand window were killings to be seen, and less mercy than History supposes, yet some of the fighters were merciful, and mercy was sometimes a part of Death's courtly pose, which went with the cloak and the plume. But in the other window through that deep, beautiful blue Rodriguez saw Man make a new ally, an ally who was only cruel and strong and had no purpose but killing, who had no pretences or pose, no mask and no manner, but was only the slave of Death and had no care but for his business. He saw it grow bigger and stronger. Heart it had none, but he saw its cold steel core scheming methodical plans and dreaming always destruction. Before it faded men and their fields and their houses. Rodriguez saw the machine.

Many a proud invention of ours that Rodriguez saw raging on that ruinous plain he might have anticipated, but not for all Spain would he have done so: it was for the sake of Spain that he was silent about much that he saw through that window. As he looked from war to war he saw almost the same men fighting, men with always the same attitude to the moment and with similar dim conception of larger, vaguer things; grandson differed imperceptibly from grandfather; he saw them fight sometimes mercifully, sometimes murderously, but in all the wars beyond that twinkling window he saw the machine spare nothing.

Then he looked farther, for the wars that were farthest from him in time were farther away from the window. He looked farther and saw the ruins of Peronne. He saw them all alone with their doom at night, all drenched in white moonlight, sheltering huge darkness in their stricken hollows. Down the white street, past darkness after darkness as he went by the gaping rooms that the moon left mourning alone, Rodriguez saw a captain going back to the wars in that far-future time, who turned his head a moment as he passed, looking Rodriguez in the face, and so went on through the ruins to find a floor on which to lie down for the night. When he was gone the street was all alone with disaster, and moonlight pouring down, and the black gloom in the houses.

Rodriguez lifted his eyes and glanced from city to city, to Albert, Bapaume, and Arras, his gaze moved over a plain with its harvest of desolation lying forlorn and ungathered, lit by the flashing clouds and the moon and peering rockets. He turned from the window and wept.

The deep round window glowed with serene blue glory. It seemed a foolish thing to weep by that beautiful glass. Morano tried to comfort him. That calm, deep blue, he felt, and those little lights, surely, could hurt no one.

What had Rodriguez seen? Morano asked. But that Rodriguez would not answer, and told no man ever after what he had seen through that window.

The Professor stood silent still: he had no comfort to offer; indeed his magical wisdom had found none for the world.

You wonder perhaps why the Professor did not give long ago to the world some of these marvels that are the pride of our age. Reader, let us put aside my tale for a moment to answer this. For all the darkness of his sinister art there may well have been some good in the Slave of Orion; and any good there was, and mere particle even, would surely have spared the world many of those inventions that our age has not spared it. Blame not the age, it is now too late to stop; it is in the grip of inventions now, and has to go on; we cannot stop content with mustard-gas; it is the age of Progress, and our motto is Onwards. And if there was no good in this magical man, then may it not have been he who in due course, long after he himself was safe from life, caused our inventions to be so deadly divulged? Some evil spirit has done it, then why not he?

He stood there silent: let us return to our story.

Perhaps the efforts of poor clumsy Morano to comfort him cheered Rodriguez and sent him back to the window, perhaps he turned from them to find comfort of his own; but, however he came by it, he had a hope that this was a passing curse that had come on the world, whose welfare he cared for whether he lived or died, and that looking a little farther into the future he would see Mother Earth smiling and her children happy again. So he looked through the deep-blue luminous window once more, beyond the battles we know. From this he turned back shuddering.

Again he saw the Professor smile with his lips, though whether at his own weakness, or whether with cynical mirth at the fate of the world, Rodriguez could not say.

The Fourth Chronicle

HOW HE CAME TO THE MOUNTAINS OF THE SUN

The Professor said that in curiosity alone had been found the seeds of all that is needful for our damnation. Nevertheless, he said, if Rodriguez cared to see more of his mighty art the mysteries of Saragossa were all at his guest's disposal.

Rodriguez, sad and horrified though he was, forgot none of his courtesy. He thanked the Professor and praised the art of Saragossa, but his faith in man and his hope for the world having been newly disappointed, he cared little enough for the things we should care to see or for any of the amusements that are usually dear to youth.

"I shall be happy to see anything, senor," he said to the Slave of Orion, "that is further from our poor Earth, and to study therein and admire your famous art."

The Professor bowed. He drew small curtains over the windows, matching his cloak. Morano sought a glimpse through the right-hand window before the curtains covered it. Rodriguez held him back. Enough had been seen already, he thought, through that window for the peace of mind of the world: but he said no word to Morano. He held him by the arm, and the Professor covered the windows. When the little mauve curtains were drawn it seemed to Rodriguez that the windows behind them disappeared and were there no more; but this he only guessed from uncertain indications.

Then the Professor drew forth his wand and went to his cupboard of wonder. Thence he brought condiments, oils, and dews of amazement. These he poured into a vessel that was in the midst of the room, a bowl of agate standing alone on a table. He lit it and it all welled up in flame, a low broad flame of the colour of pale emerald. Over this he waved his wand, which was of exceeding blackness. Morano watched as children watch the dancer, who goes from village to village when spring is come, with some new dance out of Asia or some new song.[*] Rodriguez sat and waited. The Professor explained that to leave this Earth alive, or even dead, was prohibited to our bodies, unless to a very few, whose names were hidden. Yet the spirits of men could by incantation be liberated, and being liberated, could be directed on journeys by such minds as had that power passed down to them from of old. Such journeys, he said, were by no means confined by the hills of Earth. "The Saints," exclaimed Morano, "guard us utterly!" But Rodriguez smiled a little. His faith was given to the Saints of Heaven. He wondered

---

[*] He doesn't, but why shouldn't he?

at their wonders, he admired their miracles, he had little faith to spare for other marvels; in fact he did not believe the Slave of Orion.

"Do you desire such a journey?" said the Professor.

"It will delight me," answered Rodriguez, "to see this example of your art."

"And you?" he said to Morano.

The question seemed to alarm the placid Morano, but "I follow my master," he said.

At once the Professor stretched out his ebony wand, calling the green flame higher. Then he put out his hands over the flame, without the wand, moving them slowly with constantly tremulous fingers. And all at once they heard him begin to speak. His deep voice flowed musically while he scarcely seemed to be speaking but seemed only to be concerned with moving his hands. It came soft, as though blown faint from fabulous valleys, illimitably far from the land of Spain. It seemed full not so much of magic as mere sleep, either sleep in an unknown country of alien men, or sleep in a land dreamed sleeping a long while since. As the travellers heard it they thought of things far away, of mythical journeys and their own earliest years.

They did not know what he said or what language he used. At first Rodriguez thought Moorish, then he deemed it some secret language come down from magicians of old, while Morano merely wondered; and then they were lulled by the rhythm of those strange words, and so enquired no more. Rodriguez pictured some sad wandering angel, upon some mountain-peak of African lands, resting a moment and talking to the solitudes, telling the lonely valley the mysteries of his home. While lulled though Morano was he gave up his alertness uneasily. All the while the green flame flooded upwards: all the while the tremulous fingers made curious shadows. The shadow seemed to run to Rodriguez and beckon him thence: even Morano felt them calling. Rodriguez closed his eyes. The voice and the Moorish spells made now a more haunting melody: they were now like a golden organ on undiscoverable mountains. Fear came on Morano at the thought: who had power to speak like this? He grasped Rodriguez by the wrist. "Master!" he said, but at that moment on one of those golden spells the spirit of Rodriguez drifted away from his body, and out of the greenish light of the curious room; unhampered by weight, or fatigue, or pain, or sleep; and it rose above the rocks and over the mountain, an unencumbered spirit: and the spirit of Morano followed.

The mountain dwindled at once; the Earth swept out all round them and grew larger, and larger still, and then began to dwindle. They saw then that they were launched upon some astounding journey. Does my reader wonder they saw when they had no eyes? They saw as they had never seen before, with sight beyond what they had ever thought to be possible. Our eyes gather in light, and with the little rays of light that they bring us we gather a few images of things as we suppose them to be. Pardon me, reader, if I call them things as we suppose them to be; call them by all means Things As They Really Are, if you wish. These images then, this tiny little brainful that we gather from the immensities, are all brought in by our eyesight upside-down, and the brain corrects them again; and so, and so we know something. An oculist will tell you how it all works. He may admit it is all a little clumsy, or for the dignity of his profession he may say it is not at all. But be this as it may, our eyes are but barriers between us and the immensities. All our five senses that grope a little here and touch a little there, and seize, and compare notes, and get a little knowledge sometimes, they are only barriers between us and what there is to know. Rodriguez and Morano were outside these barriers. They saw without the imperfections of eyesight; they heard on that journey what would have deafened ears; they went through our atmosphere unburned by speed, and were unchilled in the bleak of the outer spaces. Thus freed of the imperfections of the body they sped, no less upon a terrible journey, whose direction as yet Rodriguez only began to fear.

They had seen the stars pale rapidly and then the flash of dawn. The Sun rushed up and at once began to grow larger. Earth, with her curved sides still diminishing violently, was soon a small round garden in blue and filmy space, in which mountains were planted. And still the Sun was growing wider and wider. And now Rodriguez, though he knew nothing of Sun or planets, perceived the obvious truth of their terrible journey: they were heading straight for the Sun. But the spirit of Morano was merely astounded; yet, being free of the body he suffered none of those inconveniences that perturbation may bring to us: spirits do not gasp, or palpitate, or weaken, or sicken.

The dwindling Earth seemed now no more than the size of some unmapped island seen from a mountain-top, an island a hundred yards or so across, looking like a big table.

Speed is comparative: compared to sound, their pace was beyond comparison; nor could any modern projectile attain any velocity comparable to it; even the speed of explosion was slow to it. And yet for spirits they were moving slowly, who being independent of all material things, travel with such velocities as that, for instance, of thought. But they were controlled by one still dwelling on Earth, who used material things, and the material that the Professor was using to hurl them upon their journey was light, the adaptation of which to this purpose he had learned at Saragossa. At the pace of light they were travelling towards the Sun.

They crossed the path of Venus, far from where Venus then was, so that she scarcely seemed larger to them; Earth was but little bigger than the Evening Star, looking dim in that monstrous daylight.

Crossing the path of Mercury, Mercury appeared huger than our Moon, an object weirdly unnatural; and they saw ahead of them the terrific glare in which Mercury basks, from a Sun whose withering orb had more than doubled its width since they came from the hills of Earth. And after this the Sun grew terribly larger, filling the centre of the sky, and spreading and spreading and spreading. It was now that they saw what would have dazzled eyes, would have burned up flesh and would have shrivelled every protection that our scientists' ingenuity could have devised even today. To speak of time there is meaningless. There is nothing in the empty space between the Sun and Mercury with which time is at all concerned. Far less is there meaning in time wherever the spirits of men are under stress. A few minutes' bombardment in a trench, a few hours in a battle, a few weeks' travelling in a trackless country; these minutes, these hours, these weeks can never be few.

Rodriguez and Morano had been travelling about six or seven minutes, but it seems idle to say so.

And then the Sun began to fill the whole sky in front of them. And in another minute, if minutes had any meaning, they were heading for a boundless region of flame that, left and right, was everywhere, and now towered above them, and went below them into a flaming abyss.

And now Morano spoke to Rodriguez. He thought towards him, and Rodriguez was aware of his thinking: it is thus that spirits communicate.

"Master," he said, "when it was all spring in Spain, years ago when I was thin and young, twenty years gone at least; and the butterflies were come, and song was everywhere; there came a maid bare-footed over a stream, walking through flowers, and all to pluck the anemones." How fair she seemed even now, how bright that far spring day. Morano told Rodriguez not with his blundering lips: they were closed and resting deeply millions of miles away: he told him as spirits tell. And in that clear communication Rodriguez saw all that shone in Morano's memory, the grace of the young girl's ankles, the thrill of Spring, the anemones larger and brighter than anemones ever were, the hawks still in clear sky; earth happy and heaven blue, and the dreams of youth between. You would not have said, had you seen Morano's coarse fat body, asleep in a chair in the Professor's room, that his spirit treasured such delicate, nymph-like, pastoral memories as now shone clear to Rodriguez. No words the blunt man had ever been able to utter had ever hinted that he sometimes thought like a dream of pictures by Watteau. And now in that awful space before the power of the terrible Sun, spirit communed with spirit, and Rodriguez saw the beauty of that far day, framed all about the beauty of one young girl, just as it had been for years in Morano's memory. How shall I tell with words what spirit sang wordless to spirit? We poets may compete with each other in words; but when spirits give up the purest gold of their store, that has shone far down the road of their earthly journey, cheering tired hearts and guiding mortal feet, our words shall barely interpret.

Love, coming long ago over flowers in Spain, found Morano; words did not tell the story, words cannot tell it; as a lake reflects a cloud in the blue of heaven, so Rodriguez understood and felt and knew this memory out of the days of Morano's youth. "And so, master," said Morano, "I sinned, and would indeed repent, and yet even now at this last dread hour I cannot abjure that day; and this is indeed Hell, as the good father said."

Rodriguez tried to comfort Morano with such knowledge as he had of astronomy, if knowledge it could be called. Indeed, if he had known anything he would have perplexed Morano more, and his little pieces of ignorance were well adapted for comfort. But Morano had given up hope, having long been taught to expect this very fire: his spirit was no wiser than it had been on Earth, it was merely freed of the imperfections of the five senses and so had observation and expression beyond those of any artist the world has known. This was the natural result of being freed of the body; but he was not suddenly wiser; and so, as he moved towards this boundless flame, he expected every moment to see Satan charge out to meet him: and having no hope for the future he turned to the past and fondled the memory of that one spring day. His was a backsliding, unrepentant spirit.

As that monstrous sea of flame grew ruthlessly larger Rodriguez felt no fear, for spirits have no fear of material things: but Morano feared. He feared as spirits fear spiritual things; he thought he neared the home of vast spirits of evil and that the arena of conflict was eternity. He feared with a fear too great to be borne by bodies. Perhaps the fat body that slept on a chair on earth was troubled in dreams by some echo of that fear that gripped the spirit so sorely. And it may be from such far fears that all our nightmares come.

When they had travelled nearly ten minutes from Earth and were about to pass into the midst of the flame, that magician who controlled their journey halted them suddenly in Space, among the upper mountain-peaks of the Sun. There they hovered as the clouds hover that leave their companions and drift among crags of the Alps: below them those awful mountains heaved and thundered. All Atlas, and Teneriffe, and lonely Kenia might have lain amongst them unnoticed. As often as the earthquake rocked their bases it loosened from near their summits wild avalanches of gold that swept down their flaming slopes with unthinkable tumult. As they watched, new mountains rode past them, crowned with their frightful flames; for, whether man knew it or not, the Sun was rotating, but the force of its gravity that swung the planets had no grip upon spirits, who were held by the power of that tremendous spell that the Professor had learned one midnight at Saragossa from one of that dread line who have their secrets from a source that we do not know in a distant age.

There is always something tremendous in the form of great mountains; but these swept by, not only huger than anything Earth knows, but troubled by horrible commotions, as though overtaken in flight by some ceaseless calamity.

Rodriguez and Morano, as they looked at them, forgetting the gardens of Earth, forgetting Spring and Summer and the sweet beneficence of sunshine, felt that the purpose of Creation was evil! So shocking a thought may well astound us here, where green hills slope to lawns or peer at a peaceful sea; but there among the flames of those dreadful peaks the Sun seemed not the giver of joy and colour and life, but only a catastrophe huger than everlasting war, a centre of hideous violence and ruin and anger and terror. There came by mountains of copper burning everlasting, hurling up to unthinkable heights their mass of emerald flame. And mountains of iron raged by and mountains of salt, quaking and thundering and clothed with their colours, the iron always scarlet and the salt blue. And sometimes there came by pinnacles a thousand miles high that from base to summit were fire, mountains of pure flame that had no other substance. And these explosive mountains, born of thunder and earthquake, hurling down avalanches the size of our continents, and drawing upward out of the deeps of the Sun new material for splendour and horror, this roaring waste, this extravagant destruction, were necessary for every tint that our butterflies wear on their wings. Without those flaming ranges of mountains of iron they would have no red to show; even the poppy could have no red for her petals: without the flames that were blasting the mountains of salt there could be no answering blue in any wing, or one blue flower for all the bees of Earth: without the nightmare light of those frightful canyons of copper that awed the two spirits watching their ceaseless ruin, the very leaves of the woods we love would be without their green with which to welcome Spring; for from the flames of the various metals and wonders that for ever blaze in the Sun, our sunshine gets all its colours that it conveys to us almost unseen, and thence the wise little insects and patient flowers softly draw the gay tints that they glory in; there is nowhere else to get them.

And yet to Rodriguez and Morano all that they saw seemed wholly and hideously evil.

How long they may have watched there they tried to guess afterwards, but as they looked on those ter-rific scenes they had no way to separate days from minutes: nothing about them seemed to escape de-struction, and time itself seemed no calmer than were those shuddering mountains.

Then the thundering ranges passed; and afterwards there came a gleaming mountain, one huge and lonely peak, seemingly all of gold. Had our whole world been set beside it and shaped as it was shaped, that golden mountain would yet have towered above it: it would have taken our moon as well to reach that flashing peak. It rode on toward them in its golden majesty, higher than all the flames, save now and then when some wild gas seemed to flee from the dread earth-quakes of the Sun, and was overtaken in the height by fire, even above that mountain.

As that mass of gold that was higher than all the world drew near to Rodriguez and Morano they felt

its unearthly menace; and though it could not overcome their spirits they knew there was a hideous terror about it. It was in its awful scale that its terror
lurked for any creature of our planet. Though they
could not quake or tremble they felt that terror. The
mountain dwarfed Earth.

Man knows his littleness, his own mountains remind him; many countries are small, and some na-
tions: but the dreams of Man make up for our faults
and failings, for the brevity of our lives, for the nar-
rowness of our scope; they leap over boundaries and
are away and away. But this great mountain belittled
the world and all: who gazed on it knew all his dreams
to be puny. Before this mountain Man seemed a trivial thing, and Earth, and all the dreams Man had of
himself and his home.

The golden mass drew opposite those two watchers
and seemed to challenge with its towering head the
pettiness of the tiny world they knew. And then the
whole gleaming mountain gave one shudder and fell
into the awful plains of the Sun. Straight down before
Rodriguez and Morano it slipped roaring, till the gold-
en peak was gone, and the molten plain closed over it;
and only ripples remained, the size of Europe, as when
a tumbling river strikes the rocks of its bed and on its
surface heaving circles widen and disappear. And then,
as though this horror left nothing more to be shown,
they felt the Professor beckon to them from Earth.

Over the plains of the Sun a storm was sweeping
in gusts of howling flame as they felt the Professor's

spell drawing them home. For the magnitude of that storm there are no words in use among us; its velocity, if expressed in figures, would have no meaning; its heat was immeasurable. Suffice it to say that if such a tempest could have swept over Earth for a second, both the poles would have boiled. The travellers left it galloping over that plain, rippled from underneath by the restless earthquake and whipped into flaming foam by the force of the storm. The Sun already was receding from them, already growing smaller. Soon the storm seemed but a cloud of light sweeping over the empty plain, like a murderous mourner rushing swiftly away from the grave of that mighty mountain.

And now the Professor's spell gripped them in earnest: rapidly the Sun grew smaller. As swiftly as he had sent them upon that journey he was now drawing them home. They overtook thunders that they had heard already, and passed them, and came again to the silent spaces which the thunders of the Sun are unable to cross, so that even Mercury is undisturbed by them.

I have said that spirits neither fade nor weary. But a great sadness was on them; they felt as men feel who come whole away from periods of peril. They had seen cataclysms too vast for our imagination, and a mournfulness and a satiety were upon them. They could have gazed at one flower for days and needed no other experience, as a wounded man may be happy staring at the flame of a candle.

Crossing the paths of Mercury and Venus, they saw that these planets had not appreciably moved, and Rodriguez, who knew that planets wander in the night, guessed thereby that they had not been absent from Earth for many hours.

They rejoiced to see the Sun diminishing steadily. Only for a moment as they started their journey had they seen that solar storm rushing over the plains of the Sun; but now it appeared to hang halted in its mid anger, as though blasting one region eternally.

Moving on with the pace of light, they saw Earth, soon after crossing the path of Venus, beginning to grow larger than a star. Never had home appeared more welcome to wanderers, who see their house far off, returning home.

And as Earth grew larger, and they began to see forms that seemed like seas and mountains, they looked for their own country, but could not find it: for, travelling straight from the Sun, they approached that part of the world that was then turned towards it, and were heading straight for China, while Spain lay still in darkness.

But when they came near Earth and its mountains were clear, then the Professor drew them across the world, into the darkness and over Spain; so that those two spirits ended their marvellous journey much as the snipe ends his, a drop out of heaven and a swoop low over marshes. So they came home, while Earth seemed calling to them with all her voices; with memories, sights and scents, and little sounds; calling anxiously, as though they had been too long away and must be home soon. They heard a cock crow on the edge of the night; they heard more little sounds than words can say; only the organ can hint at them. It was Earth calling. For, talk as we may of our dreams that transcend this sphere, or our hopes that build beyond it, Mother Earth has yet a mighty hold upon us; and her myriad sounds were blending in one cry now, knowing that it was late and that these two children of hers were nearly lost. For our spirits that sometimes cross the path of the angels, and on rare evenings hear a word of their talk, and have brief equality with the Powers of Light, have the duty also of moving fingers and toes, which freeze if our proud spirits forget their task for too long.

And just as Earth was despairing they reached the Professor's mountain and entered the room in which their bodies were.

Blue and cold and ugly looked the body of Morano, but for all its pallor there was beauty in the young face of Rodriguez.

The Professor stood before them as he had stood when their spirits left, with the table between him and the bodies, and the bowl on the table which held the green flame, now low and flickering desperately, which the Professor watched as it leaped and failed, with an air of anxiety that seemed to pinch his thin features.

With an impatience strange to him he waved a swift hand towards each of the two bodies where they sat stiff, illumined by the last of the green light; and at those rapid gestures the travellers returned to their habitations.

They seemed to be just awakening out of deep sleep. Again they saw the Professor standing before them. But they saw him only with blinking eyes, they saw him only as eyes can see, guessing at his mind from the lines of his face, at his thoughts from the movements of his hands, guessing as men guess, blindly: only a moment before they had known him utterly. Now they were dazed and forgetting: slow blood began to creep again to their toes and to come again to its place under fingernails: it came with intense pain: they forgot their spirits. Then all the woes of Earth crowded their minds at once, so that they wished to weep, as infants weep.

The Professor gave this mood time to change, as change it presently did. For the warm blood came back and lit their cheeks, and a tingling succeeded the pain in their fingers and toes, and a mild warmth succeeded the tingling: their thoughts came back to the things of every day, to mundane things and the affairs of the body. Therein they rejoiced, and Morano no less than Rodriguez; though it was a coarse and common body that Morano's spirit inhabited. And when the Professor saw that the first sorrow of Earth, which all spirits feel when they land here, had passed away, and that they were feeling again the joy of mundane things, only then did he speak.

"Senor," he said, "beyond the path of Mars run many worlds that I would have you know. The greatest of these is Jupiter, towards whom all that follow my most sacred art show reverent affection. The smallest are those that sometimes strike our world, flaming all green upon November nights, and are even as small as apples." He spoke of our world with a certain air and a pride, as though, through virtue of his transcendent art, the world were only his. "The world that we name Argola," he said, "is far smaller than Spain and, being invisible from Earth, is only known to the few who have spoken to spirits whose wanderings have surpassed the path of Mars. Nearly half of Argola you shall find covered with forests, which though very dense are no deeper than moss, and the elephants in them are not larger than beetles. You shall see many wonders of smallness in this world of Argola, which I desire in especial to show you, since it is the orb with which we who study the Art are most familiar, of all the worlds that the vulgar have not known. It is indeed the prize of our traffic in those things that far transcend the laws that have forbidden them."

And as he said this the green flame in the bowl before him died, and he moved towards his cupboard of wonder. Rodriguez hastily thanked the Professor for his great courtesy in laying bare before him secrets that the centuries hid, and then he referred to his own great unworthiness, to the lateness of the hour, to the fatigue of the Professor, and to the importance to Learning of adequate rest to refresh his illustrious mind. And all that he said the Professor parried with bows, and drew enchantments from his cupboard of wonder to replenish the bowl on the table. And Rodriguez saw that he was in the clutch of a collector, one who having devoted all his days to a hobby will exhibit his treasures to the uttermost, and that the stars that magic knows were no less to the Professor than all the whatnots that a man collects and insists on showing to whomsoever enters his house. He feared some terrible journey, perhaps some bare escape; for though no material thing can quite encompass a spirit, he knew not what wanderers he might not meet in lonely spaces beyond the path of Mars. So when his last polite remonstrance failed, being turned aside with a pleasant phrase and a smile from the grim lips, and looking at Morano he saw that he shared his fears, then he determined to show whatever resistance were needed to keep himself and Morano in this old world that we know, or that youth at least believes that it knows.

He watched the Professor return with his packets of wonder; dust from a fallen star, phials of tears of lost lovers, poison and gold out of elf-land, and all manner of things. But the moment that he put them into the bowl Rodriguez' hand flew to his sword- hilt. He heaved up his elbow, but no sword came forth, for it lay magnetised to its scabbard by the grip of a current of magic. When Rodriguez saw this he knew not what to do.

The Professor went on pouring into the bowl. He added an odour distilled out of dream-roses, three drops from the gall-bladder of a fabulous beast, and a little dust that had been man. More too he added, so that my reader might wonder were I to tell him all; yet it is not so easy to free our spirits from the gross grip of our bodies. Wonder not then, my reader, if the Professor exerted strange powers. And all the while Morano was picking at a nail that fastened on the handle to his frying-pan.

And just as the last few mysteries were shaken into the bowl,—and there were two among them of which even Asia is ignorant,—just as the dews were blended with the powers in a grey-green sinister harmony, Morano untwisted his nail and got the handle loose.

The Professor kindled the mixture in the bowl; again green flame arose, again that voice of his began to call to their spirits, and its beauty and the power of its spell were as of some fallen angel. The spirit of Rodriguez was nearly passing helplessly forth again on some frightful journey, when Morano losed his scabbard and sword from its girdle and tied the handle of his frying-pan across it a little below the hilt with a piece of string. Across the table the Professor intoned his spell, across a narrow table, but it seemed to come from the far side of the twilight, a twilight red and golden in long layers, of an evening wonderfully long ago. It seemed to take its music out of the lights that it flowed through and to call Rodriguez from immediately far away, with a call which it were sacrilege to refuse, and anguish even, and hard toil such as there was no strength to do. And then Morano held up the sword in its scabbard with the handle of the frying-pan tied across. Rodriguez, disturbed by a stammer in the spell, looked up and saw the Professor staring at the sword where Morano held it up before his face in the green light of the flame from the bowl. He did not seem like a fallen angel now. His spell had stopped. He seemed like a professor who had forgotten the theme of his lecture, while the class waits. For Morano was holding up the sign of the cross.

"You have betrayed me!" shouted the Slave of Orion: the green flame died, and he strode out of the room, his purple cloak floating behind him.

"Master," Morano said, "it was always good against magic."

The sword was loose in the scabbard as Rodriguez took it back; there was no longer a current of magic gripping the steel.

A little uneasily Rodriguez thanked Morano: he was not sure if Morano had behaved as a guest's servant should. But when he thought of the Professor's terrible spells, which had driven them to the awful crags of the sun, and might send them who knows where to hob-nob with who knows what, his second thoughts perceived that Morano was right to cut short those arts that the Slave of Orion loved, even by so extreme a step: and he praised Morano as his ready shrewdness deserved.

"We were very nearly too late back from that outing, master," remarked Morano.

"How know you that?" said Rodriguez.

"This old body knew," said Morano. "Those heart-thumpings, this warmness, and all the things that make a fat body comfortable, they were stopping, master, they were spoiling, they were getting cold and strange: I go no more errands for that senor."

A certain diffidence about criticising his host even now; and a very practical vein that ran through his nature, now showing itself in anxiety for a bed at so late an hour; led Rodriguez to change the subject. He wanted that aged butler, yet dare not ring the bell; for he feared lest with all the bells there might be in use that frightful practice that he had met by the outer door, a chain connected with some hideous hook that gave anguish to something in the basement whenever one touched the handle, so that the menials of that grim Professor were shrilly summoned by screams. And therefore Rodriguez sought counsel of Morano, who straightway volunteered to find the butler's quarters, by a certain sense that he had of the fitness of things: and forth he went, but would not leave the room without the scabbard and the handle of the frying-pan lashed to it, which he bore high before him in both his hands as though he were leading some austere procession. And even so he returned with that aged man the butler, who led them down dim corridors of stone; but, though he showed the way, Morano would go in front, still holding up that scabbard and handle before him, while Rodriguez held the bare sword. And so they came to a room lit by the flare of one candle, which their guide told them the Professor had prepared for his guest. In the vastness of it was a great bed. Shadows and a whir as of wings passed out of the door as they entered. "Bats," said the ancient guide. But Morano believed he had routed powers of evil with the handle of his frying-pan and his master's scabbard. Who could say what they were in such a house, where bats and evil spirits sheltered perennially from the brooms of the just? Then that ancient man with the lips of some woodland thing departed, and Rodriguez went to the great bed. On a pile of straw that had been cast into the room Morano lay down across the door, setting the scabbard upright in a rat-hole near his head, while Rodriguez lay down with the bare sword in his hand. There was only one door in the room, and this Morano guarded. Windows there were, but they were shuttered with raw oak of enormous thickness. He had already enquired with his sword behind the velvet curtains. He felt secure in the bulk of Morano across the only door, at least from creatures of this world: and Morano feared no longer either spirit or spell, believing that he had vanquished the Professor with his symbol, and all such allies as he may have had here or elsewhere. But not thus easily do we overcome the powers of evil.

A step was heard such as man walks with at the close of his later years, coming along the corridor of stone; and they knew it for the Professor's butler returning. The latch of the door trembled and lifted, and the great oak door bumped slowly against Morano, who arose grumbling, and the old man appeared.

"The Professor," he said, while Morano watched him grudgingly, "returns with all his household to Saragossa at once, to resume those studies for which his name resounds, a certain conjunction of the stars having come favourably."

Even Morano doubted that so suddenly the courses of the stars, which he deemed to be gradual, should have altered from antagonism towards the Professor's art into a favourable aspect. Rodriguez sleepily acknowledged the news and settled himself to sleep, still sword in hand, when the servitor repeated with as much emphasis as his aged voice could utter, "With all his household, senor."

"Yes," muttered Rodriguez. "Farewell."

And repeating again, "He takes his household with him," the old man shuffled back from the room and hesitatingly closed the door. Before the sound of his slow footsteps had failed to reach the room Morano was asleep under his cross. Rodriguez still watched for a while the shadows leaping and shuddering away from the candle, riding over the ceiling, striding hugely along the walls, towards him and from him, as draughts swayed the ruddy flame; then, gripping his sword still firmer in his hand, as though that could avail against magic, he fell into the sleep of tired men.

No sound disturbed Rodriguez or Morano till both awoke in late morning upon the rocks of the mountain. The sun had climbed over the crags and now shone on their faces. Rodriguez was still lying with his sword gripped in his hand, but the cross had fallen by Morano and now lay on the rocks beside him with the handle of the frying-pan still tied in its place by string. A young, wild, woodland squirrel gambolled near, though there were no woods for it anywhere within sight: it leaped and played as though rejoicing in youth, with such merriment as though youth had but come to it newly or been lost and restored again.

All over the mountain they looked but there was no house, nor any sign of dwelling of man or spirit.

The Fifth Chronicle

HOW HE RODE IN THE TWILIGHT
AND SAW SERAFINA

Rodriguez, who loved philosophy, turned his mind at once to the journey that lay before him, deciding which was the north; for he knew that it was by the north that he must leave Spain, which he still desired to leave since there were no wars in that country.

Morano knew not clearly what philosophy was, yet he wasted no thoughts upon the night that was gone; and, fitting up his frying- pan immediately, he brought out what was left of his bacon and began to look for material to make a fire. The bacon lay waiting in the frying-pan for some while before this material was gathered, for nothing grew on the mountain but a heath; and of that there were few bushes, scattered here and there.

Rodriguez, far from ruminating upon the events of the previous night, realised as he watched these preparations that he was enormously hungry. And when Morano had kindled a fire and the smell of cooking arose, he who had held the chair of magic at Saragossa was banished from both their minds, although upon this very spot they had spent so strange a night; but where bacon is, and there be hungry men, the things of yesterday are often forgotten.

"Morano," said Rodriguez, "we must walk far to-day."

"Indeed, master," said Morano, "we must push on to these wars; for you have no castle, master, no lands, no fortune ..."

"Come," said Rodriguez.

Morano slung his frying-pan behind him: they had eaten up the last of his bacon: he stood up, and they were ready for the journey. The smoke from their meagre fire went thinly into the air, the small grey clouds of it went slowly up: nothing beside remained to bid them farewell, or for them to thank for their strange night's hospitality. They climbed till they reached the rugged crest of the mountain; thence they saw a wide plain and the morning: the day was waiting for them.

The northern slope of the mountain was wholly different from that black congregation of angry rocks through which they had climbed by night to the House of Wonder.

The slope that now lay before them was smooth and grassy, flowing before them far, a gentle slope that was soon to lend speed to Rodriguez' feet, adding nimbleness even to youth. Soon, too, it was to lift onward the dull weight of Morano as he followed his master towards unknown wars, youth going before him like a spirit and the good slope helping behind. But before they gave themselves to that waiting journey they stood a moment and looked at the shining plain that lay before them like an open page, on which was the whole chronicle of that day's wayfaring. There was the road they should travel by, there were the streams it crossed and narrow woods they might rest in, and dim on the farthest edge was the place they must spend that night. It was all, as it were written, upon the plain they watched, but in a writing not intended for them, and, clear although it be, never to be interpreted by one of our race. Thus they saw clear, from a height, the road they would go by, but not one of all the events to which it would lead them.

"Master," said Morano, "shall we have more adventures to-day?"

"I trust so," said Rodriguez. "We have far to go, and it will be dull journeying without them."

Morano turned his eyes from his master's face and looked back to the plain. "There, master," he said, "where our road runs through a wood, will our adventure be there, think you? Or there, perhaps," and he waved his hand widely farther.

"No," said Rodriguez, "we pass that in bright daylight."

"Is that not good for adventure?" said Morano.

"The romances teach," said Rodriguez, "that twilight or night are better. The shade of deep woods is favourable, but there are no such woods on this plain. When we come to evening we shall doubtless meet some adventure, far over there." And he pointed to the grey rim of the plain where it started climbing towards hills.

"These are good days," said Morano. He forgot how short a time ago he had said regretfully that these days were not as the old days. But our race, speaking generally, is rarely satisfied with the present, and Morano's cheerfulness had not come from his having risen suddenly superior to this everyday trouble of ours; it came from his having shifted his gaze to the future. Two things are highly tolerable to us, and even alluring, the past and the future. It was only with the present that Morano was ever dissatisfied.

When Morano said that the days were good Rodriguez set out to find them, or at least that one that for some while now lay waiting for them on the plain. He strode down the slope at once and, endowing nature with his own impatience, he felt that he heard the morning call to him wistfully. Morano followed.

For an hour these refugees escaping from peace went down the slope; and in that hour they did five swift miles, miles that seemed to run by them as they walked, and so they came lightly to the level plain. And in the next hour they did four miles more. Words were few, either because Morano brooded mainly upon one thought, the theme of which was his lack of bacon, or because he kept his breath to follow his master who, with youth and the morning, was coming out of the hills at a pace not tuned to Morano's forty years or so. And at the end of these nine miles Morano perceived a house, a little way from the road, on the left, upon rising ground. A mile or so ahead they saw the narrow wood that they had viewed in the morning from the mountain running across the plain. They saw now by the lie of the ground that it probably followed a stream, a pleasant place in which to take the rest demanded by Spain at noon. It was just an hour to noon; so Rodriguez, keeping the road, told Morano to join him where it entered the wood when he had acquired his bacon. And then as they parted a thought occurred to Rodriguez, which was that bacon cost money. It was purely an afterthought, an accidental fancy, such as inspirations are, for he had never had to buy bacon. So he gave Morano a fifth part of his money, a large gold coin the size of one of our five-shilling pieces, engraved of course upon one side with the glories and honours of that golden period of Spain, and upon the other with the head of the lord the King. It was only by chance he had brought any at all; he was not what our newspapers will call, if they ever care to notice him, a level-headed business man. At the sight of the gold piece Morano bowed, for he felt this gift of gold to be an occasion; but he trusted more for the purchase of the bacon to some few small silver coins of his own that he kept among lumps of lard and pieces of string.

And so they parted for a while, Rodriguez looking for some great shadowy oak with moss under it near a stream, Morano in quest of bacon.

When Rodriguez entered the wood he found his oak, but it was not such an oak as he cared to rest beneath during the heat of the day, nor would you have done so, my reader, even though you have been to the wars and seen many a pretty mess; for four of la Garda were by it and were arranging to hang a man from the best of the branches.

"La Garda again," said Rodriguez nearly aloud.

His eye drooped, his look was listless, he gazed at other things; while a glance that you had not noticed, flashed slantingly at la Garda, satisfied Rodriguez that all four were strangers: then he walked straight towards them merrily. The man they proposed to hang was a stranger too. He appeared at first to be as stout as Morano, and he was nearly half a foot taller, but his stoutness turned out to be sheer muscle. The broad man was clothed in old brown leather and had blue eyes.

Now there was something about the poise of Rodriguez' young head which gave him an air not unlike that which the King himself sometimes wore when he went courting. It suited his noble sword and his merry plume. When la Garda saw him they were all politeness at once, and invited him to see the hanging, for which Rodriguez thanked them with amplest courtesy.

"It is not a bull-fight," said the chief of la Garda almost apologetically. But Rodriguez waved aside his deprecations and declared himself charmed at the prospect of a hanging.

Bear with me, reader, while I champion a bad cause and seek to palliate what is inexcusable. As we travel about the world on our way through life we meet and pass here and there, in peace or in war, other men, fellow-travellers: and sometimes there is no more than time for a glance, eye to eye. And in that glance you see the sort of man: and chiefly there are two sorts. The one sort always brooding, always planning; mean, silent men, collecting properties and money; keeping the law on their side, keeping everything on their side; except women and heaven, and the late, leisurely judgment of simple people: and the others merry folk, whose eyes twinkle, whose money flies, who will sooner laugh than plan, who seem to inherit rightfully the happiness that the others plot for, and fail to come by with all their schemes. In the man who was to provide the entertainment Rodriguez recognised the second kind.

Now even though the law had caught a saint that had strayed too far outside the boundary of Heaven, and desired to hang him, Rodriguez knew that it was his duty to help the law while help was needed, and to applaud after the thing was done. The law to Rodriguez was the most sacred thing man had made, if indeed it were not divine; but since the privilege that two days ago had afforded him of studying it more closely, it appeared to him the blindest, silliest thing with which he had had to do since the kittens were drowned that his cat Tabitharina had had at Arguento Harez.

It was in this deplorable state of mind that Rodriguez' glance fell on the merry eyes and the solemn

predicament of the man in the leather coat, standing pinioned under a long branch of the oak-tree:
and he determined from that moment to disappoint
la Garda and, I fear also, my reader, perhaps to disappoint you, of the hanging that they at least had
promised themselves.

"Think you," said Rodriguez, "that for so stout a
knave this branch of yours suffices?"

Now it was an excellent branch. But it was not so
much Rodriguez' words as the anxious way in which
he looked at the branch that aroused the anxieties of
la Garda: and soon they were looking about to find a
better tree; and when four men start doing this in a
wood time quickly passes. Meanwhile Morano drew
near, and Rodriguez went to meet him.

"Master," said Morano, all out of breath, "they had
no bacon. But I got these two bottles of wine. It is
strong wine, which is a rare deluder of the senses,
which will need to be deluded if we are to go hungry."

Rodriguez was about to cut short Morano's chatter
when he thought of a use for the wine, and was silent
a moment. And as he pondered Morano looked up
and saw la Garda and at the same time perceived the
situation, for he had as quick an eye for a bad business
as any man.

"No one with the horses," was his comment; for
they were tethered a little apart. But Rodriguez' mind
had already explored a surer method than the one that
Morano seemed to be contemplating. This method he
told Morano. And now, from little tugs that they were

giving to the doubled rope that hung over the branch of the oak- tree, it was clear enough that the men of the law were returning to their confidence in that very sufficient branch.

They looked up with questions ripe to drop from their lips when they saw Rodriguez returning with Morano. But before one of them spoke Morano flung to them from far off a little piece of his wisdom: for cast a truth into an occasion and it will always trouble the waters, usually stirring up contradiction, but always bringing something to the surface.

"Senores," he said, "no man can enjoy a hanging with a dry throat."

Thus he turned their attention a while from the business in hand, changing their thoughts from the stout neck of the prisoner to their own throats, wondering were they dry; and you do not wonder long about this in the south without finding that what you feared is true. And then he let them see the two great bottles, all full of wine, for the invention of the false bottom that gives to our champagne-bottles the place they rightly hold among famous deceptions had not as yet been discovered.

"It is true," said la Garda. And Rodriguez made Morano put one of the bottles away in a piece of a sack that he carried: and when la Garda saw one of the two bottles disappear it somehow decided them to have the other, though how this came to be so there is no saying; and thus the hanging was postponed again.

Now the drink was a yellow wine, sweet and heavy and stronger than our port; only our whisky could out-triumph it, but there in the warm south it answered its purpose. Rodriguez beckoned Morano up and offered the bottle to one of la Garda; but scarcely had he put it to his lips when Rodriguez bade him stop, saying that he had had his share. And he did the same with the next man.

Now there be few things indeed which la Garda resent more than meagre hospitality in the matter of drink, and with all their wits striving to cope with this vicious defect in Rodriguez, as they rightly or wrongly regarded it, how should they have any to spare for obvious precautions? As the third man drank, Rodriguez turned to speak to Morano; and the representative of the law took such advantage of an opportunity that he feared to be fleeting, that when Rodriguez turned round again the bottle was just half empty. Rodriguez had timed it very nicely.

Next Rodriguez put the bottle to his lips and held it there a little time, while the fourth man of the law, who was guarding the prisoner, watched Rodriguez wistfully, and afterwards Morano, who took the bottle next. Yet neither Rodriguez nor Morano drank.

"You can finish the bottle," said Rodriguez to this anxious watcher, who came forward eagerly though full of doubts, which changed to warm feelings of exuberant gratitude when he found how much remained. Thus he obtained not much less than two tumblerfuls of wine that, as I have said, was stronger than port;

and noon was nearing and it was spring in Spain. And then he returned to guard his prisoner under the oak-tree and lay down there on the moss, remembering that it was his duty to keep awake. And afterwards with one hand he took hold of a rope that bound the prisoner's ankles, so that he might still guard his prisoner even though he should fall asleep.

Now two of the men had had little more than the full of a sherry glass each. To these Morano made signs that there was another bottle, and, coming round behind his master, he covertly uncorked it and gave them their heart's desire; and a little was left over for the man who drank third on the first occasion. And presently the spirits of all four of la Garda grew haughty and forgot their humble bodies, and would fain have gone forth to dwell with the sons of light, while their bodies lay on the moss and the sun grew warmer and warmer, shining dappled in amongst the small green leaves. All seemed still but for the winged insects flashing through shafts of the sunlight out of the gloom of the trees and disappearing again like infinitesimal meteors. But our concern is with the thoughts of man, of which deeds are but the shadows: wherever these are active it is wrong to say all is still; for whether they cast their shadows, which are actions, or whether they remain a force not visibly stirring matter, they are the source of the tales we write and the lives we lead; it is they that gave History her material and they that bade her work it up into books.

And thoughts were very active about that oak-tree. For while the thoughts of la Garda arose like dawn, and disappeared into mists, their prisoner was silently living through the sunny days of his life, which are at no time quite lost to us, and which flash vivid and bright and near when memory touches them, herself awakened by the nearness of death. He lived again days far from the day that had brought him where he stood. He drew from those days (that is to say) that delight, that essence of hours, that something which we call life. The sun, the wind, the rough sand, the splash of the sea, on the star-fish, and all the things that it feels during its span, are stored in something like its memory, and are what we call its life: it is the same with all of us. Life is feeling. The prisoner from the store of his memory was taking all he had. His head was lifted, he was gazing northwards, far further than his eyes could see, to shining spaces in great woods; and there his threatened being walked in youth, with steps such as spirits take, over immortal flowers, which were dim and faint but unfading because they lived on in memory. In memory he walked with some who were now far from his footsteps. And, seen through the gloaming of that perilous day, how bright did those far days appear! Did they not seem sunnier than they really were? No, reader; for all the radiance that glittered so late in his mind was drawn from those very days; it was their own brightness that was shining now: we are not done with the days that were as soon as their sunsets have faded, but a light remains from them and grows fairer and fairer, like an afterglow lingering among tremendous peaks above immeasurable slopes of snow.

The prisoner had scarcely noticed Rodriguez or his servant, any more than he noticed his captors; for there come an intensity to those who walk near death that makes them a little alien from other men, life flaring up in them at the last into so grand a flame that the lives of the others seem a little cold and dim where they dwell remote from that sunset that we call mortality. So he looked silently at the days that were as they came dancing back again to him from where they had long lain lost in chasms of time, to which they had slipped over dark edges of years. Smiling they came, but all wistfully anxious, as though their errand were paramount and their span short: he saw them cluster about him, running now, bringing their tiny gifts, and scarcely heard the heavy sigh of his guard as Rodriguez gagged him and Morano tied him up.

Had Rodriguez now released the prisoner they could have been three to three, in the event of things going wrong with the sleep of la Garda; but, since in the same time they could gag and bind another, the odds would be the same at two to two, and Rodriguez preferred this to the slight uncertainties that would be connected with the entry of another partner. They accordingly gagged the next man and bound his wrists and ankles. And that Spanish wine held good with the other two and bound them far down among the deeps of dreams: and so it should, for it was of a vine that grew in the vales of Spain and had ripened in one of the years of the golden age.

They bound one as easily as they had bound the other two; and the last Rodriguez watched while Morano cut the ropes off the prisoner, for he had run out of bits of twine and all other improvisations. With these ropes he ran back to his master, and they tied up the last prisoner but did not gag him.

"Shall we gag him, master, like the rest?" said Morano.

"No," said Rodriguez. "He has nothing to say."

And though this remark turned out to be strictly untrue, it well enough answered its purpose.

And then they saw standing before them the man they had freed. And he bowed to Rodriguez like one that had never bowed before. I do not mean that he bowed with awkwardness, like imitative men unused to politeness, but he bowed as the oak bows to the woodman; he stood straight, looking Rodriguez in the eyes, then he bowed as though he had let his spirit break, which allowed him to bow to never a man before. Thus, if my pen has been able dimly to tell of it, thus bowed the man in the old leathern jacket. And Rodriguez bowed to him in answer with the elegance that they that had dwelt at Arguento Harez had slowly drawn from the ages.

"Senor, your name," said the stranger.

"Lord of Arguento Harez," said Rodriguez.

"Senor," he said, "being a busy man, I have seldom time to pray. And the blessed Saints, being more busy than I, I think seldom hear my prayers: yet your name shall go up to them. I will often tell it them quietly in the forest, and not on their holy days when bells are ringing and loud prayers fill Heaven. It may be ..."

"Senor," Rodriguez said, "I profoundly thank you."

Even in these days, when bullets are often thicker than prayers, we are not quite thankless for the prayers of others: in those days they were what "closing quotations" are on the Stock Exchange, ink in Fleet Street, machinery in the Midlands; common but valued; and Rodriguez' thanks were sincere.

And now that the curses of the ungagged one of la Garda were growing monotonous, Rodriguez turned to Morano.

"Ungag the rest," he said, "and let them talk to each other."

"Master," Morano muttered, feeling that there was enough noise already for a small wood, but he went and did as he was ordered. And Rodriguez was justified of his humane decision, for the pent thoughts of all three found expression together and, all four now talking at once, mitigated any bitterness there may have been in those solitary curses. And now Rodriguez could talk undisturbed.

"Whither?" said the stranger.

"To the wars," said Rodriguez, "if wars there be."

"Aye," said the stranger, "there be always wars somewhere. By which road go you?"

"North," said Rodriguez, and he pointed. The stranger turned his eyes to the way Rodriguez pointed.

"That brings you to the forest," he said, "unless you go far around, as many do."

"What forest?" said Rodriguez.

"The great forest named Shadow Valley," said the stranger.

"How far?" said Rodriguez.

"Forty miles," said the stranger.

Rodriguez looked at la Garda and then at their horses, and thought. He must be far from la Garda by nightfall.

"It is not easy to pass through Shadow Valley," said the stranger.

"Is it not?" said Rodriguez.

"Have you a gold great piece?" the stranger said.

Rodriguez held out one of his remaining four: the stranger took it. And then he began to rub it on a stone, and continued to rub while Rodriguez watched in silence, until the image of the lord the King was gone and the face of the coin was scratchy and shiny and flat. And then he produced from a pocket or pouch in his jacket a graving tool with a round wooden handle, which he took in the palm of his hand, and the edge of the steel came out between his forefinger and thumb: and with this he cut at the coin. And Morano rejoined them from his merciful mission and stood and wondered at the cutting. And while he cut they talked.

They did not ask him how he came to be chosen for hanging, because in every country there are about a hundred individualists, varying to perhaps half a hundred in poor ages. They go their hundred ways, or their half-dozen ways; and there is a hundred and first way, or a seventh way, which is the way that is cut for the rest: and if some of the rest catch one of the hundred, or one of the six, they naturally hang him, if they have a rope, and if hanging is the custom of the country, for different countries use different methods. And you saw by this man's eyes that he was one of the hundred. Rodriguez therefore only sought to know how he came to be caught.

"La Garda found you, senor?" he said.

"As you see," said the stranger. "I came too far from my home."

"You were travelling?" said Rodriguez.

"Shopping," he said.

At this word Morano's interest awakened wide. "Senor," he said, "what is the right price for a bottle of this wine that la Garda drink?"

"I know not," said the man in the brown jacket; "they give me these things."

"Where is your home, senor?" Rodriguez asked.

"It is Shadow Valley," he said.

One never saw Rodriguez fail to understand any-thing: if he could not clear a situation up he did not struggle with it. Morano rubbed his chin: he had heard of Shadow Valley only dimly, for all the travellers he had known out of the north had gone round it. Rodriguez and Morano bent their heads and watched a design that was growing out of the gold. And as the design grew under the hand of the strange worker he began to talk of the horses. He spoke as though his plans had been clearly established by edict, and as though no others could be.

"When I have gone with two horses," he said, "ride hard with the other two till you reach the village named Lowlight, and take them to the forge of Fernandez the smith, where one will shoe them who is not Fernandez."

And he waved his hand northwards. There was only one road. Then all his attention fell back again to his work on the gold coin; and when those blue eyes were turned away there seemed nothing left to question. And now Rodriguez saw the design was a crown, a plain gold circlet with oak leaves rising up from it. And this woodland emblem stood up out of the gold, for the worker had hollowed the coin away all around it, and was sloping it up to the edge. Little was said by the watchers in the wonder of seeing the work, for no craft is very far from the line beyond which is magic, and the man in the leather coat was clearly a craftsman: and he said nothing for he worked at a craft. And when the arboreal crown was finished, and its edges were straight and sharp, an hour had passed since he began near noon. Then he drilled a hole near the rim and, drawing a thin green ribbon from his pocket, he passed it through the hole and, rising, he suddenly hung it round Rodriguez' neck.

"Wear it thus," he said, "while you go through Shadow Valley."

As he said this he stepped back among the trees, and Rodriguez followed to thank him. Not finding him behind the tree where he thought to find him, he walked round several others, and Morano joined his search; but the stranger had vanished. When they returned again to the little clearing they heard sounds of movement in the wood, and a little way off where the four horses had grazed there were now only two, which were standing there with their heads up.

"We must ride, Morano," said Rodriguez.

"Ride, master?" said Morano dolefully.

"If we walk away," said Rodriguez, "they will walk after us."

"They" meant la Garda. It was unnecessary for him to tell Morano what I thus tell the reader, for in the wood it was hard to hear anyone else, while to think of anyone else was out of the question.

"What shall I do to them, master?" said Morano.

They were now standing close to their captives and this simple question calmed the four men's curses, all of a sudden, like shutting the door on a storm.

"Leave them," Rodriguez said. And la Garda's spirits rose and they cursed again.

"Ah. To die in the wood," said Morano. "No," said Rodriguez; and he walked towards the horses. And something in that "No" sounding almost contemptuous, Morano's feelings were hurt, and he blurted out to his master "But how can they get away to get their food?? It is good knots that I tie, master."

"Morano," Rodriguez said, "I remember ten ways in the books of romance whereby bound men untie themselves; and doubtless one or two more I have read and forgot; and there may be other ways in the books that I have not read, besides any way that there be of which no books tell. And in addition to these ways, one of them may draw a comrade's sword with his teeth and thus ..."

"Shall I pull out their teeth?" said Morano.

"Ride," said Rodriguez, for they were now come to the horses. And sorrowfully Morano looked at the horse that was to be his, as a man might look at a small, uncomfortable boat that is to carry him far upon a stormy day. And then Rodriguez helped him into the saddle.

"Can you stay there?" Rodriguez said. "We have far to go."

"Master," Morano answered, "these hands can hold till evening."

And then Rodriguez mounted, leaving Morano gripping the high front of the saddle with his large brown hands. But as soon as the horses started he got a grip with his heels as well, and later on with his knees. Rodriguez led the way on to the straggling road and was soon galloping northwards, while Morano's heels kept his horse up close to his master's. Morano rode as though trained in the same school that some while later taught Macaulay's equestrian, who rode with "loose rein and bloody spur." Yet the miles went swiftly by as they galloped on soft white dust, which lifted and settled, some of it, back on the lazy road, while some of it was breathed by Morano. The gold coin on the green silk ribbon flapped up and down as Rodriguez rode, till he stuffed it inside his clothing and remembered no more about it. Once they saw before them the man they had snatched from the noose: he was going hard and leading a loose horse. And then where the road bent round a low hill he galloped out of sight and they saw him no more. He had the loose horse to change on to as soon as the other was tired: they had no prospect of overtaking him. And so he passed out of their minds as their host had done who went away with his household to Saragossa.

At first Rodriguez' mandolin, that was always slung on his back, bumped up and down uncomfortably; but he eased it by altering the strap: small things like this bring contentment. And then he settled down to ride. But no contentment came near Morano nor did he look for it. On the first day of his wanderings he had worn his master's clothes, which has been an experience standing somewhat where toothache does, which is somewhere about half-way between discomfort and agony. On the second day he had climbed at the end of a weary journey over those sharp rocks whose shape was adapted so ill to his body. On the third day he was riding. He did not look for comfort. But he met discomfort with an easy resignation that almost defeated the intention of Satan who sends it, unless—as is very likely—it be from Heaven. And in spite of all discomforts he gaily followed Rodriguez. In a thousand days at the Inn of the Dragon and Knight no two were so different to Morano that one stood out from the other, or any from the rest. It was all as though one day were repeated again and again; and at some point in this monotonous repetition, like a milestone shaped as the rest on a perfectly featureless road, life would end and the meaningless repetition stop: and looking back on it there would only be one day to see, or, if he could not look back, it would be all gone for nothing. And then, into that one day that he was living on in the gloaming of that grim inn, Rodriguez had appeared, and Morano had known him for one of those wandering lights that sometimes make sudden day among the stars. He knew—no, he felt—that by following him, yesterday today and tomorrow would be three separate possessions in memory. Morano gladly gave up that one dull day he was living for the new strange days through which Rodriguez was sure to lead him. Gladly he left it: if this be not true how then has a man with a dream led thousands to follow his fancy, from the Crusades to whatever gay madness be the fashion when this is read? As they galloped the scent of the flowers rushed into Rodriguez' nostrils, while Morano mainly breathed the dust from the hooves of his master's horse. But the quest was favoured the more by the scent of the flowers inspiring its leader's fancies. So Morano gained even from this.

In the first hour they shortened by fifteen miles the length of their rambling quest. In the next hour they did five miles; and in the third hour ten.

After this they rode slowly. The sun was setting. Morano regarded the sunset with delight, for it seemed to promise jovially the end of his sufferings, which except for brief periods when they went on foot, to rest—as Rodriguez said—the horses, had been continuous and even increasing since they started. Rodriguez, perhaps a little weary too, drew from the sunset a more sombre feeling, as sensitive minds do: he responded to its farewell, he felt its beauty, and as little winds turned cool and the shine of blades of grass faded, making all the plain dimmer, he heard, or believed he heard, further off than he could see, sounds on the plain beyond ridges, in hollows, behind clumps of bushes; as though small creatures all unknown to his learning played instruments cut from reeds upon unmapped streams. In this hour, among these fancies, Rodriguez saw clear on a hill the white walls of the village of Lowlight. And now they began to notice that a great round moon was shining. The sunset grew dimmer and the moonlight stole in softly, as a cat might walk through great doors on her silent feet into a throne-room just as the king had gone: and they entered the village slowly in the perfect moment of twilight.

The round horizon was brimming with a pale but magical colour, welling up to the tips of trees and the battlements of white towers. Earth seemed a mysterious cup overfull of this pigment of wonder. Clouds wandering low, straying far from their azure fields, were dipped in it. The towers of Lowlight turned slowly rose in that light, and glowed together with the infinite gloaming, so that for this brief hour the things of man were wed with the things of eternity. It was into this wide, pale flame of aetherial rose that the moon came stealing like a magician on tip- toe, to enchant the tips of the trees, low clouds and the towers of Lowlight. A blue light from beyond our world touched the pink that is Earth's at evening: and what was strange and a matter for hushed voices, marvellous but yet of our earth, became at that touch unearthly. All in a moment it was, and Rodriguez gasped to see it. Even Morano's eyes grew round with the coming of wonder, or with some dim feeling that an unnoticed moment had made all things strange and new.

For some moments the spell of moonlight on sunlight hovered: the air was brimming and quivering with it: magic touched earth. For some moments, some thirty beats of a heron's wing, had the angels sung to men, had their songs gone earthward into that rosy glow, gliding past layers of faintly tinted cloud, like moths at dusk towards a briar-rose; in those few moments men would have known their language. Rodriguez reined in his horse in the heavy silence and waited. For what he waited he knew not: some unearthly answer perhaps to his questioning thoughts that had wandered far from earth, though no words came to him with which to ask their question and he did not know what question they would ask. He was all vibrating with the human longing: I know not what it is, but perhaps philosophers know.

He sat there waiting while a late bird sailed home-ward, sat while Morano wondered. And nothing spake from anywhere.

And now a dog began to notice the moon: now a child cried suddenly that had been dragged back from the street, where it had wandered at bedtime: an old dog rose from where it had lain in the sun and feebly yet confidently scratched at a door: a cat peered round a corner: a man spoke: Rodriguez knew there would be no answer now.

Rodriguez hit his horse, the tired animal went for-ward, and he and Morano rode slowly up the street.

Dona Serafina of the Valley of Dawnlight had left the heat of the room that looked on the fields, and into which the sun had all day been streaming, and had gone at sunset to sit in the balcony that looked along the street. Often she would do this at sunset; but she rather dreamed as she sat there than watched the street, for all that it had to show she knew with-out glancing. Evening after evening as soon as winter was over the neighbour would come from next door and stretch himself and yawn and sit on a chair by his doorway, and the neighbour from opposite would saunter across the way to him, and they would talk with eagerness of the sale of cattle, and sometimes, but more coldly, of the affairs of kings. She knew, but cared not to know, just when the two old men would begin their talk. She knew who owned every dog that stretched itself in the dust until chilly winds blew in the dusk and they rose up dissatisfied. She knew the affairs of that street like an old, old lesson taught drearily, and her thoughts went far away to vales of an imagination where they met with many another maiden fancy, and they all danced there together through the long twilight in Spring. And then her mother would come and warn her that the evening grew cold, and Serafina would turn from the mystery of evening into the house and the candle-light. This was so evening after evening all through spring and summer for two long years of her youth. And then, this evening, just as the two old neighbours began to discuss whether or not the subjugation of the entire world by Spain would be for its benefit, just as one of the dogs in the road was rising slowly to shake itself, neighbours and dogs all raised their heads to look, and there was Rodriguez riding down the street and Morano coming behind him. When Serafina saw this she brought her eyes back from dreams, for she dreamed not so deeply but that the cloak and plume of Rodriguez found some place upon the boundaries of her day-dream. When she saw the way he sat his horse and how he carried his head she let her eyes flash for a little moment along the street from her balcony. And if some critical reader ask how she did it I answer, "My good sir, I can't tell you, because I don't know," or "My dear lady, what a question to ask!" And where she learned to do it I cannot think, but nothing was easier. And then she smiled to think that she had done the very thing that her mother had warned her there was danger in doing.

"Serafina," her mother said in that moment at the large window, "the evening grows cold. It might be dangerous to stay there longer." And Serafina entered the house, as she had done at the coming of dusk on many an evening.

Rodriguez missed as much of that flash of her eyes, shot from below the darkness of her hair, as youth in its first glory and freedom misses. For at the point on the road called life at which Rodriguez was then, one is high on a crag above the promontories of watchmen, lower only than the peaks of the prophets, from which to see such things. Yet it did not need youth to notice Serafina. Beggars had blessed her for the poise of her head.

She turned that head a little as she went between the windows, till Rodriguez gazing up to her saw the fair shape of her neck: and almost in that moment the last of the daylight died. The windows shut; and Rodriguez rode on with Morano to find the forge that was kept by Fernandez the smith. And presently they came to the village forge, a cottage with huge, high roof whose beams were safe from sparks; and its fire was glowing redly into the moonlight through the wide door made for horses, although there seemed no work to be done, and a man with a swart moustache was piling more logs on. Over the door was burned on oak in ungainly great letters—

"FERNANDEZ"

"For whom do you seek, senor?" he said to Rodriguez, who had halted before him with his horse's nose inside the doorway sniffing.

"I look," he said, "for him who is not Fernandez."

"I am he," said the man by the fire.

Rodriguez questioned no further but dismounted, and bade Morano lead the horses in. And then he saw in the dark at the back of the forge the other two horses that he had seen in the wood. And they were shod as he had never seen horses shod before. For the front pair of shoes were joined by a chain riveted stoutly to each, and the hind pair also; and both horses were shod alike. The method was equally new to Morano. And now the man with the swart moustache picked up another bunch of horseshoes hanging in pairs on chains. And Rodriguez was not far out when he guessed that whenever la Garda overtook their horses they would find that Fernandez was far away making holiday, while he who shod them now would be gone upon other business. And all this work seemed to Rodriguez not to be his affair.

"Farewell," he said to the smith that was not Fernandez; and with a pat for his horse he left it, having obtained a promise of oats. And so Rodriguez and Morano went on foot again, Morano elated in spite of fatigue and pain, rejoicing to feel the earth once more, flat under the soles of his feet; Rodriguez a little humbled.

The Sixth Chronicle

HOW HE SANG TO HIS MANDOLIN AND WHAT CAME OF HIS SINGING

They walked back slowly in silence up the street down which they had ridden. Earth darkened, the moon grew brighter: and Rodriguez gazing at the pale golden disk began to wonder who dwelt in the lunar valleys; and what message, if folk were there, they had for our peoples; and in what language such message could ever be, and how it could fare across that limpid remoteness that wafted light on to the coasts of Earth and lapped in silence on the lunar shores. And as he wondered he thought of his mandolin.

"Morano," he said, "buy bacon."

Morano's eyes brightened: they were forty-five miles from the hills on which he had last tasted bacon. He selected his house with a glance, and then he was gone. And Rodriguez reflected too late that he had forgotten to tell Morano where he should find him, and this with night coming on in a strange village. Scarcely, Rodriguez reflected, he knew where he was going himself. Yet if old tunes lurking in its hollows, echoing though imperceptibly from long-faded evenings, gave the mandolin any knowledge of human affairs that other inanimate things cannot possess, the mandolin knew.

Let us in fancy call up the shade of Morano from that far generation. Let us ask him where Rodriguez is going. Those blue eyes, dim with the distance over which our fancy has called them, look in our eyes with wonder.

"I do not know," he says, "where Don Rodriguez is going. My master did not tell me."

Did he notice nothing as they rode by that balcony?

"Nothing," Morano answers, "except my master riding."

We may let Morano's shade drift hence again, for we shall discover nothing: nor is this an age to which to call back spirits.

Rodriguez strolled slowly on the deep dust of that street as though wondering all the while where he should go; and soon he and his mandolin were below that very balcony whereon he had seen the white neck of Serafina gleam with the last of the daylight. And now the spells of the moon charmed Earth with their full power.

The balcony was empty. How should it have been otherwise? And yet Rodriguez grieved. For between the vision that had drawn his footsteps and that bare balcony below shuttered windows was the difference between a haven, sought over leagues of sea, and sheer, uncharted cliff. It brought a wistfulness into the music he played, and a melancholy that was all new to Rodriguez, yet often and often before had that mandolin sent up through evening against unheeding Space that cry that man cannot utter; for the spirit of man needs a mandolin as a comrade to face the verdict of the chilly stars as he needs a bulldog for more mundane things.

Soon out of the depth of that stout old mandolin, in which so many human sorrows had spun tunes out of themselves, as the spiders spin misty grey webs, till it was all haunted with music, soon the old cry went up to the stars again, a thread of supplication spun of the matter which else were distilled in tears, beseeching it knew not what. And, but that Fate is deaf, all that man asks in music had been granted then.

What sorrows had Rodriguez known in his life that he made so sad a melody? I know not. It was the mandolin. When the mandolin was made it knew at once all the sorrows of man, and all the old unnamed longings that none defines. It knew them as the dog knows the alliance that its forefathers made with man. A mandolin weeps the tears that its master cannot shed, or utters the prayers that are deeper than its master's lips can draw, as a dog will fight for his master with teeth that are longer than man's. And if the moonlight streamed on untroubled, and though Fate was deaf, yet beauty of those fresh strains going starward from under his fingers touched at least the heart of Rodriguez and gilded his dreams and gave to his thoughts a mournful autumnal glory, until he sang all newly as he never had sung before, with limpid voice along the edge of tears, a love-song old as the woods of his father's valleys at whose edge he had heard it once drift through the evening. And as he played and sang with his young soul in the music he fancied (and why not, if they care aught for our souls in Heaven?) he fancied the angles putting their hands each one on a star and leaning out of Heaven through the constellations to listen.

"A vile song, senor, and a vile tune with it," said a voice quite close.

However much the words hurt his pride in his mandolin Rodriguez recognised in the voice the hidalgo's accent and knew that it was an equal that now approached him in the moonlight round a corner of the house with the balcony; and he knew that the request he courteously made would be as courteously granted.

"Senor," he said, "I pray you to permit me to lean my mandolin against the wall securely before we speak of my song."

"Most surely, senor," the stranger replied, "for there is no fault with the mandolin."

"Senor," Rodriguez said, "I thank you profoundly." And he bowed to the gallant, whom he now perceived to be young, a youth tall and lithe like himself, one whom we might have chosen for these chronicles had we not found Rodriguez.

Then Rodriguez stepped back a short way and placed his kerchief on the ground; and upon this he put his mandolin and leaned it against the wall. When the mandolin was safe from dust or accident he approached the stranger and drew his sword.

"Senor," he said, "we will now discuss music."

"Right gladly, senor," said the young man, who now drew his sword also. There were no clouds; the moon was full; the evening promised well.

Scarcely had the flash of thin rapiers crossing each other by moonlight begun to gleam in the street when Morano appeared beside them and stood there watching. He had bought his bacon and gone straight to the house with the balcony. For though he knew no Latin he had not missed the silent greeting that had welcomed his master to that village, or failed to interpret the gist of the words that Rodriguez' dumb glance would have said. He stood there watching while each combatant stood his ground.

And Rodriguez remembered all those passes and feints that he had had from his father, and which Sevastiani, a master of arms in Madrid, had taught in his father's youth: and some were famous and some were little known. And all these passes, as he tried them one by one, his unknown antagonist parried. And for a moment Rodriguez feared that Morano would see those passes in which he trusted foiled by that unknown sword, and then he reflected that Morano knew nothing of the craft of the rapier, and with more content at that thought he parried thrusts that were strange to him. But something told Morano that in this fight the stranger was master and that along that pale-blue, moonlit, unknown sword lurked a sure death for Rodriguez. He moved from his place of vantage and was soon lost in large shadows; while the rapiers played and blade rippled on blade with a sound as though Death were gently sharpening his scythe in the dark. And now Rodriguez was giving ground, now his antagonist pressed him; thrusts that he believed invincible had failed; now he parried wearily and had at once to parry again; the unknown pressed on, was upon him, was scattering his weakening parries; drew back his rapier for a deadlier pass, learned in a secret school, in a hut on mountains he knew, and practised surely; and fell in a heap upon Rodriguez' feet, struck full on the back of the head by Morano's frying-pan.

"Most vile knave," shouted Rodriguez as he saw Morano before him with his frying-pan in his hand, and with something of the stupid expression that you see on the face of a dog that has done some foolish thing which it thinks will delight its master.

"Master! I am your servant," said Morano.

"Vile, miserable knave," replied Rodriguez.

"Master," Morano said plaintively, "shall I see to your comforts, your food, and not to your life?"

"Silence," thundered Rodriguez as he stooped anxiously to his antagonist, who was not unconscious but only very giddy and who now rose to his feet with the help of Rodriguez.

"Alas, senor," said Rodriguez, "the foul knave is my servant. He shall be flogged. He shall be flayed. His vile flesh shall be cut off him. Does the hurt pain you, senor? Sit and rest while I beat the knave, and then we will continue our meeting."

And he ran to his kerchief on which rested his mandolin and laid it upon the dust for the stranger.

"No, no," said he. "My head clears again. It is nothing."

"But rest, senor, rest," said Rodriguez. "It is always well to rest before an encounter. Rest while I punish the knave."

And he led him to where the kerchief lay on the ground. "Let me see the hurt, senor," he continued. And the stranger removed his plumed hat as Rodriguez compelled him to sit down. He straightened out the hat as he sat, and the hurt was shown to be of no great consequence.

"The blessed Saints be praised," Rodriguez said. "It need not stop our encounter. But rest awhile, senor."

"Indeed, it is nothing," he answered.

"But the indignity is immeasurable," sighed Rodriguez. "Would you care, senor, when you are well rested to give the chastisement yourself?"

"As far as that goes," said the stranger, "I can chastise him now."

"If you are fully recovered, senor," Rodriguez said, "my own sword is at your disposal to beat him sore with the flat of it, or how you will. Thus no dishonour shall touch your sword from the skin of so vile a knave."

The stranger smiled: the idea appealed to him.

"You make a noble amend, senor," he said as he bowed over Rodriguez' proffered sword.

Morano had not moved far, but stood near, wondering. "What should a servant do if not work for his master?" he wondered. And how work for him when dead? And dead, as it seemed to Morano, through his own fault if he allowed any man to kill him when he perceived him about to do so. He stood there puzzled. And suddenly he saw the stranger coming angrily towards him in the clear moonlight with a sword. Morano was frightened.

As the hidalgo came up to him he stretched out his left hand to seize Morano by the shoulder. Up went the frying-pan, the stranger parried, but against a stroke that no school taught or knew, and for the second time he went down in the dust with a reeling head. Rodriguez turned toward Morano and said to him ... No, realism is all very well, and I know that my duty as author is to tell all that happened, and I could win mighty praise as a bold, unconventional writer; at the same time, some young lady will be reading all this next year in some far country, or in twenty years in England, and I would sooner she should not read what Rodriguez said. I do not, I trust, disappoint her. But the gist of it was that he should leave that place now and depart from his service for ever. And hearing those words Morano turned mournfully away and was at once lost in the darkness. While Rodriguez ran once more to help his fallen antagonist. "Senor, senor," he said with an emotion that some wearing centuries and a cold climate have taught us not to show, and beyond those words he could find no more to say.

"Giddy, only giddy," said the stranger.

A tear fell on his forehead as Rodriguez helped him to his feet.

"Senor," Rodriguez said fervently, "we will finish our encounter come what may. The knave is gone and ..."

"But I am somewhat giddy," said the other.

"I will take off one of my shoes," said Rodriguez, "leaving the other on. It will equalise our unsteadiness, and you shall not be disappointed in our encounter. Come," he added kindly.

"I cannot see so clearly as before," the young hidalgo murmured.

"I will bandage my right eye also," said Rodriguez, "and if this cannot equalise it ..."

"It is a most fair offer," said the young man.

"I could not bear that you should be disappointed of your encounter," Rodriguez said, "by this spirit of Hell that has got itself clothed in fat and dares to usurp the dignity of man."

"It is a right fair offer," the young man said again.

"Rest yourself, senor," said Rodriguez, "while I take off my shoe," and he indicated his kerchief which was still on the ground.

The stranger sat down a little wearily, and Rodriguez sitting upon the dust took off his left shoe. And now he began to think a little wistfully of the face that had shone from that balcony, where all was dark now in black shadow unlit by the moon. The emptiness of the balcony and its darkness oppressed him;

for he could scarcely hope to survive an encounter with that swordsman, whose skill he now recognised as being of a different class from his own, a class of which he knew nothing. All his own feints and passes were known, while those of his antagonist had been strange and new, and he might well have even others. The stranger's giddiness did not alter the situation, for Rodriguez knew that his handicap was fair and even generous. He believed he was near his grave, and could see no spark of light to banish that dark belief; yet more chances than we can see often guard us on such occasions. The absence of Serafina saddened him like a sorrowful sunset.

Rodriguez rose and limped with his one shoe off to the stranger, who was sitting upon his kerchief.

"I will bandage my right eye now, senor," he said.

The young man rose and shook the dust from the kerchief and gave it to Rodriguez with a renewed expression of his gratitude at the fairness of the strange handicap. When Rodriguez had bandaged his eye the stranger returned his sword to him, which he had held in his hand since his effort to beat Morano, and drawing his own stepped back a few paces from him. Rodriguez took one hopeless look at the balcony, saw it as empty and as black as ever, then he faced his antagonist, waiting.

"Bandage one eye, indeed!" muttered Morano as he stepped up behind the stranger and knocked him down for the third time with a blow over the head from his frying-pan.

The young hidalgo dropped silently.

Rodriguez uttered one scream of anger and rushed at Morano with his sword. Morano had already started to run; and, knowing well that he was running for his life, he kept for awhile the start that he had of the rapier. Rodriguez knew that no plump man of over forty could last against his lithe speed long. He saw Morano clearly before him, then lost sight of him for a moment and ran confidently on pursuing. He ran on and on. And at last he recognised that Morano had slipped into the darkness, which lies always so near to the moonlight, and was not in front of him at all. So he returned to his fallen antagonist and found him breathing heavily where he fell, scarcely conscious. The third stroke of the frying-pan had done its work surely. Rodriguez' fury died down, only because it is difficult to feel two emotions at once: it died down as pity took its place, though every now and then it would suddenly flare and fall again. He returned his sword and lifted the young hidalgo and carried him to the door of the house under which they had fought.

With one fist he beat on the door without putting the hurt man down, and continued to hit it until steps were heard, and bolts began to grumble, as though disturbed too early from their rusty sleep in stone sockets.

The door of the house with the balcony was opened by a servant who, when he saw who it was that Rodriguez carried, fled into the house in alarm, as one who runs with bad news. He carried one candle and, when

148

he had disappeared with the steaming flame, Rodriguez found himself in a long hall lit by the moonlight only, which was looking in through the small contorted panes of the upper part of a high window. Alone with echoes and shadows Rodriguez carried the hurt man through the hall, who was muttering now as he came back to consciousness. And, as he went, there came to Rodriguez thoughts between wonder and hope, for he had had no thought at all when he beat on the door except to get shelter and help for the hurt man. At the end of the hall they came to an open door that led into a chamber partly shining with moonlight.

"In there," said the man that he carried.

Rodriguez carried him in and laid him on a long couch at the end of the room. Large pictures of men in the blackness, out of the moon's rays, frowned at Rodriguez mysteriously. He could not see their faces in the darkness, but he somehow knew they frowned. Two portraits that were clear in the moonlight eyed him with absolute apathy. So cold a welcome from that house's past generations boded no good to him from those that dwelt there today. Rodriguez knew that in carrying the hurt man there he helped at a Christian deed; and yet there was no putting the merits of the case against the omens that crowded the chamber, lurking along the edge of moonlight and darkness, disappearing and reappearing till the gloom was heavy with portent. The omens knew. In a weak voice and few words the hurt man thanked him, but the apathetic faces seemed to say What of that? And the frowning faces that he could not see still filled the darkness with anger.

And then from the end of the chamber, dressed in white, and all shining with moonlight, came Serafina.

Rodriguez in awed silence watched her come. He saw her pass through the moonlight and grow dimmer, and glide to the moonlight again that streamed through another window. A great dim golden circle appeared at the far end of the chamber whence she had come, as the servent returned with his candle and held it high to give light for Dona Serafina. But that one flame seemed to make the darkness only blacker; and for any cheerfulness it brought to the gloom it had better never have challenged those masses of darkness at all in that high chamber among the brooding portraits it seemed trivial, ephemeral, modern, ill able to cope with the power of ancient things, dead days and forgotten voices, which make their home in the darkness because the days that have usurped them have stolen the light of the sun.

And there the man stood holding his candle high, and the rays of the moon became more magical still beside that little mundane, flickering thing. And Serafina was moving through the moonlight as though its rays were her sisters, which she met noiselessly and brightly upon some island, as it seemed to Rodriguez, beyond the costs of Earth, so quietly and so brightly did her slender figure move and so aloof from him appeared her eyes. And there came on Rodriguez that feeling that some deride and that others explain away, the feeling of which romance is mainly made and which is the aim and goal of all the earth. And his love for Serafina seemed to him not only to be an event in his life but to have some part in veiled and shadowy destinies and to have the blessing of most distant days: grey beards seemed to look out of graves in forgotten places to wag approval: hands seemed to beckon to him out of far-future times, where faces were smiling quietly: and, dreaming on further still, this vast approval that gave benediction to his heart's youthful fancy seemed to widen and widen like the gold of a summer's evening or, the humming of bees in summer in endless rows of limes, until it became a part of the story of man. Spring days of his earliest memory seemed to have their part in it, as well as wonderful evenings of days that were yet to be, till his love for Serafina was one with the fate of earth; and, wandering far on their courses, he knew that the stars blessed it. But Serafina went up to the man on the couch with no look for Rodriguez.

With no look for Rodriguez she bent over the stricken hidalgo. He raised himself a little on one elbow. "It is nothing," he said, "Serafina."

Still she bent over him. He laid his head down again, but now with open and undimmed eyes. She put her hand to his forehead, she spoke in a low voice to him; she lavished upon him sympathy for which Rodriguez would have offered his head to swords; and all, thought Rodriguez for three blows from a knave's frying-pan: and his anger against Morano flared up again fiercely. Then there came another thought to him out of the shadows, where Serafina was standing all white, a figure of solace. Who was this man who so mysteriously blended with the other unknown things that haunted the gloom of that chamber? Why had he fought him at night? What was he to Serafina? Thoughts crowded up to him from the interior of the darkness, sombre and foreboding as the shadows that nursed them. He stood there never daring to speak to Serafina; looking for permission to speak, such as a glance might give. And no glance came.

And now, as though soothed by her beauty, the hurt man closed his eyes. Serafina stood beside him anxious and silent, gleaming in that dim place. The servant at the far end of the chamber still held his one candle high, as though some light of earth were needed against the fantastic moon, which if unopposed would give everything over to magic. Rodriguez stood there, scarcely breathing. All was silent. And then through the door by which Serafina had come, past that lonely, golden, moon-defying candle, all down the long room across moonlight and blackness, came the lady of the house, Serafina's mother. She came, as Serafina came, straight toward the man on the couch, giving no look to Rodriguez, walking something as Serafina walked, with the same poise, the same dignity, though the years had carried away from her the grace Serafina had: so that, though you saw that they were mother and daughter, the elder lady called to mind the lovely things of earth, large gardens at evening, statues dim in the dusk, summer and whatsoever binds us to earthly things; but Serafina turned Rodriguez' thoughts to the twilight in which he first saw her, and he pictured her native place as far from here, in mellow fields near the moon, wherein she had walked on twilight outlasting any we know, with all delicate things of our fancy, too fair for the rugged earth.

As the lady approached the couch upon which the young man was lying, and still no look was turned towards Rodriguez, his young dreams fled as butterflies sailing high in the heat of June that are suddenly plunged in night by a total eclipse of the sun. He had never spoken to Serafina, or seen before her mother, and they did not know his name; he knew that he, Rodriguez, had no claim to a welcome. But his dreams had flocked so much about Serafina's face, basking so much in her beauty, that they now fell back dying; and when a man's dreams die what remains, if he lingers awhile behind them?

Rodriguez suddenly felt that his left shoe was off and his right eye still bandaged, things that he had not noticed while his only thought was for the man he carried to shelter, but torturing his consciousness now that he thought of himself. He opened his lips to explain; but before words came to him, looking at the face of Serafina's mother, standing now by the couch, he felt that, not knowing how, he had somehow wronged the Penates of this house, or whatever was hid in the dimness of that long chamber, by carrying in this young man there to rest from his hurt.

Rodriguez' depression arose from these causes, but having arisen, it grew of its own might: he had had nothing to eat since morning, and in the favouring atmosphere of hunger his depression grew gigantic. He opened his lips once more to say farewell, was oppressed by all manner of thoughts that held him dumb, and turned away in silence and left the house. Outside he recovered his mandolin and his shoe. He was tired with the weariness of defeated dreams that slept in his spirit exhausted, rather than with any fatigue his young muscles had from the journey. He needed sleep; he looked at the shuttered houses; then at the soft dust of the road in which dogs lay during the daylight. But the dust was near to his mood, so he lay down where he had fought the unknown hidalgo. A light wind wandered the street like a visitor come to the village out of a friendly valley, but Rodriguez' four days on the roads had made him familiar with all wandering things, and the breeze on his forehead troubled him not at all: before it had wearied of wandering in the night Rodriguez had fallen asleep. Just by the edge of sleep, upon which side he knew not, he heard the window of the balcony creak, and looked up wide awake all in a moment. But nothing stirred in the darkness of the balcony and the window was fast shut. So whatever sound came from the window came not from its opening but shutting: for a while he wondered; and then his tired thoughts rested, and that was sleep.

A light rain woke Rodriguez, drizzling upon his face; the first light rain that had fallen in a romantic tale. Storms there had been, lashing oaks to terrific shapes seen at night by flashes of lightning, through which villains rode abroad or heroes sought shelter at midnight; hurricanes there had been, flapping huge cloaks, fierce hail and copious snow; but until now no drizzle. It was morning; dawn was old; and pale and grey and unhappy.

The balcony above him, still empty, scarcely even held romance now. Rain dripped from it sadly. Its cheerless bareness seemed worse than the most sinister shadows of night.

And then Rodriguez saw a rose lying on the ground beside him. And for all the dreams, fancies, and hopes that leaped up in Rodriguez' mind, rising and falling and fading, one thing alone he knew and all the rest was mystery: the rose had lain there before the rain had fallen. Beneath the rose was white dust, while all around it the dust was turning grey with rain.

Rodriguez tried to guess how long the rain had fallen. The rose may have lain beside him all night long. But the shadows of mystery receded no farther than this one fact that the rose was there before the rain began. No sign of any kind came from the house.

Rodriguez put the rose safe under his coat, wrapped in the kerchief that had guarded the mandolin, to carry it far from Lowlight, through places familiar with roses and places strange to them; but it remained for him a thing of mystery until a day far from then.

Sadly he left the house in the sad rain, marching away alone to look for his wars.

The Seventh Chronicle

HOW HE CAME TO SHADOW VALLEY

Rodriguez still believed it to be the duty of any Christian man to kill Morano. Yet, more than comfort, more than dryness, he missed Morano's cheerful chatter, and his philosophy into which all occasions so easily slipped. Upon his first day's journey all was new; the very anemones kept him company; but now he made the discovery that lonely roads are long.

When he had suggested food or rest Morano had fallen in with his wishes; when he had suggested winning a castle in vague wars Morano had agreed with him. Now he had dismissed Morano and had driven him away at the rapier's point. There was no one now either to cook his food or to believe in the schemes his ambition made. There was no one now to speak of the wars as the natural end of the journey. Alone in the rain the wars seemed far away and castles hard to come by. The unromantic rain in which no dreams thrive fell on and on.

The village of Lowlight was some way behind him, as he went with mournful thoughts through the drizzling rain, when he caught the smell of bacon. He looked for a house but the plain was bare except for small bushes. He looked up wind, which was blowing from the west, whence came the unmistakable smell of bacon: and there was a small fire smoking greyly against a bush; and the fat figure crouching beside it, although the face was averted, was clearly none but Morano. And when Rodriguez saw that he was tenderly holding the infamous frying-pan, the very weapon that had done the accursed deed, then he almost felt righteous anger; but that frying-pan held other memories too, and Rodriguez felt less fury than what he thought he felt. As for killing Morano, Rodriguez believed, or thought he believed, that he was too far from the road for it to be possible to overtake him to mete out his just punishment. As for the bacon, Rodriguez scorned it and marched on down the road. Now one side of the frying-pan was very hot, for it was tilted a little and the lard had run sideways. By tilting it back again slowly Morano could make the fat run back bit by bit over the heated metal, and whenever it did so it sizzled. He now picked up the frying-pan and one log that was burning well and walked parallel with Rodriguez. He was up-wind of him, and whenever the bacon-fat sizzled Rodriguez caught the smell of it. A small matter to inspire thoughts; but Rodriguez had eaten nothing since the morning before, and

ideas surged through his head; and though they began with moral indignation they adapted themselves
more and more to hunger, until there came the idea
that since his money had bought the bacon the food
was rightfully his, and he had every right to eat it
wherever he found it. So much can slaves sometimes
control the master, and the body rule the brain.

So Rodriguez suddenly turned and strode up to
Morano. "My bacon," he said.

"Master," Morano said, for it was beginning to cool,
"let me make another small fire."

"Knave, call me not master," said Rodriguez.

Morano, who knew when speech was good, was silent now, and blew on the smouldering end of the log
he carried and gathered a handful of twigs and shook
the rain off them; and soon had a small fire again,
warming the bacon. He had nothing to say which bacon could not say better. And when Rodriguez had
finished up the bacon he carefully reconsidered the
case of Morano, and there were points in it which he
had not thought of before. He reflected that for the
execution of knaves a suitable person was provided.
He should perhaps give Morano up to la Garda. His
next thought was where to find la Garda. And easily enough another thought followed that one, which
was that although on foot and still some way behind
four of la Garda were trying to find him. Rodriguez'
mind, which was looking at life from the point of
view of a judge, changed somewhat at this thought.
He reflected next that, for the prevention of crime, to

make Morano see the true nature of his enormity so that he should never commit it again might after all be as good as killing him. So what we call his better nature, his calmer judgment, decided him now to talk to Morano and not to kill him: but Morano, looking back upon this merciful change, always attributed it to fried bacon.

"Morano," said Rodriguez' better nature, "to offend the laws of Chivalry is to have against you the swords of all true men."

"Master," Morano said, "that were dreadful odds."

"And rightly," said Rodriguez.

"Master," said Morano, "I will keep those laws henceforth. I may cook bacon for you when you are hungry, I may brush the dust from your cloak, I may see to your comforts. This Chivalry forbids none of that. But when I see anyone trying to kill you, master; why, kill you he must, and welcome."

"Not always," said Rodriguez somewhat curtly, for it struck him that Morano spoke somehow too lightly of sacred things.

"Not always?" asked Morano.

"No," said Rodriguez.

"Master, I implore you tell me," said Morano, "when they may kill you and when they may not, so that I may never offend again."

Rodriguez cast a swift glance at him but found his face so full of puzzled anxiety that he condescended to do what Morano had asked, and began to explain to him the rudiments of the laws of Chivalry.

"In the wars," he said, "you may defend me whoever assails me, or if robbers or any common persons attack me, but if I arrange a meeting with a gentleman, and any knave basely interferes, then is he damned hereafter as well as accursed now; for, the laws of Chivalry being founded on true religion, the penalty for their breach is by no means confined to this world."

"Master," replied Morano thoughtfully, "if I be not damned already I will avoid those fires of Hell; and none shall kill you that you have not chosen to kill you, and those that you choose shall kill you whenever you have a mind."

Rodriguez opened his lips to correct Morano but reflected that, though in his crude and base-born way, he had correctly interpreted the law so far as his mind was able.

So he briefly said "Yes," and rose and returned to the road, giving Morano no order to follow him; and this was the last concession he made to the needs of Chivalry on account of the sin of Morano. Morano gathered up the frying-pan and followed Rodriguez, and when they came to the road he walked behind him in silence.

For three or four miles they walked thus, Morano knowing that he followed on sufferance and calling no attention to himself with his garrulous tongue. But at the end of an hour the rain lifted; and with the coming out of the sun Morano talked again.

"Master," he said, "the next man that you choose to kill you, let him be one too base-born to know the tricks of the rapier, too ignorant to do aught but wish you well, some poor fat fool over forty who shall be too heavy to elude your rapier's point and too elderly for it to matter when you kill him at your Chivalry, the best of life being gone already at forty-five."

"There is timber here," said Rodriguez. "We will have some more bacon while you dry my cloak over a fire."

Thus he acknowledged Morano again for his servant but never acknowledged that in Morano's words he had understood any poor sketch of Morano's self, or that the words went to his heart.

"Timber, Master?" said Morano, though it did not need Rodriguez to point out the great oaks that now began to stand beside their journey, but he saw that the other matter was well and thus he left well alone.

Rodriguez waved an arm towards the great trees. "Yes, indeed," said Morano, and began to polish up the frying-pan as he walked.

Rodriguez, who missed little, caught a glimpse of tears in Morano's eyes, for all that his head was turned downward over the frying-pan; yet he said nothing, for he knew that forgiveness was all that Morano needed, and that he had now given him: and it was much to give, reflected Rodriguez, for so great a crime, and dismissed the matter from his mind.

And now their road dipped downhill, and they passed a huge oak and then another. More and more often now they met these solitary giants, till their view began to be obscured by them. The road dwindled till it was no better than a track, the earth beside it was wild and rocky; Rodriguez wondered to what manner of land he was coming. But continually the branches of some tree obscured his view and the only indication he had of it was from the road he trod, which seemed to tell him that men came here seldom. Beyond every huge tree that they passed as they went downhill Rodriguez hoped to get a better view, but always there stood another to close the vista. It was some while before he realised that he had entered a forest. They were come to Shadow Valley.

The grandeur of this place, penetrated by shafts of sunlight, coloured by flashes of floating butterflies, filled by the chaunt of birds rising over the long hum of insects, lifted the fallen spirits of Rodriguez as he walked on through the morning.

He still would not have exchanged his rose for the whole forest; but in the mighty solemnity of the forest his mourning for the lady that he feared he had lost no longer seemed the only solemn thing: indeed, the sombre forest seemed well attuned to his mood; and what complaint have we against Fate wherever this is so. His mood was one of tragic loss, the defeat of an enterprise that his hopes had undertaken, to seize victory on the apex of the world, to walk all his days only just outside the edge of Paradise, for no less than that his hopes and his first love promised each other; and then he walked despairing in small rain. In this mood Fate had led him to solemn old oaks standing huge among shadows; and the grandeur of their grey grip on the earth that had been theirs for centuries was akin to the grandeur of the high hopes he had had, and his despair was somehow soothed by the shadows. And then the impudent birds seemed to say "Hope again."

They walked for miles into the forest and lit a fire before noon, for Rodriguez had left Lowlight very early. And by it Morano cooked bacon again and dried his master's cloak. They ate the bacon and sat by the fire till all their clothes were dry, and when the flames from the great logs fell and only embers glowed they sat there still, with hands spread to the warmth of the embers; for to those who wander a fire is food and rest and comfort. Only as the embers turned grey did they throw earth over their fire and continue their journey. Their road grew smaller and the forest denser.

They had walked some miles from the place where they lit their fire, when a somewhat unmistakable sound made Rodriguez look ahead of him. An arrow had struck a birch tree on the right side, ten or twelve paces in front of him; and as he looked up another struck it from the opposite side just level with the first; the two were sticking in it ten feet or so from the ground. Rodriguez drew his sword. But when a third arrow went over his head from behind and struck the birch tree, whut! just between the other two, he perceived, as duller minds could have done, that it was a hint, and he returned his sword and stood still. Morano questioned his master with his eyes, which were asking what was to be done next. But Rodriguez shrugged his shoulders: there was no fighting with an invisible foe that could shoot like that. That much Morano knew, but he did not know that there might not be some law of Chivalry that would demand that Rodriguez should wave his sword in the air or thrust at the birch tree until someone shot him. When there seemed to be no such rule Morano was well content. And presently men came quietly on to the road from different parts of the wood. They were dressed in brown leather and wore leaf-green hats, and round each one's neck hung a disk of engraved copper. They came up to the travellers carrying bows, and the leader said to Rodriguez:

"Senor, all travellers here bring tribute to the King of Shadow Valley," at the mention of whom all touched hats and bowed their heads. "What do you bring us?"

Rodriguez thought of no answer; but after a moment he said, for the sake of loyalty: "I know one king only."

"There is only one king in Shadow Valley," said the bowman.

"He brings a tribute of emeralds," said another, looking at Rodriguez' scabbard. And then they searched him and others search Morano. There were eight or nine of them, all in their leaf-green hats, with ribbons round their necks of the same colour to hold the copper disks. They took a gold coin from Morano and grey greasy pieces of silver. One of them took his frying-pan; but he looked so pitifully at them as he said simply, "I starve," that the frying-pan was restored to him.

They unbuckled Rodriguez' belt and took from him sword and scabbard and three gold pieces from his purse. Next they found the gold piece that was hanging round his neck, still stuffed inside his clothes where he had put it when he was riding. Having examined it they put it back inside his clothes, while the leader rebuckled his sword-belt about his waist and returned him his three gold-pieces.

Others returned his money to Morano. "Master," said the leader, bowing to Rodriguez, his green hat in hand, "under our King, the forest is yours."

Morano was pleased to hear this respect paid to his master, but Rodriguez was so surprised that he who was never curt without reason found no more to say than "Why?"

"Because we are your servants," said the other.

"Who are you?" asked Rodriguez.

"We are the green bowmen, master," he said, "who hold this forest against all men for our King."

"And who is he?" said Rodriguez.

And the bowman answered: "The King of Shadow Valley," at which the others all touched hats and bowed heads again. And Rodriguez seeing that the mystery would grow no clearer for any information to be had from them said: "Conduct me to your king."

"That, master, we cannot do," said the chief of the bowmen. "There be many trees in this forest, and behind any one of them he holds his court. When he needs us there is his clear horn. But when men need him who knows which shadow is his of all that lie in the forest?" Whether or not there was anything interesting in the mystery, to Rodriguez it was merely annoying; and finding it grew no clearer he turned his attention to shelter for the night, to which all travellers give a thought at least once, between noon and sunset.

"Is there any house on this road, senor," he said, "in which we could rest the night?"

"Ten miles from here," said he, "and not far from the road you take is the best house we have in the forest. It is yours, master, for as long as you honour it."

"Come then," said Rodriguez, "and I thank you, senor."

So they all started together, Rodriguez with the leader going in front and Morano following with all the bowmen. And soon the bowmen were singing songs of the forest, hunting songs, songs of the winter; and songs of the long summer evenings, songs of love. Cheered by this merriment, the miles slipped by.

And Rodriguez gathered from the songs they sang something of what they were and of how they lived in the forest, living amongst the woodland creatures till these men's ways were almost as their ways; killing what they needed for food but protecting the woodland things against all others; straying out amongst the villages in summer evenings, and always welcome; and owning no allegiance but to the King of the Shadow Valley.

And the leader told Rodriguez that his name was Miguel Threegeese, given him on account of an exploit in his youth when he lay one night with his bow by one of the great pools in the forest, where the geese come in winter. He said the forest was a hundred miles long, lying mostly along a great valley, which they were crossing. And once they had owned allegiance to kings of Spain, but now to none but the King of the Shadow Valley, for the King of Spain's men had once tried to cut some of the forest down, and the forest was sacred.

Behind him the men sang on of woodland things, and of cottage gardens in the villages: with singing and laughter they came to their journey's end. A cottage as though built by peasants with boundless material stood in the forest. It was a thatched cottage built in the peasant's way but of enormous size. The leader entered first and whispered to those within, who rose and bowed to Rodriguez as he entered, twenty more bowmen who had been sitting at a table. One does not speak of the banqueting-hall of a cottage, but such it appeared, for it occupied more than half of the cottage and was as large as the banqueting-hall of any castle. It was made of great beams of oak, and high at either end just under the thatch were windows with their little square panes of bulging bluish glass, which at that time was rare in Spain. A table of oak ran down the length of it, cut from a single tree, polished and dark from the hands of many men that had sat at it. Boar spears hung on the wall, great antlers and boar's tusks and, carved in the oak of the wall and again on a high, dark chair that stood at the end of the long table empty, a crown with oak leaves that Rodriguez recognised. It was the same as the one that was cut on his gold coin, which he had given no further thought to, riding to Lowlight, and which the face of Serafina had driven from his mind altogether. "But," he said, and then was silent, thinking to learn more by watching than by talking. And his companions of the road came in and all sat down on the benches beside the ample table, and a brew was brought, a kind of pale mead, that they called forest water. And all drank; and, sitting at the table, watching them more closely than he could as he walked in the forest, Rodriguez saw by the sunlight that streamed in low through one window that on the copper disks they wore round their necks on green ribbon the design was again the same. It was much smaller than his on the gold coin but the same strange leafy crown. "Wear it as you go through Shadow Valley," he now seemed to remember the man saying to him who put it round his neck. But why? Clearly because it was the badge of this band of men. And this other man was one of them.

His eyes strayed back to the great design on the wall. "The crown of the forest," said Miguel as he saw his eyes wondering at it, "as you doubtless know, senor."

Why should he know? Of course because he bore the design himself. "Who wears it?" said Rodriguez.

"The King of Shadow Valley."

Morano was without curiosity; he did not question good drink; he sat at the table with a cup of horn in his hand, as happy as though he had come to his master's castle, though that had not yet been won.

The sun sank under the oaks, filling the hall with a ruddy glow, turning the boar spears scarlet and reddening the red faces of the merry men of the bow.

A dozen of the men went out; to relieve the guard in the forest, Miguel explained. And Rodriguez learned that he had come through a line of sentries without ever seeing one. Presently a dozen others came in from their posts and unslung their bows and laid them on pegs on the wall and sat down at the table. Whereat there were whispered words and they all rose and bowed to Rodriguez. And Rodriguez had caught the words "A prince of the forest." What did it mean?

Soon the long hall grew dim, and his love for the light drew Rodriguez out to watch the sunset. And there was the sun under indescribable clouds, turning huge and yellow among the trunks of the trees and casting glory munificently down glades. It set, and the western sky became blood-red and lilac: from the other end of the sky the moon peeped out of night. A hush came and a chill, and a glory of colour, and a dying away of light; and in the hush the mystery of the great oaks became magical. A blackbird blew a tune less of this earth than of fairy-land.

Rodriguez wished that he could have had a less ambition than to win a castle in the wars, for in those glades and among those oaks he felt that happiness might be found under roofs of thatch. But having come by his ambition he would not desert it.

Now rushlights were lit in the great cottage and the window of the long room glowed yellow. A fountain fell in the stillness that he had not heard before. An early nightingale tuned a tentative note. "The forest is fair, is it not?" said Miguel.

Rodriguez had no words to say. To turn into words the beauty that was now shining in his thoughts, reflected from the evening there, was no easier than for wood to reflect all that is seen in the mirror.

"You love the forest," he said at last.

"Master," said Miguel, "it is the only land in which we should live our days. There are cities and roads but man is not meant for them. I know not, master, what God intends about us; but in cities we are against the intention at every step, while here, why, we drift along with it."

"I, too, would live here always," said Rodriguez.

"The house is yours," said Miguel. And Rodriguez answered: "I go tomorrow to the wars."

They turned round then and walked slowly back to the cottage, and entered the candlelight and the loud talk of many men out of the hush of the twilight. But they passed from the room at once by a door on the left, and came thus to a large bedroom, the only other room in the cottage.

"Your room, master," said Miguel Threegeese.

It was not so big as the hall where the bowmen sat, but it was a goodly room. The bed was made of carved wood, for there were craftsmen in the forest, and a hunt went all the way round it with dogs and deer. Four great posts held a canopy over it: they were four young birch-trees seemingly still wearing their bright bark, but this had been painted on their bare timber by some woodland artist. The chairs had not the beauty of the great ages of furniture, but they had a dignity that the age of commerce has not dreamed of. Each one was carved out of a single block of wood: there was no join in them anywhere. One of them lasts to this day.

The skins of deer covered the long walls. There were great basins and jugs of earthenware. All was forest-made. The very shadows whispering among themselves in corners spoke of the forest. The room was rude; but being without ornament, except for the work of simple craftsmen, it had nothing there to offend the sense of right of anyone entering its door, by any jarring conflict with the purposes and traditions of the land in which it stood. All the woodland spirits might have entered there, and slept—if spirits sleep—in the great bed, and left at dawn unoffended. In fact that age had not yet learned vulgarity.

When Miguel Threegeese left Morano entered.

"Master," he said, "they are making a banquet for you."

"Good," said Rodriguez. "We will eat it." And he waited to hear what Morano had come to say, for he could see that it was more than this.

"Master," said Morano, "I have been talking with the bowman. And they will give you whatever you ask. They are good people, master, and they will give you all things, whatever you asked of them."

Rodriguez would not show to his servant that it all still puzzled him.

"They are very amiable men," he said.

"Master," said Morano, coming to the point, "that Garda, they will have walked after us. They must be now in Lowlight. They have all to-night to get new shoes on their horses. And to-morrow, master, to-morrow, if we be still on foot..."

Rodriguez was thinking. Morano seemed to him to be talking sense.

"You would like another ride?" he said to Morano.

"Master," he answered, "riding is horrible. But the public garrotter, he is a bad thing too." And he meditatively stroked the bristles under his chin.

"They would give us horses?" said Rodriguez.

"Anything, master, I am sure of it. They are good people."

"They'll have news of the road by which they left Lowlight," said Rodriguez reflectively. "They say la Garda dare not enter the forest," Morano continued, "but thirty miles from here the forest ends. They could ride round while we go through."

"They would give us horses?" said Rodriguez again.

"Surely," said Morano.

And then Rodriguez asked where they cooked the banquet, since he saw that there were only two rooms in the great cottage and his inquiring eye saw no preparations for cooking about the fireplace of either. And Morano pointed through a window at the back of the room to another cottage among the trees, fifty paces away. A red glow streamed from its windows, growing strong in the darkening forest.

"That is their kitchen, master," he said. "The whole house is kitchen." His eyes looked eagerly at it, for, though he loved bacon, he welcomed the many signs of a dinner of boundless variety.

As he and his master returned to the long hall great plates of polished wood were being laid on the table. They gave Rodriguez a place on the right of the great chair that had the crown of the forest carved on the back.

"Whose chair is that?" said Rodriguez.

"The King of Shadow Valley," they said.

"He is not here then," said Rodriguez.

"Who knows?" said a bowman.

"It is his chair," said another; "his place is ready. None knows the ways of the King of Shadow Valley."

"He comes sometimes at this hour," said a third, "as the boar comes to Heather Pool at sunset. But not always. None knows his ways."

"If they caught the King," said another, "the forest would perish. None loves it as he, none knows its ways as he, no other could so defend it."

"Alas," said Miguel, "some day when he be not here they will enter the forest." All knew whom he meant by they. "And the goodly trees will go." He spoke as a man foretelling the end of the world; and, as men to whom no less was announced, the others listened to him. They all loved Shadow Valley.

In this man's time, so they told Rodriguez, none entered the forest to hurt it, no tree was cut except by his command, and venturous men claiming rights from others than him seldom laid axe long to tree before he stood near, stepping noiselessly from among shadows of trees as though he were one of their spirits coming for vengeance on man.

All this they told Rodriguez, but nothing definite they told of their king, where he was yesterday, where he might be now; and any questions he asked of such things seemed to offend a law of the forest.

And then the dishes were carried in, to Morano's great delight: with wide blue eyes he watched the produce of that mighty estate coming in through the doorway cooked. Boars' heads, woodcock, herons, plates full of fishes, all manner of small eggs, a roe-deer and some rabbits, were carried in by procession. And the men set to with their ivory-handled knives, each handle being the whole tusk of a boar. And with their eating came merriment and tales of past hunt-ings and talk of the forest and stories of the King of Shadow Valley.

And always they spoke of him not only with re-spect but also with the discretion, Rodriguez thought, of men that spoke of one who might be behind them at that moment, and one who tolerated no trifling with his authority. Then they sang songs again, such as Rodriguez had heard on the road, and their merry lives passed clearly before his mind again, for we live in our songs as no men live in histories. And again Rodriguez lamented his hard ambition and his long, vague journey, turning away twice from happiness; once in the village of Lowlight where happiness deserted him, and here in the goodly forest where he jilted happiness. How well could he and Morano live as two of this band, he thought; leaving all cares in cities: for there dwelt cares in cities even then. Then he put the thought away. And as the evening wore away with merry talk and with song, Rodriguez turned to Miguel and told him how it was with la Garda and broached the matter of horses. And while the others sang Miguel spoke sadly to him. "Master," he said, "la Garda shall never take you in Shadow Valley, yet if you must leave us to make your fortune in the wars, though your fortune waits you here, there be many horses in the forest, and you and your servant shall have the best."

"Tomorrow morning, senor?" said Rodriguez.

"Even so," said Miguel.

"And how shall I send them to you again?" said Rodriguez.

"Master, they are yours," said Miguel.

But this Rodriguez would not have, for as yet he only guessed what claim at all he had upon Shadow Valley, his speculations being far more concerned with the identity of the hidalgo that he had fought the night before, how he concerned Serafina, who had owned the rose that he carried: in fact his mind was busy with such studies as were proper to his age. And at last they decided between them on the house of a lowland smith, who was the furthest man that the bowmen knew who was secretly true to their king. At his house Rodriguez and Morano should leave the horses. He dwelt sixty miles from the northern edge of the forest, and would surely give Rodriguez fresh horses if he possessed them, for he was a true man to the bowman. His name was Gonzalez and he dwelt in a queer green house.

They turned then to listen a moment to a hunting song that all the bowmen were singing about the death of a boar. Its sheer merriment constrained them. Then Miguel spoke again. "You should not leave the forest," he said sadly.

Rodriguez sighed: it was decided. Then Miguel told him of his road, which ran north-eastward and would one day bring him out of Spain. He told him how towns on the way, and the river Ebro, and with awe and reverence he spoke of the mighty Pyrenees. And then Rodriguez rose, for the start was to be at dawn, and walked quietly through the singing out of the hall to the room where the great bed was. And soon he slept, and his dreams joined in the endless hunt through Shadow Valley that was carved all round the timbers of his bed.

All too soon he heard voices, voices far off at first, to which he drew nearer and nearer; thus he woke grudgingly out of the deeps of sleep. It was Miguel and Morano calling him.

When at length he reached the hall all the merriment of the evening was gone from it but the sober beauty of the forest flooded in through both windows with early sunlight and bird-song; so that it had not the sad appearance of places in which we have rejoiced, when we revisit them next day or next generation and find them all deserted by dance and song.

Rodriguez ate his breakfast while the bowmen waited with their bows all strung by the door. When he was ready they all set off in the early light through the forest.

Rodriguez did not criticise his ambition; it sailed too high above his logic for that; but he regretted it, as he went through the beauty of the forest among these happy men. But we must all have an ambition, and Rodriguez stuck to the one he had. He had another, but it was an ambition with weak wings that could not come to hope. It depended upon the first. If he could win a castle in the wars he felt that he might even yet hope towards Lowlight.

Little was said, and Rodriguez was all alone with his thoughts. In two hours they met a bowman holding two horses. They had gone eight miles.

"Farewell to the forest," said Miguel to Rodriguez. There was almost a query in his voice. Would Rodriguez really leave them? it seemed to say.

"Farewell," he answered.

Morano too had looked sideways towards his master, seeming almost to wonder what his answer would be: when it came he accepted it and walked to the horses. Rodriguez mounted: willing hands helped up Morano. "Farewell," said Miguel once more. And all the bowmen shouted "Farewell."

"Make my farewell," said Rodriguez, "to the King of Shadow Valley."

A twig cracked in the forest.

"Hark," said Miguel. "Maybe that was a boar."

"I cannot wait to hunt," said Rodriguez, "for I have far to go."

"Maybe," said Miguel, "it was the King's farewell to you."

Rodriguez looked into the forest and saw nothing.

"Farewell," he said again. The horses were fresh and he let his go. Morano lumbered behind him. In two miles they came to the edge of the forest and up a rocky hill, and so to the plains again, and one more adventure lay behind them. Rodriguez turned round once on the high ground and took a long look back on the green undulations of peace. The forest slept there as though empty of men.

Then they rode. In the first hour, easily cantering, they did ten miles. Then they settled down to what those of our age and country and occupation know as a hound-jog, which is seven miles an hour. And after two hours they let the horses rest. It was the hour of the frying-pan. Morano, having dismounted, stretched himself dolefully; then he brought out all manner of meats. Rodriguez looked wonderingly at them.

"For the wars, master," said Morano. To whatever wars they went, the green bowmen seemed to have supplied an ample commissariat.

They ate. And Rodriguez thought of the wars, for the thought of Serafina made him sad, and his rejection of the life of the forest saddened him too; so he sought to draw from the future the comfort that he could not get from the past.

They mounted again and rode again for three hours, till they saw very far off on a hill a village that Miguel had told them was fifty miles from the forest.

"We rest the night there," said Rodriguez pointing, though it was yet seven or eight miles away.

"All the Saints be praised," said Morano.

They dismounted then and went on foot, for the horses were weary. At evening they rode slowly into the village. At an inn whose hospitable looks were as cheerfully unlike the Inn of the Dragon and Knight as possible, they demanded lodging for all four. They went first to the stable, and when the horses had been handed over to the care of a groom they returned to the inn, and mine host and Rodriguez had to help Morano up the three steps to the door, for he had walked nine miles that day and ridden fifty and he was too weary to climb the steps.

And later Rodriguez sat down alone to his supper at a table well and variously laden, for the doors of mine hosts' larder were opened wide in his honour; but Rodriguez ate sparingly, as do weary men.

And soon he sought his bed. And on the old echoing stairs as he and mine host ascended they met Morano leaning against the wall. What shall I say of Morano? Reader, your sympathy is all ready to go out to the poor, weary man. He does not entirely deserve it, and shall not cheat you of it. Reader, Morano was drunk. I tell you this sorry truth rather than that the knave should have falsely come by your pity. And yet he is dead now over three hundred years, having had his good time to the full. Does he deserve your pity on that account? Or your envy? And to whom or what would you give it? Well, anyhow, he deserved no pity for being drunk. And yet he was thirsty, and too tired to eat, and sore in need of refreshment, and had had no more cause to learn to shun good wine than he had had to shun the smiles of princesses; and there the good wine had been, sparkling beside him merrily.

And now, why now, fatigued as he had been an hour or so ago (but time had lost its tiresome, restless meaning), now he stood firm while all things and all men staggered.

"Morano," said Rodriguez as he passed that foolish figure, "we go sixty miles to-morrow."

"Sixty, master?" said Morano. "A hundred: two hundred."

"It is best to rest now," said his master.

"Two hundred, master, two hundred," Morano replied.

And then Rodriguez left him, and heard him muttering his challenge to distance still, "Two hundred, two hundred," till the old stairway echoed with it.

And so he came to his chamber, of which he remembered little, for sleep lurked there and he was soon with dreams, faring further with them than my pen can follow.

The Eighth Chronicle

HOW HE TRAVELLED FAR

One blackbird on a twig near Rodriguez' window sang, then there were fifty singing, and morning arose over Spain all golden and wonderful.

Rodriguez descended and found mine host rubbing his hands by his good table, with a look on his face that seemed to welcome the day and to find good auguries concerning it. But Morano looked as one that, having fallen from some far better place, is ill-content with earth and the mundane way.

He had scorned breakfast; but Rodriguez breakfasted. And soon the two were bidding mine host farewell. They found their horses saddled, they mounted at once, and rode off slowly in the early day. The horses were tired and, slowly trotting and walking, and sometimes dismounting and dragging the horses on, it was nearly two hours before they had done ten miles and come to the house of the smith in a rocky village: the street was cobbled and the houses were all of stone.

The early sparkle had gone from the dew, but it was still morning, and many a man but now sat down to his breakfast, as they arrived and beat on the door.

Gonzalez the smith opened it, a round and ruddy man past fifty, a citizen following a reputable trade, but once, ah once, a bowman.

"Senor," said Rodriguez, "our horses are weary. We have been told you will change them for us."

"Who told you that?" said Gonzalez.

"The green bowmen in Shadow Valley," the young man answered.

As a meteor at night lights up with its greenish glare flowers and blades of grass, twisting long shadows behind them, lights up lawns and bushes and the deep places of woods, scattering quiet night for a moment, so the unexpected answer of Rodriguez lit memories in the mind of the smith all down the long years; and a twinkle and a sparkle of those memories dancing in woods long forsaken flashed from his eyes.

"The green bowmen, senor," said Gonzalez. "Ah, Shadow Valley!"

"We left it yesterday," said Rodriguez.

When Gonzalez heard this he poured forth questions. "The forest, senor; how is it now with the forest? Do the boars still drink at Heather Pool? Do the geese go still to Greatmarsh? They should have come early this year. How is it with Larios, Raphael, Migada? Who shoots woodcock now?"

The questions flowed on past answering, past remembering: he had not spoken of the forest for years.

And Rodriguez answered as such questions are always answered, saying that all was well, and giving Gonzalez some little detail of some trifling affair of the forest, which he treasured as small shells are treasured in inland places when travellers bring them from the sea; but all that he heard of the forest seemed to the smith like something gathered on a far shore of time. Yes, he had been a bowman once.

But he had no horses. One horse that drew a cart, but no horses for riding at all. And Rodriguez thought of the immense miles lying between him and the foreign land, keeping him back from his ambition; they all pressed on his mind at once. The smith was sorry, but he could not make horses.

"Show him your coin, master," said Morano.

"Ah, a small token," said Rodriguez, drawing it forth still on its green ribbon under his clothing. "The bowman's badge, is it not?"

Gonzalez looked at it, then looked at Rodriguez.

"Master," he said, "you shall have your horses. Give me time: you shall have them. Enter, master." And he bowed and widely opened the door. "If you will breakfast in my house while I go to the neighbours you shall have some horses, master."

So they entered the house, and the smith with many bows gave the travellers over to the care of his wife, who saw from her husband's manner that these were persons of importance and as such she treated them both, and as such entertained them to their second breakfast. And this meant they ate heartily, as

183

travellers can, who can go without a breakfast or eat two; and those who dwell in cities can do neither.

And while the plump dame did them honour they spoke no word of the forest, for they knew not what place her husband's early years had in her imagination. They had barely finished their meal when the sound of hooves on cobbles was heard and Gonzalez beat on the door. They all went to the door and found him there with two horses. The horses were saddled and bridled. They fixed the stirrups to please them, then the travellers mounted at once. Rodriguez made his grateful farewell to the wife of the smith: then, turning to Gonzalez, he pointed to the two tired horses which had waited all the while with their reins thrown over a hook on the wall.

"Let the owner of these have them till his own come back," he said, and added: "How far may I take these?"

"They are good horses," said the smith.

"Yes," said Rodriguez.

"They could do fifty miles to-day," Gonzalez continued, "and to- morrow, why, forty, or a little more."

"And where will that bring me?" said Rodriguez, pointing to the straight road which was going his way, north-eastward.

"That," said Gonzalez, "that should bring you some ten or twenty miles short of Saspe."

"And where shall I leave the horses?" Rodriguez asked.

"Master," Gonzalez said, "in any village where there be a smith, if you say 'these are the horses of the smith

Gonzalez, who will come for them one day from here,' they will take them in for you, master."

"But," and Gonzalez walked a little away from his wife, and the horses walked and he went beside them, "north of here none knows the bowmen. You will get no fresh horses, master. What will you do?"

"Walk," said Rodriguez.

Then they said farewell, and there was a look on the face of the smith almost such as the sons of men might have worn in Genesis when angels visited them briefly.

They settled down into a steady trot and trotted thus for three hours. Noon came, and still there was no rest for Morano, but only dust and the monotonous sight of the road, on which his eyes were fixed: nearly an hour more passed, and at last he saw his master halt and turn round in his saddle.

"Dinner," Rodriguez said.

All Morano's weariness vanished: it was the hour of the frying-pan once more.

They had done more than twenty-one miles from the house of Gonzalez. Nimbly enough, in his joy at feeling the ground again, Morano ran and gathered sticks from the bushes. And soon he had a fire, and a thin column of grey smoke going up from it that to him was always home.

When the frying-pan warmed and lard sizzled, when the smell of bacon mingled with the smoke, then Morano was where all wise men and all unwise try to be, and where some of one or the other some times come for awhile, by unthought paths and are gone again; for that smoky, mixed odour was happiness.

Not for long men and horses rested, for soon Rodriguez' ambition was drawing him down the road again, of which he knew that there remained to be travelled over two hundred miles in Spain, and how much beyond that he knew not, nor greatly cared, for beyond the frontier of Spain he believed there lay the dim, desired country of romance where roads were long no more and no rain fell. They mounted again and pushed on for this country. Not a village they saw but that Morano hoped that here his affliction would end and that he would dismount and rest; and always Rodriguez rode on and Morano followed, and with a barking of dogs they were gone and the village rested behind them. For many an hour their slow trot carried them on; and Morano, clutching the saddle with worn arms, already was close to despair, when Rodriguez halted in a little village at evening before an inn. They had done their fifty miles from the house of Gonzalez, and even a little more.

Morano rolled from his horse and beat on the small green door. Mine host came out and eyed them, preening the point of his beard; and Rodriguez sat his horse and looked at him. They had not the welcome here that Gonzalez gave them; but there was a room to spare for Rodriguez, and Morano was promised what he asked for, straw; and there was shelter to be had for the horses. It was all the travellers needed.

Children peered at the strangers, gossips peeped out of doors to gather material concerning them, dogs noted their coming, the eyes of the little village watched them curiously, but Rodriguez and Morano passed into the house unheeding; and past those two tired men the mellow evening glided by like a dream. Tired though Rodriguez was he noticed a certain politeness in mine host while he waited at supper, which had not been noticeable when he had first received him, and rightly put this down to some talk of Morano's; but he did not guess that Morano had opened wide blue eyes and, babbling to his host, had guilelessly told him that his master a week ago had killed an uncivil inn-keeper.

Scarcely were late birds home before Rodriguez sought his bed, and not all of them were sleeping before he slept.

Another morning shone, and appeared to Spain, and all at once Rodriguez was wide awake. It was the eighth day of his wanderings.

When he had breakfasted and paid his due in silver he and Morano departed, leaving mine host upon his doorstep bowing with an almost perplexed look on his shrewd face as he took the points of moustachios and beard lightly in turn between finger and thumb: for we of our day enter vague details about ourselves in the book downstairs when we stay at inns, but it was mine host's custom to gather all that with his sharp eyes. Whatever he gathered, Rodriguez and Morano were gone.

But soon their pace dwindled, the trot slackening and falling to a walk; soon Rodriguez learned what it is to travel with tired horses. To Morano riding was merely riding, and the discomforts of that were so great that he noticed no difference. But to Rodriguez, his continual hitting and kicking his horse's sides, his dislike of doing it, the uselessness of it when done, his ambition before and the tired beast underneath, the body always some yards behind the beckoning spirit, were as great vexation as a traveller knows. It came to dismounting and walking miles on foot; even then the horses hung back. They halted an hour over dinner while the horses grazed and rested, and they returned to their road refreshed by the magic that was in the frying-pan, but the horses were no fresher.

When our bodies are slothful and lie heavy, never responding to the spirit's bright promptings, then we know dullness: and the burden of it is the graver for hearing our spirits call faintly, as the chains of a buccaneer in some deep prison, who hears a snatch of his comrades' singing as they ride free by the coast, would grow more unbearable than ever before. But the weight of his tired horse seemed to hang heavier on the fanciful hopes that Rodriguez' dreams had made. Farther than ever seemed the Pyrenees, huger than ever their barrier, dimmer and dimmer grew the lands of romance.

If the hopes of Rodriguez were low, if his fancies were faint, what material have I left with which to make a story with glitter enough to hold my readers' eyes to the page: for know that mere dreams and idle fancies, and all amorous, lyrical, unsubstantial things, are all that we writers have of which to make a tale, as they are all that the Dim Ones have to make the story of man.

Sometimes riding, sometimes going on foot, with the thought of the long, long miles always crowding upon Rodriguez, overwhelming his hopes; till even the castle he was to win in the wars grew too pale for his fancy to see, tired and without illusions, they came at last by starlight to the glow of a smith's forge. He must have done forty-five miles and he knew they were near Caspe.

The smith was working late, and looked up when Rodriguez halted. Yes, he knew Gonzalez, a master in the trade: there was a welcome for his horses.

But for the two human travellers there were excuses, even apologies, but no spare beds. It was the same in the next three or four houses that stood together by the road. And the fever of Rodriguez' ambition drove him on, though Morano would have lain down and slept where they stood, though he himself was weary. The smith had received his horses; after that he cared not whether they gave him shelter or not, the alternative being the road, and that bringing nearer his wars and the castle he was to win. And that fancy that led his master Morano allowed always to lead him too, though a few more miles and he would have fallen asleep as he walked and dropped by the roadside and slept on. Luckily they had gone barely two miles from the forge where the horses rested, when they saw a high, dark house by the road and knocked on the door and found shelter. It was an old woman who let them in, a farmer's wife, and she had room for them and one mattress, but no bed. They were too tired to eat and did not ask for food, but at once followed her up the booming stairs of her house, which were all dark but for her candle, and so came among huge minuetting shadows to the long loft at the top. There was a mattress there which the old woman laid out for Rodriguez, and a heap of hay for Morano. Just for a moment, as Rodriguez climbed the last step of the stair and entered the loft where the huge shadows twirled between the one candle's light and the unbeaten darkness in corners, just for a moment romance seemed to beckon to him; for a moment, in spite of his fatigue and dejection, in spite of the possibility of his quest being crazy, for a moment he felt that great shadows and echoing boards, the very cobwebs even that hung from the black rafters, were all romantic things; he felt that his was a glorious adventure and that all these things that filled the loft in the night were such as should fitly attend on youth and glory. In a moment that feeling was gone he knew not why it had come. And though he remembered it till grey old age, when he came to know the causes of many things, he never knew what romance might have to do with shadows or echoes at night in an empty room, and only knew of such fancies that they came from beyond his understanding, whether from wisdom or folly.

Morano was first asleep, as enormous snores testified, almost before the echoes had died away of the footsteps of the old woman descending the stairs; but soon Rodriguez followed him into the region of dreams, where fantastic ambitions can live with less of a struggle than in the broad light of day: he dreamed he walked at night down a street of castles strangely colossal in an awful starlight, with doors too vast for any human need, whose battlements were far in the heights of night; and chose, it being in time of war, the one that should be his; but the gargoyles on it were angry and spoiled the dream.

Dream followed dream with furious rapidity, as the dreams of tired men do, racing each other, jostling and mingling and dancing, an ill-assorted company: myriads went by, a wild, grey, cloudy multitude; and with the last walked dawn.

Rodriguez rose more relieved to quit so tumultuous a rest than refreshed by having had it.

He descended, leaving Morano to sleep on, and not till the old dame had made a breakfast ready did he return to interrupt his snores.

Even as he awoke upon his heap of hay Morano remained as true to his master's fantastic quest as the camel is true to the pilgrimage to Mecca. He awoke grumbling, as the camel grumbles at dawn when the packs are put on him where he lies, but never did he doubt that they went to victorious wars where his master would win a castle splendid with towers.

Breakfast cheered both the travellers. And then the old lady told Rodriguez that Caspe was but a three hours' walk, and that cheered them even more, for Caspe is on the Ebro, which seemed to mark for Rodriguez a stage in his journey, being carried easily in his imagination, like the Pyrenees. What road he would take when he reached Caspe he had not planned. And soon Rodriguez expressed his gratitude, full of fervour, with many a flowery phrase which lived long in the old dame's mind; and the visit of those two travellers became one of the strange events of that house and was chief of the memories that faintly haunted the rafters of the loft for years.

They did not reach Caspe in three hours, but went lazily, being weary; for however long a man defies fatigue the hour comes when it claims him. The knowledge that Caspe lay near with sure lodging for the night, soothed Rodriguez' impatience. And as they loitered they talked, and they decided that la Garda must now be too far behind to pursue any longer. They came in four hours to the bank of the Ebro and there saw Caspe near them; but they dined once more on the grass, sitting beside the river, rather than enter the town at once, for there had grown in both travellers a liking for the wanderers' green table of earth.

It was a time to make plans. The country of romance was far away and they were without horses.

"Will you buy horses, master?" said Morano.

"We might not get them over the Pyrenees," said Rodriguez, though he had a better reason, which was that three gold pieces did not buy two saddled horses. There were no more friends to hire from. Morano grew thoughtful. He sat with his feet dangling over the bank of the Ebro.

"Master," he said after a while, "this river goes our way. Let us come by boat, master, and drift down to France at our ease."

To get a river over a range of mountains is harder than to get horses. Some such difficulty Rodriguez implied to him; but Morano, having come slowly by an idea, parted not so easily with it.

"It goes our way, master," he repeated, and pointed a finger at the Ebro.

At this moment a certain song that boatmen sing on that river, when the current is with them and they have nothing to do but be idle and their lazy thoughts run to lascivious things, came to the ears of Rodriguez and Morano; and a man with a bright blue sash steered down the Ebro. He had been fishing and was returning home.

"Master," Morano said, "that knave shall row us there."

Rodriguez seeing that the idea was fixed in Morano's mind determined that events would move it sooner than argument, and so made no reply.

"Shall I tell him, master?" asked Morano.

"Yes," said Rodriguez, "if he can row us over the Pyrenees."

This was the permission that Morano sought, and a hideous yell broke from his throat hailing the boat-man. The boatman looked up lazily, a young man with strong brown arms, turning black moustaches towards Morano. Again Morano hailed him and ran along the bank, while the boat drifted down and the boatman steered in towards Morano. Somehow Morano persuaded him to come in to see what he wanted; and in a creek he ran his boat aground, and there he and Morano argued and bargained. But Rodriguez remained where he was, wondering why it took so long to turn his servant's mind from that curious fancy. At last Morano returned.

"Well?" said Rodriguez.

"Master," said Morano, "he will row us to the Pyrenees."

"The Pyrenees!" said Rodriguez. "The Ebro runs into the sea." For they had taught him this at the college of San Josephus.

"He will row us there," said Morano, "for a gold piece a day, rowing five hours each day."

Now between them they had but four gold pieces; but that did not make the Ebro run northward. It seemed that the Ebro, after going their way, as Morano had said, for twenty or thirty miles, was joined by the river Segre, and that where the Ebro left them, turning eastwards, the course of the Segre took them on their way: but it would be rowing against the current.

"How far is it?" said Rodriguez.

"A hundred miles, he says," answered Morano. "He knows it well."

Rodriguez calculated swiftly. First he added thirty miles; for he knew that his countrymen took a cheerful view of distance, seldom allowing any distance to oppress them under its true name at the out set of a journey; then he guessed that the boatman might row five miles an hour for the first thirty miles with the stream of the Ebro, and he hoped that he might row three against the Segre until they came near the mountains, where the current might grow too strong.

"Morano," he said, "we shall have to row too."

"Row, master?" said Morano.

"We can pay him for four days," said Rodriguez. "If we all row we may go far on our way."

"It is better than riding," replied Morano with entire resignation.

And so they walked to the creek and Rodriguez greeted the boatman, whose name was Perez; and they entered the boat and he rowed them down to Caspe. And, in the house of Perez, Rodriguez slept that night in a large dim room, untidy with diverse wares: they slept on heaps of things that pertained to the river and fishing. Yet it was late before Rodriguez slept, for in sight of his mind came glimpses at last of the end of his journey; and, when he slept at last, he saw the Pyrenees. Through the long night their mighty heads rejected him, staring immeasurably beyond him in silence, and then in happier dreams they beckoned him for a moment. Till at last a bird that had entered the city of Caspe sang clear and it was dawn. With that first light Rodriguez arose and awoke Morano. Together they left that long haven of lumber and found Perez already stirring. They ate hastily and all went down to the boat, the unknown that waits at the end of all strange journeys quickening their steps as they went through the early light.

Perez rowed first and the others took their turns and so they went all the morning down the broad flood of the Ebro, and came in the afternoon to its meeting place with the Segre. And there they landed and stretched their limbs on shore and lit a fire and feasted, before they faced the current that would be henceforth against them. Then they rowed on.

When they landed by starlight and unrolled a sheet of canvas that Perez had put in the boat, and found what a bad time starlight is for pitching a tent, Rodriguez and Morano had rowed for four hours each and Perez had rowed for five. They carried no timber in the boat but used the oars for tent-poles and cut tent-pegs with a small hatchet that Perez had brought.

They stumbled on rocks, tore the canvas on bushes, lost the same thing over and over again; in fact they were learning the craft of wandering. Yet at last their tent was up and a good fire comforting them outside, and Morano had cooked the food and they had supped and talked, and after that they slept. And over them sleeping the starlight faded away, and in the greyness that none of them dreamed was dawn five clear notes were heard so shrill in the night that Rodriguez half waking wondered what bird of the darkness called, and learned from the answering chorus that it was day.

He woke Morano who rose in that chilly hour and, striking sparks among last night's embers, soon had a fire: they hastily made a meal and wrapped up their tent and soon they were going onward against the tide of the Segre. And that day Morano rowed more skilfully; and Rodriguez unwrapped his mandolin and played, reclining in the boat while he rested from rowing. And the mandolin told them all, what the words of none could say, that they fared to adventure in the land of Romance, to the overthrow of dullness and the sameness of all drear schemes and the conquest of discontent in the spirit of man; and perhaps it sang of a time that has not yet come, or the mandolin lied.

That evening three wiser men made their camp before starlight. They were now far up the Segre.

For thirteen hours next day they toiled at the oars or lay languid. And while Rodriguez rested he played on his mandolin. The Segre slipped by them.

They seemed like no men on their way to war, but seemed to loiter as the bright river loitered, which slid seaward in careless ease and was wholly freed from time.

On this day they heard men speak of the Pyrenees, two men and a woman walking by the river; their voices came to the boat across the water, and they spoke of the Pyrenees. And on the next day they heard men speak of war. War that some farmers had fled from on the other side of the mountain. When Rodriguez heard these chance words his dreams came nearer till they almost touched the edges of reality.

It was the last day of Perez' rowing. He rowed well although they neared the cradle of the Segre and he struggled against them in his youth. Grey peaks began to peer that had nursed that river. Grey faces of stone began to look over green hills. They were the Pyrenees.

When Rodriguez saw at last the Pyrenees he drew a breath and was unable to speak. Soon they were gone again below the hills: they had but peered for a moment to see who troubled the Segre.

And the sun set and still they did not camp, but Perez rowed on into the starlight. That day he rowed six hours.

They pitched their tent as well as they could in the darkness; and, breathing a clear new air all crisp from the Pyrenees, they slept outside the threshold of adventure.

Rodriguez awoke cold. Once more he heard the first blackbird who sings clear at the edge of night all alone in the greyness, the nightingale's only rival; a rival like some unknown in the midst of a crowd who for a moment leads some well-loved song, in notes more liquid than a master-singer's; and all the crowd joins in and his voice is lost, and no one learns his name. At once a host of birds answered him out of dim bushes, whose shapes had barely as yet emerged from night. And in this chorus Perez awoke, and even Morano.

They all three breakfasted together, and then the wanderers said good-bye to Perez. And soon he was gone with his bright blue sash, drifting homewards with the Segre, well paid yet singing a little sadly as he drifted; for he had been one of a quest, and now he left it at the edge of adventure, near solemn mountains and, beyond them, romantic, near-unknown lands. So Perez left and Rodriguez and Morano turned again to the road, all the more lightly because they had not done a full day's march for so long, and now a great one unrolled its leagues before them.

The heads of the mountains showed themselves again. They tramped as in the early days of their quest. And as they went the mountains, unveiling themselves slowly, dropping film after film of distance that hid their mighty forms, gradually revealed to the wanderers the magnificence of their beauty. Till at evening Rodriguez and Morano stood on a low hill, looking at that tremendous range, which lifted far above the fields of Earth, as though its mountains were no earthly things but sat with Fate and watched us and did not care.

Rodriguez and Morano stood and gazed in silence. They had come twenty miles since morning, they were tired and hungry, but the mountains held them: they stood there looking neither for rest nor food. Beyond them, sheltering under the low hills, they saw a little village. Smoke straggled up from it high into the evening: beyond the village woods sloped away upwards. But far above smoke or woods the bare peaks brooded. Rodriguez gazed on their austere solemnity, wondering what secret they guarded there for so long, guessing what message they held and hid from man; until he learned that the mystery they guarded among them was of things that he knew not and could never know.

Tinkle-ting said the bells of a church, invisible among the houses of that far village. Tinkle-ting said the crescent of hills that sheltered it. And after a while, speaking out of their grim and enormous silences with all the gravity of their hundred ages, Tinkle-ting said the mountains. With this trivial message Echo returned from among the homes of the mighty, where she had run with the small bell's tiny cry to trouble their crowned aloofness.

Rodriguez and Morano pressed on, and the mountains cloaked themselves as they went, in air of many colours; till the stars came out and the lights of the village gleamed. In darkness, with surprise in the tones of the barking dogs, the two wanderers came to the village where so few ever came, for it lay at the end of Spain, cut off by those mighty rocks, and they knew not much of what lands lay beyond.

They beat on a door below a hanging board, on which was written "The Inn of the World's End": a wandering scholar had written it and had been well paid for his work, for in those days writing was rare. The door was opened for them by the host of the inn, and they entered a room in which men who had supped were sitting at a table. They were all of them men from the Spanish side of the mountains, farmers come into the village on the affairs of Mother Earth; next day they would be back at their farms again; and of the land the other side of the mountains that was so near now they knew nothing, so that it still remained for the wanderers a thing of mystery wherein romance could dwell: and because they knew nothing of that land the men at the inn treasured all the more the rumours that sometimes came from it, and of these they talked, and mine host listened eagerly, to whom all tales were brought soon or late; and most he loved to hear tales from beyond the mountains.

Rodriguez and Morano sat still and listened, and the talk was all of war. It was faint and vague like fable, but rumour clearly said War, and the other side of the mountains. It may be that no man has a crazy ambition without at moments suspecting it; but prove it by the touchstone of fact and he becomes at once as a woman whose invalid son, after years of seclusion indoors, wins unexpectedly some athletic prize. When Rodriguez heard all this talk of wars quite near he thought of his castle as already won; his thoughts went further even, floating through Lowlight in the glowing evening, and drifting up and down past Serafina's house below the balcony where she sat for ever.

Some said the Duke would never attack the Prince because the Duke's aunt was a princess from the Troubadour's country. Another said that there would surely be war. Others said that there was war already, and too late for man to stop it. All said it would soon be over.

And one man said that it was the last war that would come, because gunpowder made fighting impossible. It could smite a man down, he said, at two hundred paces, and a man be slain not knowing whom he fought. Some loved fighting and some loved peace, he said, but gunpowder suited none.

"I like not the sound of that gunpowder, master," said Morano to Rodriguez.

"Nobody likes it," said the man at the table. "It is the end of war." And some sighed and some were glad. But Rodriguez determined to push on before the last war was over.

Next morning Rodriguez paid the last of his silver pieces and set off with Morano before any but mine host were astir. There was nothing but the mountains in front of them.

They climbed all the morning and they came to the fir woods. There they lit a good fire and Morano brought out his frying-pan. Over the meal they took stock of their provisions and found that, for all the store Morano had brought from the forest, they had now only food for three days; and they were quite without money. Money in those uplifted wastes seemed trivial, but the dwindling food told Rodriguez that he must press on; for man came among those rocky monsters supplied with all his needs, or perished unnoticed before their stony faces. All the afternoon they passed through the fir woods, and as shadows began to grow long they passed the last tree. The village and all the fields about it and the road by which they had come were all spread out below them like little trivial things dimly remembered from very long ago by one whose memory weakens. Distance had dwarfed them, and the cold regard of those mighty peaks ignored them. And then a shadow fell on the village, then tiny lights shone out. It was night down there. Still the two wanderers climbed on in the daylight. With their faces to the rocks they scarce saw night climb up behind them. But when Rodriguez looked up at the sky to see how much light was left, and met the calm gaze of the evening star, he saw that Night and the peaks were met together, and understood all at once how puny an intruder is man.

"Morano," said Rodriguez, "we must rest here for the night."

Morano looked round him with an air of discontent, not with his master's words but with the rocks' angular hardness. There was scarce a plant of any kind near them now. They were near the snow, which had flushed like a wild rose at sunset but was now all grey. Grey cliffs seemed to be gazing sheer at eternity; and here was man, the creature of a moment, who had strayed in the cold all homeless among his betters. There was no welcome for them there: whatever feeling great mountains evoke, THAT feeling was clear in Rodriguez and Morano. They were all amongst those that have other aims, other ends, and know naught of man. A bitter chill from the snow and from starry space drove this thought home.

They walked on looking for a better place, as men will, but found none. And at last they lay down on the cold earth under a rock that seemed to give shelter from the wind, and there sought sleep; but cold came instead, and sleep kept far from the tremendous presences of the peaks of the Pyrenees that gazed on things far from here.

An ageing moon arose, and Rodriguez touched Morano and rose up; and the two went slowly on, tired though they were. Picture the two tiny figures, bent, shivering and weary, walking with clumsy sticks cut in the wood, amongst the scorn of those tremendous peaks, which the moon showed all too clearly.

They got little warmth from walking, they were too weary to run; and after a while they halted and burned their sticks, and got a little warmth for some moments from their fire, which burned feebly and strangely in those inhuman solitudes.

Then they went on again and their track grew steeper. They rested again for fatigue, and rose and climbed again because of the cold; and all the while the peaks stared over them to spaces far beyond the thought of man.

Long before Spain knew anything of dawn a monster high in heaven smiled at the sun, a peak out-towering all its aged children. It greeted the sun as though this lonely thing, that scorned the race of man since ever it came, had met a mighty equal out in Space.

The vast peak glowed, and the rest of its grey race took up the greeting leisurely one by one. Still it was night in all Spanish houses.

Rodriguez and Morano were warmed by that cold peak's glow, though no warmth came from it at all; but the sight of it cheered them and their pulses rallied, and so they grew warmer in that bitter hour.

And then dawn came, and showed them that they were near the top of the pass. They had come to the snow that gleams there everlastingly.

There was no material for a fire but they ate cold meats, and went wearily on. They passed through that awful assemblage of peaks. By noon they were walking upon level ground.

In the afternoon Rodriguez, tired with the journey and with the heat of the sun, decided that it was possible to sleep, and, wrapping his cloak around him, he lay down, doing what Morano would have done, by instinct. Morano was asleep at once and Rodriguez soon after. They awoke with the cold at sunset.

Refreshed amazingly they ate some food and started their walk again to keep themselves warm for the night. They were still on level ground and set out with a good stride in their relief at being done with climbing. Later they slowed down and wandered just to keep warm. And some time in the starlight they felt their path dip, and knew that they were going downward now to the land of Rodriguez' dreams.

When the peaks glowed again, first meeting day in her earliest dancing-grounds of filmy air, they stood now behind the wanderers. Below them still in darkness lay the land of their dream, but hitherto it had always faded at dawn. Now hills put up their heads one by one through films of mist; woods showed, then hedges, and afterwards fields, greyly at first and then, in the cold hard light of morning, becoming more and more real. The sight of the land so long sought, at moments believed by Morano not to exist on earth, perhaps to have faded away when fables died, swept their fatigue from the wanderers, and they stepped out helped by the slope of the Pyrenees and cheered by the rising sun. They came at last to things that welcome man, little shrubs flowering, and—at noon—to the edge of a fir wood. They entered the wood and lit a merry fire, and heard birds singing, at which they both rejoiced, for the great peaks had said nothing.

They ate the food that Morano cooked, and drew warmth and cheer from the fire, and then they slept a little: and, rising from sleep, they pushed on through the wood, downward and downward toward the land of their dreams, to see if it was true.

They passed the wood and came to curious paths, and little hills, and heath, and rocky places, and wandering vales that twisted all awry. They passed through them all with the slope of the mountain behind them. When level rays from the sunset mellowed the fields of France the wanderers were walking still, but the peaks were far behind them, austerely gazing on the remotest things, forgetting the footsteps of man. And walking on past soft fields in the evening, all tilted a little about the mountain's feet, they had scarcely welcomed the sight of the evening star, when they saw before them the mild glow of a window and knew they were come again to the earth that is mother to man. In their cold savagery the inhuman mountains decked themselves out like gods with colours they took from the sunset; then darkened, all those peaks, in brooding conclave and disappeared in the night. And the hushed night heard the tiny rap of Morano's hands on the door of the house that had the glowing window.

The Ninth Chronicle

HOW HE WON A CASTLE IN SPAIN

The woman that came to the door had on her face a look that pleased Morano.

"Are you soldiers?" she said. And her scared look portended war.

"My master is a traveller looking for the wars," said Morano. "Are the wars near?"

"Oh, no, not near," said the woman; "not near."

And something in the anxious way she said "not near" pleased Morano also.

"We shall find those wars, master," he said.

And then they both questioned her. It seemed the wars were but twenty miles away. "But they will move northward," she said. "Surely they will move farther off?"

Before the next night was passed Rodriguez' dream might come true!

And then the man came to the door anxious at hearing strange voices; and Morano questioned him too, but he understood never a word. He was a French farmer that had married a Spanish girl, out of the wonderful land beyond the mountains: but whether he understood her or not he never understood Spanish. But both Rodriguez and the farmer's wife knew the two languages, and he had no difficulty in asking for lodging for the night; and she looked wistfully at him going to the wars, for in those days wars were small and not every man went. The night went by with dreams that were all on the verge of waking, which passed like ghosts along the edge of night almost touched by the light of day. It was Rodriguez whom these dreams visited. The farmer and his wife wondered awhile and then slept; Morano slept with all his wonted lethargy; but Rodriguez with his long quest now on the eve of fulfilment slept a tumultuous sleep. Sometimes his dreams raced over the Pyrenees, running south as far as Lowlight; and sometimes they rushed forward and clung like bats to the towers of the great castle that he should win in the war. And always he lay so near the edge of sleep that he never distinguished quite between thought and dream.

Dawn came and he put by all the dreams but the one that guided him always, and went and woke Morano. They ate hurriedly and left the house, and again the farmer's wife looked curiously at Rodriguez, as though there were something strange in a man that went to wars: for those days were not as these days. They followed the direction that had been given them, and never had the two men walked so fast. By the end of four hours they had done sixteen miles. They halted then, and Morano drew out his frying-pan with a haughty flourish, and cooked in the grand manner, every movement he made was a triumphant gesture; for they had passed refugees! War was now obviously close: they had but to take the way that the refugees were not taking. The dream was true: Morano saw himself walking slowly in splendid dress along the tapestried corridors of his master's castle. He would have slept after eating and would have dreamed more of this, but Rodriguez commanded him to put the things together: so what remained of the food disappeared again in a sack, the frying-pan was slung over his shoulders, and Morano stood ready again for the road.

They passed more refugees: their haste was unmistakable, and told more than their lips could have told had they tarried to speak: the wars were near now, and the wanderers went leisurely.

As they strolled through the twilight they came over the brow of a hill, a little fold of the earth disturbed eras ago by the awful rushing up of the Pyrenees; and they saw the evening darkening over the fields below them and a white mist rising only just clear of the grass, and two level rows of tents greyish-white like the mist, with a few more tents scattered near them. The tents had come up that evening with the mist, for there were men still hammering pegs. They were lighting fires now as evening settled in. Two hundred paces or so separated each row. It was two armies facing each other.

The gloaming faded: mist and the tents grew greyer: camp-fires blinked out of the dimness and grew redder and redder, and candles began to be lit beside the tents till all were glowing pale golden: Rodriguez and Morano stood there wondering awhile as they looked on the beautiful aura that surrounds the horrors of war.

They came by starlight to that tented field, by twinkling starlight to the place of Rodriguez' dream.

"For which side will you fight, master?" said Morano in his ear.

"For the right," said Rodriguez and strode on towards the nearest tents, never doubting that he would be guided, though not trying to comprehend how this could be.

They met with an officer going among his tents. "Where do you go?" he shouted.

"Senor," Rodriguez said, "I come with my mandolin to sing songs to you."

And at this the officer called out and others came from their tents; and Rodriguez repeated his offer to them not without confidence, for he knew that he had a way with the mandolin. And they said that they fought a battle on the morrow and could not listen to song: they heaped scorn on singing for they said they must needs prepare for the fight: and all of them looked with scorn on the mandolin. So Rodriguez bowed low to them with doffed hat and left them; and Morano bowed also, seeing his master bow; and the men of that camp returned to their preparations. A short walk brought Rodriguez and his servant to the other camp, over a flat field convenient for battle. He went up to a large tent well lit, the door being open towards him; and, having explained his errand to a sentry that stood outside, he entered and saw three persons of quality that were sitting at a table. To them he bowed low in the tent door, saying: "Senors, I am come to sing songs to you, playing the while upon my mandolin."

And they welcomed him gladly, saying: "We fight tomorrow and will gladly cheer our hearts with the sound of song and strengthen our men thereby."

And so Rodriguez sang among the tents, standing by a great fire to which they led him; and men came from the tents and into the circle of light, and in the darkness outside it were more than Rodriguez saw. And he sang to the circle of men and the vague glimmer of faces. Songs of their homes he sang them, not in their language, but songs that were made by old poets about the homes of their infancy, in valleys under far mountains remote from the Pyrenees. And in the song the yearnings of dead poets lived again, all streaming homeward like swallows when the last of the storms is gone: and those yearnings echoed in the hearts that beat in the night around the campfire, and they saw their own homes. And then he began to touch his mandolin; and he played them the tunes that draw men from their homes and that march them away to war. The tunes flowed up from the firelight: the mandolin knew. And the men heard the mandolin saying what they would say.

In the late night he ended, and a hush came down on the camp while the music floated away, going up from the dark ring of men and the fire-lit faces, touching perhaps the knees of the Pyrenees and drifting thence wherever echoes go. And the sparks of the camp- fire went straight upwards as they had done for hours, and the men that sat around it saw them go: for long they had not seen the sparks stream upwards, for their thoughts were far away with the mandolin. And all at once they cheered. And Rodriguez bowed to the one whose tent he had entered, and sought permission to fight for them in the morning.

With good grace this was accorded him, and while he bowed and well expressed his thanks he felt Morano touching his elbow. And as soon as he had gone aside with Morano that fat man's words bubbled over and were said.

"Master, fight not for these men," he exclaimed, "for they listen to song till midnight while the others prepare for battle. The others will win the fight, master, and where will your castle be?"

"Morano," said Rodriguez, "there seems to be truth in that. Yet must we fight for the right. For how would it be if those that have denied song should win and thrive? The arm of every good man must be against them. They have denied song, Morano! We must fight against them, you and I, while we can lay sword to head."

"Yes, indeed, master," said Morano. "But how shall you come by your castle?"

"As for that," said Rodriguez, "it must some day be won, yet not by denying song. These have given a welcome to song, and the others have driven it forth. And what would life be if those that deny song are to be permitted to thrive unmolested by all good men?"

"I know not, master," said Morano, "but I would have that castle."

"Enough," said Rodriguez. "We must fight for the right."

And so Rodriguez remained true to those that had heard him sing. And they gave him a casque and breast-plate, proof, they said, against any sword, and offered a sword that they said would surely cleave any breast-plate. For they fought not in battle with the nimble rapier. But Rodriguez did not forsake that famous exultant sword whose deeds he knew from many an ancient song; which he had brought so far to give it its old rich drink of blood. He believed it the bright key of the castle he was to win.

And they gave Rodriguez a good bed on the ground in the tent of the three leaders, the tent to which he first came; for they honoured him for the gift of song that he had, and because he was a stranger, and because he had asked permission to fight for them in their battle. And Rodriguez took one look by the light of a lantern at the rose he had carried from Lowlight, then slept a sleep through whose dreams loomed up the towers of castles.

Dawn came and he slept on still; but by seven all the camp was loudly astir, for they had promised the

enemy to begin the battle at eight. Rodriguez breakfasted lightly; for, now that the day of his dreams was
come at last and all his hopes depended on the day,
an anxiety for many things oppressed him. It was as
though his castle, rosy and fair in dreams, chilled with
its huge cold rocks all the air near it: it was as though
Rodriguez touched it at last with his hands and felt a
dankness of which he had never dreamed.

Then it came to the hour of eight and his anxieties passed.

The army was now drawn up before its tents in
line, but the enemy was not yet ready and so they
had to wait.

When the signal at length was given and the can-
noniers fired their pieces, and the musketoons were
shot off, many men fell. Now Rodriguez, with Morano, was placed on the right, and either through a
slight difference in numbers or because of an uneven-
ness in the array of battle they a little overlapped the
enemy's left. When a few men fell wounded there by
the discharge of the musketoons this overlapping was
even more pronounced.

Now the leaders of that fair army scorned all un-
knightly devices, and would never have descended to
any vile ruse de querre. The reproach can therefore
never be made against them that they ever intended
to outflank their enemy. Yet, when both armies advanced after the discharge of the musketoons and the
merry noise of the cannon, this occurred as the result
of chance, which no leader can be held accountable

for; so that those that speak of treachery in this battle, and deliberate outflanking, lie.

Now Rodriguez as he advanced with his sword, when the musketoons were empty, had already chosen his adversary. For he had carefully watched those opposite to him, before any smoke should obscure them, and had selected the one who from the splendour of his dress might be expected to possess the finest castle. Certainly this adversary outshone those amongst whom he stood, and gave fair promise of owning goodly possessions, for he wore a fine green cloak over a dress of lilac, and his helm and cuirass had a look of crafty workmanship. Towards him Rodriguez marched.

Then began fighting foot to foot, and there was a pretty laying on of swords. And had there been a poet there that day then the story of their fight had come down to you, my reader, all that way from the Pyrenees, down all those hundreds of years, and this tale of mine had been useless, the lame repetition in prose of songs that your nurses had sung to you. But they fought unseen by those that see for the Muses.

Rodriguez advanced upon his chosen adversary and, having briefly bowed, they engaged at once. And Rodriguez belaboured his helm till dints appeared, and beat it with swift strokes yet till the dints were cracks, and beat the cracks till hair began to appear: and all the while his adversary's strokes grew weaker and wilder, until he tottered to earth and Rodriguez had won. Swift then as cats, while Morano kept off others, Rodriguez leaped to his throat, and, holding up the stiletto that he had long ago taken as his legacy from the host of the Dragon and Knight, he demanded the fallen man's castle as ransom for his life.

"My castle, senor?" said his prisoner weakly.

"Yes," said Rodriguez impatiently.

"Yes, senor," said his adversary and closed his eyes for awhile.

"Does he surrender his castle, master?" asked Morano.

"Yes, indeed," said Rodriguez. They looked at each other: all at last was well.

The battle was rolling away from them and was now well within the enemy's tents.

History says of that day that the good men won. And, sitting, a Muse upon her mythical mountain, her decision must needs be one from which we may not appeal: and yet I wonder if she is ever bribed. Certainly the shrewd sense of Morano erred for once; for those for whom he had predicted victory, because they prepared so ostentatiously upon the field, were defeated; while the others, having made their preparations long before, were able to cheer themselves with song before the battle and to win it when it came.

And so Rodriguez was left undisturbed in possession of his prisoner and with the promise of his castle as a ransom. The battle was swiftly over, as must needs be where little armies meet so close. The enemy's camp was occupied, his army routed, and within an hour of beginning the battle the last of the fighting ceased.

The army returned to its tents to rejoice and to make a banquet, bringing with them captives and horses and other spoils of war. And Rodriguez had honour among them because he had fought on the right and so was one of those that had broken the enemy's left, from which direction victory had come. And they would have feasted him and done him honour, both for his work with the sword and for his songs to the mandolin; and they would have marched away soon to their own country and would have taken him with them and advanced him to honour there. But Rodriguez would not stay with them for he had his castle at last, and must needs march off at once with his captive and Morano to see the fulfilment of his dream. And therefore he thanked the leaders of that host with many a courtesy and many a well-bent bow, and explained to them how it was about his castle, and felicitated them on the victory of their good cause, and so wished them farewell. And they said farewell sorrowfully: but when they saw he would go, they gave him horses for himself and Morano, and another for his captive; and they heaped them with sacks of provender and blankets and all things that could give him comfort upon a journey: all this they brought him out of their spoils of war, and they would give him no less that the most that the horses could carry. And then Rodriguez turned to his captive again, who now stood on his feet.

"Senor," he said, "pray tell us all of your castle wherewith you ransom your life."

"Senor," he answered, "I have a castle in Spain."

"Master," broke in Morano, his eyes lighting up with delight, "there are no castles like the Spanish ones."

They got to horse then, all three; the captive on a horse of far poorer build than the other two and well-laden with sacks, for Rodriguez took no chance of his castle cantering, as it were, away from him on four hooves through the dust.

And when they heard that his journey was by way of the Pyrenees four knights of that army swore they would ride with him as far as the frontier of Spain, to bear him company and bring him fuel in the lonely cold of the mountains. They all set off and the merry army cheered. He left them making ready for their banquet, and never knew the cause for which he had fought.

They came by evening again to the house to which Rodriguez had come two nights before, when he had slept there with his castle yet to win. They all halted before it, and the man and the woman came to the door terrified. "The wars!" they said.

"The wars," said one of the riders, "are over, and the just cause has won."

"The Saints be praised!" said the woman. "But will there be no more fighting?"

"Never again," said the horseman, "for men are sick of gunpowder."

"The Saints be thanked," she said.

"Say not that," said the horseman, "for Satan invented gunpowder."

And she was silent; but, had none been there, she had secretly thanked Satan.

They demanded the food and shelter that armed men have the right to demand.

In the morning they were gone. They became a memory, which lingered like a vision, made partly of sunset and partly of the splendour of their cloaks, and so went down the years that those two folk had, a thing of romance, magnificence and fear. And now the slope of the mountain began to lift against them, and they rode slowly towards those unearthly peaks that had deserted the level fields before ever man came to them, and that sat there now familiar with stars and dawn with the air of never having known of man. And as they rode they talked. And Rodriguez talked with the four knights that rode with him, and they told tales of war and told of the ways of fighting of many men: and Morano rode behind them beside the captive and questioned him all the morning about his castle in Spain. And at first the captive answered his questions slowly, as if he were weary, or as though he were long from home and remembered its features dimly; but memory soon returned and he answered clearly, telling of such a castle as Morano had not dreamed; and the eyes of the fat man bulged as he rode beside him, growing rounder and rounder as they rode.

They came by sunset to that wood of firs in which Rodriguez had rested. In the midst of the wood they halted and tethered their horses to trees; they tied blankets to branches and made an encampment; and in the midst of it they made a fire, at first, with pine-needles and the dead lower twigs and then with great logs. And there they feasted together, all seven, around the fire. And when the feast was over and the great logs burning well, and red sparks went up slowly towards the silver stars, Morano turned to the prisoner seated beside him and "Tell the senors," he said, "of my master's castle."

And in the silence, that was rather lulled than broken by the whispering wind from the snow that sighed through the wood, the captive slowly lifted up his head and spoke in his queer accent.

"Senors, in Aragon, across the Ebro, are many goodly towers." And as he spoke they all leaned forward to listen, dark faces bright with firelight. "On the Ebro's southern bank stands," he went on, "my home."

He told of strange rocks rising from the Ebro; of buttresses built among them in unremembered times; of the great towers lifting up in multitudes from the buttresses; and of the mighty wall, windowless until it came to incredible heights, where the windows shone all safe from any ladder of war.

At first they felt in his story his pride in his lost home, and wondered, when he told of the height of his towers, how much he added in pride. And then the force of that story gripped them all and they doubted never a battlement, but each man's fancy saw between firelight and starlight every tower clear in the air. And at great height upon those marvellous towers the turrets of arches were; queer carvings grinned down from above inaccessible windows; and the towers gathered in light from the lonely air where nothing stood but they, and flashed it far over Aragon; and the Ebro floated by them always new, always amazed by their beauty.

He spoke to the six listeners on the lonely mountain, slowly, remembering mournfully; and never a story that Romance has known and told of castles in Spain has held men more than he held his listeners, while the sparks flew up toward the peaks of the Pyrenees and did not reach to them but failed in the night, giving place to the white stars.

And when he faltered through sorrow, or memory weakening, Morano always, watching with glittering eyes, would touch his arm, sitting beside him, and ask some question, and the captive would answer the question and so talk sadly on.

He told of the upper terraces, where heliotrope and aloe and oleander took sunlight far above their native earth: and though but rare winds carried the butterflies there, such as came to those fragrant terraces lingered for ever.

And after a while he spoke on carelessly, and Morano's questions ended, and none of the men in the firelight said a word; but he spoke on uninterrupted, holding them as by a spell, with his eyes fixed far away on black crags of the Pyrenees, telling of his great towers: almost it might have seemed he was speaking of mountains. And when the fire was only a deep red glow and white ash showed all round it, and he ceased speaking, having told of a castle marvellous even amongst the towers of Spain: all sitting round the embers felt sad with his sadness, for his sad voice drifted into their very spirits as white mists enter houses, and all were glad when Rodriguez said to him that one of his ten tall towers the captive should keep and should live in it for ever. And the sad man thanked him sadly and showed no joy.

When the tale of the castle and those great towers was done, the wind that blew from the snow touched all the hearers; they had seemed to be away by the bank of the Ebro in the heat and light of Spain, and now the vast night stripped them and the peaks seemed to close round on them. They wrapped themselves in blankets and lay down in their shelters. For a while they heard the wind waving branches and the thump of a horse's hoof restless at night; then they all slept except one that guarded the captive, and the captive himself who long lay thinking and thinking.

Dawn stole through the wood and waked none of the sleepers; the birds all shouted at them, still they slept on; and then the captive's guard wakened Morano and he stirred up the sparks of the fire and cooked, and they breakfasted late. And soon they left the wood and faced the bleak slope, all of them going on foot and leading their horses.

And the track crawled on till it came to the scorn of the peaks, winding over a shoulder of the Pyrenees, where the peaks gaze cold and contemptuous away from the things of man.

In the presence of those that bore them company Rodriguez and Morano felt none of the deadly majesty of those peaks that regard so awfully over the solitudes. They passed through them telling cheerfully of wars the four knights had known: and descended and came by sunset to the lower edge of the snow. They pushed on a little farther and then camped; and with branches from the last camp that they had heaped on their horses they made another great fire and, huddling round it in the blankets that they had brought, found warmth even there so far from the hearths of men.

And dawn and the cold woke them all on that treeless slope by barely warm embers. Morano cooked again and they ate in silence. And then the four knights rose sadly and one bowed and told Rodriguez how they must now go back to their own country. And grief seized on Rodriguez at his words, seeing that he was to lose four old friends at once and perhaps for ever, for when men have fought under the same banner in war they become old friends on that morning.

"Senors," said Rodriguez, "we may never meet again!"

And the other looked back to the peaks beyond which the far lands lay, and made a gesture with his hands.

"Senor, at least," said Rodriguez, "let us camp once more together."

And even Morano babbled a supplication.

"Methinks, senor," he answered, "we are already across the frontier, and when we men of the sword cross frontiers misunderstandings arise, so that it is our custom never to pass across them save when we push the frontier with us, adding the lands over which we march to those of our liege lord."

"Senors," said Rodriguez, "the whole mountain is the frontier. Come with us one day further." But they would not stay.

All the good things that could be carried they loaded on to the three horses whose heads were turned towards Spain; then turned, all four, and said farewell to the three. And long looked each in the face of Rodriguez as he took his hand in fare well, for they had fought under the same banner and, as wayfaring was in those days, it was not likely that they would ever meet again. They turned and went with their horses back towards the land they had fought for.

Rodriguez and his captive and Morano went sadly down the mountain. They came to the fir woods, and rested, and Morano cooked their dinner. And after a while they were able to ride their horses.

They came to the foot of the mountains, and rode on past the Inn of the World's End. They camped in the open; and all night long Rodriguez or Morano guarded the captive.

For two days and part of the third they followed their old course, catching sight again and again of the river Segre; and then they turned further west ward to come to Aragon further up the Ebro. All the way they avoided houses and camped in the open, for they kept their captive to themselves: and they slept warm with their ample store of blankets. And all the while the captive seemed morose or ill at ease, speaking seldom and, when he did, in nervous jerks.

Morano, as they rode, or by the camp fire at evening, still questioned him now and then about his castle; and sometimes he almost seemed to contradict himself, but in so vast a castle may have been many styles of architecture, and it was difficult to trace a contradiction among all those towers and turrets. His name was Don Alvidar-of-the-Rose-pink-Castle on-Ebro.

One night while all three sat and gazed at the camp-fire as men will, when the chilly stars are still and the merry flames are leaping, Rodriguez, seeking to cheer his captive's mood, told him some of his strange adventures. The captive listened with his sombre air. But when Rodriguez told how they woke on the mountain after their journey to the sun; and the sun was shining on their faces in the open, but the magician and his whole house were gone; then there came another look into Alvidar's eyes. And Rodriguez ended his tale and silence fell, broken only by Morano saying across the fire, "It is true," and the captive's thoughtful eyes gazed into the darkness. And then he also spoke.

"Senor," he said, "near to my rose-pink castle which looks into the Ebro dwells a magician also."

"Is it so?" said Rodriguez.

"Indeed so, senor," said Don Alvidar. "He is my enemy but dwells in awe of me, and so durst never molest me except by minor wonders."

"How know you that he is a magician?" said Rodriguez.

"By those wonders," answered his captive. "He afflicts small dogs and my poultry. And he wears a thin, high hat: his beard is also extraordinary."

"Long?" said Morano.

"Green," answered Don Alvidar.

"Is he very near the castle?" said Rodriguez and Morano together.

"Too near," said Don Alvidar.

"Is his house wonderful?" Rodriguez asked.

"It is a common house," was the answer. "A mean, long house of one story. The walls are white and it is well thatched. The windows are painted green; there are two doors in it and by one of them grows a rose tree."

"A rose tree?" exclaimed Rodriguez.

"It seemed a rose tree," said Don Alvidar.

"A captive lady chained to the wall perhaps, changed by magic," suggested Morano.

"Perhaps," said Don Alvidar.

"A strange house for a magician," said Rodriguez, for it sounded like any small farmhouse in Spain.

"He much affects mortal ways," replied Don Alvidar.

Little more was then said, the fire being low: and Rodriguez lay down to sleep while Morano guarded the captive.

And the day after that they came to Aragon, and in one day more they were across the Ebro; and then they rode west for a day along its southern bank looking all the while as they rode for Rodriguez' castle. And more and more silent and aloof, as they rode, grew Don Alvidar-of-the-Rose-pink-Castle-on-Ebro.

And just before sunset a cry broke from the captive. "He has taken it!" he said. And he pointed to just such a house as he had described, a jolly Spanish farmhouse with white walls and thatch and green shutters, and a rose tree by one of the doors just as he had told.

"The magician's house. But the castle is gone," he said.

Rodriguez looked at his face and saw real alarm in it. He said nothing but rode on in haste, a dim hope in his mind that explanations at the white cottage might do something for his lost castle.

And when the hooves were heard a woman came out of the cottage door by the rose tree leading a small child by the hand. And the captive called to the woman, "Maria, we are lost. And I gave my great castle with rose-pink towers that stood just here as ransom to this senor for my life. But now, alas, I see that that magician who dwelt in the house where you are now has taken it whither we know not."

"Yes, Pedro," said the woman, "he took it yesterday." And she turned blue eyes upon Rodriguez.

And then Morano would be silent no longer. He had thought vaguely for some days and intensely for the last few hundreds yards, and now he blurted out the thoughts that boiled in him.

"Master," he shouted, "he has sold his cattle and bought this raiment of his, and that helmet that you opened up for him, and never had any castle on the Ebro with any towers to it, and never knew any magician, but lived in this house himself, and now your castle is gone, master, and as for his life ..."

"Be silent a moment, Morano," said Rodriguez, and he turned to the woman whose eyes were on him still.

"Was there a castle in this place?" he said.

"Yes, senor. I swear it," she said. "And my husband, though a poor man, always spoke the truth."

"She lies," said Morano, and Rodriguez silenced him with a gesture.

"I will get neighbours who will swear it too," she said.

"A lousy neighbourhood," said Morano.

Again Rodriguez silenced him. And then the child spoke in a frightened voice, holding up a small cross that it had been taught to revere. "I swear it too," it said.

Rodriguez heaved a sigh and turned away. "Master," Morano cried in pained astonishment, "you will not believe their swearings."

"The child swore by the cross," he answered.

"But, master!" Morano exclaimed.

But Rodriguez would say no more. And they rode away aimless in silence.

Galloping hooves were heard and Pedro was there. He had come to give up his horse. He gave its reins to the scowling Morano but Rodriguez said never a word. Then he ran round and kissed Rodriguez' hand, who still was silent, for his hopes were lost with the castle; but he nodded his head and so parted for ever from the man whom his wife called Pedro, who called himself Don Alvidar-of-the-Rose-pink-Castle-on-Ebro.

The Tenth Chronicle

HOW HE CAME BACK TO LOWLIGHT

"**M**aster," Morano said. But Rodriguez rode ahead and would not speak.

They were riding vaguely southward. They had ample provisions on the horse that Morano led, as well as blankets, which gave them comfort at night. That night they both got the sleep they needed, now that there was no captive to guard. All the next day they rode slowly in the April weather by roads that wandered among tended fields; but a little way off from the fields there shone low hills in the sunlight, so wild, so free of man, that Rodriguez remembering them in later years, wondered if their wild shrubs just hid the frontiers of fairyland.

For two days they rode by the edge of unguessable regions. Had Pan piped there no one had marvelled, nor though fauns had scurried past sheltering clumps of azaleas. In the twilight no tiny queens had court within rings of toadstools: yet almost, almost they appeared.

And on the third day all at once they came to a road they knew. It was the road by which they had ridden when Rodriguez still had his dream, the way from Shadow Valley to the Ebro. And so they turned into the road they knew, as wanderers always will; and, still without aim or plan, they faced towards Shadow Valley. And in the evening of the day that followed that, as they looked about for a camping-ground, there came in sight the village on the hill which Rodriguez knew to be fifty miles from the forest: it was the village in which they had rested the first night after leaving Shadow Valley. They did not camp but went on to the village and knocked at the door of the inn. Habit guides us all at times, even kings are the slaves of it (though in their presence it takes the prouder name of precedent); and here were two wanderers without any plans at all; they were therefore defenceless in the grip of habit and, seeing an inn they knew, they loitered up to it. Mine host came again to the door. He cheerfully asked Rodriguez how he had fared on his journey, but Rodriguez would say nothing. He asked for lodging for himself and Morano and stabling for the horses: he ate and slept and paid his due, and in the morning was gone.

Whatever impulses guided Rodriguez as he rode and Morano followed, he knew not what they were or even that there could be any. He followed the road without hope and only travelled to change his camping-grounds. And that night he was half-way between the village and Shadow Valley.

Morano never spoke, for he saw that his master's disappointment was still raw; but it pleased him to notice, as he had done all day, that they were heading for the great forest. He cooked their evening meal in their camp by the wayside and they both ate it in silence. For awhile Rodriguez sat and gazed at the might-have- beens in the camp-fire: and when these began to be hidden by white ash he went to his blankets and slept. And Morano went quietly about the little camp, doing all that needed to be done, with never a word. When the horses were seen to and fed, when the knives were cleaned, when everything was ready for the start next morning, Morano went to his blankets and slept too. And in the morning again they wandered on.

That evening they saw the low gold rays of the sun enchanting the tops of a forest. It almost surprised Rodriguez, travelling without an aim, to recognise Shadow Valley. They quickened their slow pace and, before twilight faded, they were under the great oaks; but the last of the twilight could not pierce the dimness of Shadow Valley, and it seemed as if night had entered the forest with them.

They chose a camping-ground as well as they could in the darkness and Morano tied the horses to trees a little way off from the camp. Then he returned to Rodriguez and tied a blanket to the windward side of two trees to make a kind of bedroom for his master, for they had all the blankets they needed. And when this was done he set the emblem and banner of camps, anywhere all over the world in any time, for he gathered sticks and branches and lit a camp-fire. The first red flames went up and waved and proclaimed a camp: the light made a little circle, shadows ran away to the forest, and the circle of light on the ground and on the trees that stood round it became for that one night home.

They heard the horses stamp as they always did in the early part of the night; and then Morano went to give them their fodder. Rodriguez sat and gazed into the fire, his mind as full of thoughts as the fire was full of pictures: one by one the pictures in the fire fell in; and all his thoughts led nowhere.

He heard Morano running back the thirty or forty yards he had gone from the camp-fire "Master," Morano said, "the three horses are gone."

"Gone?" said Rodriguez. There was little more to say; it was too dark to track them and he knew that to find three horses in Shadow Valley was a task that might take years. And after more thought than might seem to have been needed he said; "We must go on foot."

"Have we far to go, master?" said Morano, for the first time daring to question him since they left the cottage in Spain.

"I have nowhere to go," said Rodriguez. His head was downcast as he sat by the fire: Morano stood and looked at him unhappily, full of a sympathy that he found no words to express. A light wind slipped through the branches and everything else was still. It was some while before he lifted his head; and then he saw before him on the other side of the fire, standing with folded arms, the man in the brown leather jacket.

"Nowhere to go!" said he. "Who needs go anywhere from Shadow Valley?"

Rodriguez stared at him. "But I can't stay here!" he said.

"There is no fairer forest known to man," said the other. "I know many songs that prove it."

Rodriguez made no answer but dropped his eyes, gazing with listless glance once more at the ground. "Come, senor," said the man in the leather jacket. "None are unhappy in Shadow Valley."

"Who are you?" said Rodriguez. Both he and Morano were gazing curiously at the man whom they had saved three weeks ago from the noose.

"Your friend," answered the stranger.

"No friend can help me," said Rodriguez.

"Senor," said the stranger across the fire, still standing with folded arms, "I remain under an obligation to no man. If you have an enemy or love a lady, and if they dwell within a hundred miles, either shall be before you within a week."

Rodriguez shook his head, and silence fell by the camp-fire. And after awhile Rodriguez, who was accustomed to dismiss a subject when it was ended, saw the stranger's eyes on him yet, still waiting for him to say more. And those clear blue eyes seemed to do more than wait, seemed almost to command, till they overcame Rodriguez' will and he obeyed and said, although he could feel each word struggling to stay unuttered, "Senor, I went to the wars to win a castle and a piece of land thereby; and might perchance have wed and ended my wanderings, with those of my servant here; but the wars are over and no castle is won."

And the stranger saw by his face in the firelight, and knew from the tones of his voice in the still night, the trouble that his words had not expressed.

"I remain under an obligation to no man," said the stranger. "Be at this place in four weeks' time, and you shall have a castle as large as any that men win by war, and a goodly park thereby."

"Your castle, master!" said Morano delighted, whose only thought up to then was as to who had got his horses. But Rodriguez only stared: and the stranger said no more but turned on his heel. And then Rodriguez awoke out of his silence and wonder. "But where?" he said. "What castle?"

"That you will see," said the stranger.

"But, but how ..." said Rodriguez. What he meant was, "How can I believe you?" but he did not put it in words.

"My word was never broken," said the other. And that is a good boast to make, for those of us who can make it; if we need boast at all.

"Whose word?" said Rodriguez, looking him in the eyes.

The smoke from the fire between them was thickening greyly as though something had been cast on it. "The word," he said, "of the King of Shadow Valley."

Rodriguez gazing through the increasing smoke saw not to the other side. He rose and walked round the fire, but the strange man was gone.

Rodriguez came back to his place by the fire and sat long there in silence. Morano was bubbling over to speak, but respected his master's silence: for Rodriguez was gazing into the deeps of the fire seeing pictures there that were brighter than any that he had known. They were so clear now that they seemed almost true. He saw Serafina's face there looking full at him. He watched it long until other pictures hid it, visions that had no meaning for Rodriguez. And not till then he spoke. And when he spoke his face was almost smiling.

"Well, Morano," he said, "have we come by that castle at last?"

"That man does not lie, master," he answered: and his eyes were glittering with shrewd conviction.

"What shall we do then?" said Rodriguez.

"Let us go to some village, master," said Morano, "until the time he said."

"What village?" Rodriguez asked.

"I know not, master," answered Morano, his face a puzzle of innocence and wonder; and Rodriguez fell back into thought again. And the dancing flames calmed down to a deep, quiet glow; and soon Rodriguez stepped back a yard or two from the fire to where Morano had prepared his bed; and, watching the fire still, and turning over thoughts that flashed and changed as fast as the embers, he went to wonderful dreams that were no more strange or elusive than that valley's wonderful king.

When he spoke in the morning the camp-fire was newly lit and there was a smell of bacon; and Morano, out of breath and puzzled, was calling to him.

"Master," he said, "I was mistaken about those horses."

"Mistaken?" said Rodriguez.

"They were just as I left them, master, all tied to the tree with my knots."

Rodriguez left it at that. Morano could make mistakes and the forest was full of wonders: anything might happen. "We will ride," he said.

Morano's breakfast was as good as ever; and, when he had packed up those few belongings that make a dwelling-place of any chance spot in the wilderness, they mounted the horses, which were surely there, and rode away through sunlight and green leaves. They rode slow, for the branches were low over the path, and whoever canters in a forest and closes his eyes against a branch has to consider whether he will open them to be whipped by the next branch or close them till he bumps his head into a tree. And it suited Rodriguez to loiter, for he thought thus to meet the King of Shadow Valley again or his green bowmen and learn the answers to innumerable questions about his castle which were wandering through his mind.

They ate and slept at noon in the forest's glittering greenness.

They passed afterwards by the old house in the wood, in which the bowmen feasted, for they followed the track that they had taken before. They knocked loud on the door as they passed but the house was empty. They heard the sound of a multitude felling trees, but whenever they approached the sound of chopping ceased. Again and again they left the track and rode towards the sound of chopping, and every time the chopping died away just as they drew close. They saw many a tree half felled, but never a green bowman. And at last they left it as one of the wonders of the forest and returned to the track lest they lose it, for the track was more important to them than curiosity, and evening had come and was filling the forest with dimness, and shadows stealing across the track were beginning to hide it away. In the distance they heard the invisible woodmen chopping.

And then they camped again and lit their fire; and night came down and the two wanderers slept.

The nightingale sang until he woke the cuckoo: and the cuckoo filled the leafy air so full of his two limpid notes that the dreams of Rodriguez heard them and went away, back over their border to dreamland. Rodriguez awoke Morano, who lit his fire: and soon they had struck their camp and were riding on.

By noon they saw that if they hurried on they could come to Lowlight by nightfall. But this was not Rodriguez' plan, for he had planned to ride into Lowlight, as he had done once before, at the hour when Serafina sat in her balcony in the cool of the evening, as Spanish ladies in those days sometimes did. So they tarried long by their resting-place at noon and then rode slowly on. And when they camped that night they were still in the forest.

"Morano," said Rodriguez over the camp-fire, "to-morrow brings me to Lowlight."

"Aye, master," said Morano, "we shall be there tomorrow."

"That senor with whom I had a meeting there," said Rodriguez, "he ..."

"He loves me not," said Morano.

"He would surely kill you," replied Rodriguez.

Morano looked sideways at his frying-pan.

"It would therefore be better," continued Rodriguez, "that you should stay in this camp while I give such greetings of ceremony in Lowlight as courtesy demands."

"I will stay, master," said Morano.

Rodriguez was glad that this was settled, for he felt that to follow his dreams of so many nights to that balconied house in Lowlight with Morano would be no better than visiting a house accompanied by a dog that had bitten one of the family.

"I will stay," repeated Morano. "But, master ..." The fat man's eyes were all supplication.

"Yes?" said Rodriguez.

"Leave me your mandolin," implored Morano.

"My mandolin?" said Rodriguez.

"Master," said Morano, "that senor who likes my fat body so ill he would kill me, he ..."

"Well?" said Rodriguez, for Morano was hesitating.

"He likes your mandolin no better, master."

Rodriguez resented a slight to his mandolin as much as a slight to his sword, but he smiled as he looked at Morano's anxious face.

"He would kill you for your mandolin," Morano went on eagerly, "as he would kill me for my frying-pan."

And at the mention of that frying-pan Rodriguez frowned, although it had given him many a good meal since the night it offended in Lowlight. And he would sooner have gone to the wars without a sword than under the balcony of his heart's desire without a mandolin.

So Rodriguez would hear no more of Morano's request; and soon he left the fire and went to lie down; but Morano sighed and sat gazing on into the embers unhappily; while thoughts plodded slow through his mind, leading to nothing. Late that night he threw fresh logs on the camp-fire, so that when they awoke there was still fire in the embers And when they had eaten their breakfast Rodriguez said farewell to Morano, saying that he had business in Lowlight that might keep him a few days. But Morano said not farewell then, for he would follow his master as far as the midday halt to cook his next meal. And when noon came they were beyond the forest.

Once more Morano cooked bacon. Then while Rodriguez slept Morano took his cloak and did all that could be done by brushing and smoothing to give back to it that air that it some time had, before it had flapped upon so many winds and wrapped Rodriguez on such various beds, and met the vicissitudes that make this story.

For the plume he could do little.

And his master awoke, late in the afternoon, and went to his horse and gave Morano his orders. He was to go back with two of the horses to their last camp in the forest and take with him all their kit except one blanket and make himself comfortable there and wait till Rodriguez came.

And then Rodriguez rode slowly away, and Morano stood gazing mournfully and warningly at the mandolin; and the warnings were not lost upon Rodriguez, though he would never admit that he saw in Morano's staring eyes any wise hint that he heeded.

And Morano sighed, and went and untethered his horses; and soon he was riding lonely back to the forest. And Rodriguez taking the other way saw at once the towers of Lowlight.

Does my reader think that he then set spurs to his horse, galloping towards that house about whose balcony his dreams flew every night? No, it was far from evening; far yet from the colour and calm in which the light with never a whisper says farewell to Earth, but with a gesture that the horizon hides takes silent leave of the fields on which she has danced with joy; far yet from the hour that shone for Serafina like a great halo round her and round her mother's house.

We cannot believe that one hour more than another shone upon Serafina, or that the dim end of the

evening was only hers: but these are the Chronicles
of Rodriguez, who of all the things that befell him
treasured most his memory of Serafina in the twilight, and who held that this hour was hers as much
as her raiment and her balcony: such therefore it is in
these chronicles.

And so he loitered, waiting for the slow sun to
set: and when at last a tint on the walls of Lowlight
came with the magic of Earth's most faery hour he
rode in slowly not perhaps wholly unwitting, for all
his anxious thoughts of Serafina, that a little air of
romance from the Spring and the evening followed
this lonely rider.

From some way off he saw that balcony that had
drawn him back from the other side of the far Pyrenees. Sometimes he knew that it drew him and
mostly he knew it not; yet always that curved balcony brought him nearer, ever since he turned from
the field of the false Don Alvidar: the balcony held
him with invisible threads, such as those with which
Earth draws in the birds at evening. And there was
Serafina in her balcony.

When Rodriguez saw Serafina sitting there in the
twilight, just as he had often dreamed, he looked
no more but lowered his head to the withered rose
that he carried now in his hand, the rose that he had
found by that very balcony under another moon. And,
gazing still at the rose, he rode on under the balcony, and passed it, until his hoof-beats were heard
no more in Lowlight and he and his horse were one

dim shape between the night and the twilight. And still he held on.

He knew not yet, but only guessed, who had thrown that rose from the balcony on the night when he slept on the dust: he knew not who it was that he fought on the same night, and dared not guess what that unknown hidalgo might be to Serafina. He had no claim to more from that house, which once gave him so cold a welcome, than thus to ride by it in silence. And he knew as he rode that the cloak and the plume that he wore scarce seemed the same as those that had floated by when more than a month ago he had ridden past that balcony; and the withered rose that he carried added one more note of autumn. And yet he hoped.

And so he rode into twilight and was hid from the sight of the village, a worn, pathetic figure, trusting vaguely to vague powers of good fortune that govern all men, but that favour youth.

And, sure enough, it was not yet wholly moonlight when cantering hooves came down the road behind him. It was once more that young hidalgo. And as soon as he drew rein beside Rodriguez both reached out merry hands as though their former meeting had been some errand of joy. And as Rodriguez looked him in the eyes, while the two men leaned over clasping hands, in light still clear though faded, he could not doubt Serafina was his sister.

"Senor," said his old enemy, "will you tarry with us, in our house a few days, if your journey is not urgent?"

Rodriguez gasped for joy; for the messenger from Lowlight, the certainty that here was no rival, the summons to the house of his dreams' pilgrimage, came all together: his hand still clasped the stranger's. Yet he answered with the due ceremony that that age and land demanded: then they turned and rode together towards Lowlight. And first the young men told each other their names; and the stranger told how he dwelt with his mother and sister in the house that Rodriguez knew, and his name was Don Alderon of the Valley of Dawnlight. His house had dwelt in that valley since times out of knowledge; but then the Moors had come and his forbears had fled to Lowlight: the Moors were gone now, for which Saint Michael and all fighting Saints be praised; but there were certain difficulties about his right to the Valley of Dawnlight. So they dwelt in Lowlight still.

And Rodriguez told of the war that there was beyond the Pyrenees and how the just cause had won, but little more than that he was able to tell, for he knew scarce more of the cause for which he had fought than History knows of it, who chooses her incidents and seems to forget so much. And as they talked they came to the house with the balcony. A waning moon cast light over it that was now no longer twilight; but was the light of wild things of the woods, and birds of prey, and men in mountains outlawed by the King, and magic, and mystery, and the quests of love. Serafina had left her place: lights gleamed now in the windows. And when the door was opened the hall seemed to Rodriguez so much less hugely hollow, so much less full of ominous whispered echoes, that his courage rose high as he went through it with Alderon, and they entered the room together that they had entered together before. In the long room beyond many candles he saw Dona Serafina and her mother rising up to greet him. Neither the ceremonies of that age nor Rodriguez' natural calm would have entirely concealed his emotion had not his face been hidden as he bowed. They spoke to him; they asked him of his travels; Rodriguez answered with effort. He saw by their manner that Don Alderon must have explained much in his favour. He had this time, to cheer him, a very different greeting; and yet he felt little more at ease than when he had stood there late at night before, with one eye bandaged and wearing only one shoe, suspected of he knew not what brawling and violence.

It was not until Dona Mirana, the mother of Serafina, asked him to play to them on his mandolin that Rodriguez' ease returned. He bowed then and brought round his mandolin, which had been slung behind him; and knew a triumphant champion was by him now, one old in the ways of love and wise in the sorrows of man, a slender but potent voice, well-skilled to tell what there were not words to say; a voice unhindered by language, unlimited even by thought, whose universal meaning was heard and understood, sometimes perhaps by wandering spirits of light, beaten far by some evil thought for their heavenly courses and passing close along the coasts of Earth.

And Rodriguez played no tune he had ever known, nor any airs that he had heard men play in lanes in Andalusia; but he told of things that he knew not, of sadnesses that he had scarcely felt and undreamed exaltations. It was the hour of need, and the mandolin knew.

And when all was told that the mandolin can tell of whatever is wistfulest in the spirit of man, a mood of merriment entered its old curved sides and there came from its hollows a measure such as they dance to when laughter goes over the greens in Spain. Never a song sang Rodriguez; the mandolin said all.

And what message did Serafina receive from those notes that were strange even to Rodriguez? Were they not stranger to her? I have said that spirits blown far out of their course and nearing the mundane coasts hear mortal music sometimes, and hearing understand. And if they cannot understand those snatches of song, all about mortal things and human needs, that are wafted rarely to them by chance passions, how much more surely a young mortal heart, so near Rodriguez, heard what he would say and understood the message however strange.

When Dona Mirana and her daughter rose, exchanging their little curtsies for the low bows of Rodriguez, and so retired for the night, the long room seemed to Rodriguez now empty of threatening omens. The great portraits that the moon had lit, and that had frowned at him in the moonlight when he came here before, frowned at him now no longer. The anger that he had known to lurk in the darkness on pictured faces of dead generations had gone with the gloom that it haunted: they were all passionless now in the quiet light of the candles. He looked again at the portraits eye to eye, remembering looks they had given him in the moonlight, and all looked back at him with ages of apathy; and he knew that whatever glimmer of former selves there lurks about portraits of the dead and gone was thinking only of their own past days in years remote from Rodriguez. Whether their anger had flashed for a moment over the ages on that night a month from now, or whether it was only the moonlight, he never knew. Their spirits were back now surely amongst their own days, whence they deigned not to look on the days that make these chronicles.

Not till then did Rodriguez admit, or even know, that he had not eaten since his noonday meal. But now he admitted this to Don Alderon's questions; and Don Alderon led him to another chamber and there regaled him with all the hospitality for which that time was famous. And when Rodriguez had eaten, Don Alderon sent for wine, and the butler brought it in an olden flagon, dark wine of a precious vintage: and soon the two young men were drinking together and talking of the wickedness of the Moors. And while they talked the night grew late and chilly and still, and the hour came when moths are fewer and young men think of bed. Then Don Alderon showed his guest to an upper room, a long room dim with red hangings, and carvings in walnut and oak, which the one candle he carried barely lit but only set queer shadows scampering. And here he left Rodriguez, who was soon in bed, with the great red hangings round him. And awhile he wondered at the huge silence of the house all round him, with never a murmur, never an echo, never a sigh; for he missed the passing of winds, branches waving, the stirring of small beasts, birds of prey calling, and the hundred sounds of the night; but soon through the silence came sleep.

He did not need to dream, for here in the home of Serafina he had come to his dreams' end.

Another day shone on another scene; for the sunlight that went in a narrow stream of gold and silver between the huge red curtains had sent away the shadows that had stalked overnight through the room, and had scattered the eeriness that had lurked on the far side of furniture, and all the dimness was gone that the long red room had harboured. And for a while Rodriguez did not know where he was; and for a while, when he remembered, he could not believe it true. He dressed with care, almost with fear, and preened his small moustachios, which at last had grown again just when he would have despaired. Then he descended, and found that he had slept late, though the three of that ancient house were seated yet at the table, and Serafina all dressed in white seemed to Rodriguez to be shining in rivalry with the morning. Ah dreams and fancies of youth!

The Eleventh Chronicle

HOW HE TURNED TO GARDENING
AND HIS SWORD RESTED

These were the days that Rodriguez always remembered; and, side by side with them, there lodged in his memory, and went down with them into his latter years, the days and nights when he went through the Pyrenees and walked when he would have slept but had to walk or freeze: and by some queer rule that guides us he treasured them both in his memory, these happy days in this garden and the frozen nights on the peaks.

For Serafina showed Rodriguez the garden that behind the house ran narrow and long to the wild. There were rocks with heliotrope pouring over them and flowers peeping behind them, and great azaleas all in triumphant bloom, and ropes of flowering creepers coming down from trees, and oleanders, and a plant named popularly Joy of the South, and small paths went along it edged with shells brought from the far sea.

There was only one street in the village, and you did not go far among the great azaleas before you lost sight of the gables; and you did not go far before the small paths ended with their shells from the distant sea, and there was the mistress of all gardeners facing you, Mother Nature nursing her children, the things of the wild. She too had azaleas and oleanders, but they stood more solitary in their greater garden than those that grew in the garden of Dona Mirana; and she too had little paths, only they were without borders and without end. Yet looking from the long and narrow garden at the back of that house in Lowlight to the wider garden that sweeps round the world, and is fenced by Space from the garden in Venus and by Space from the garden in Mars, you scarce saw any difference or noticed where they met: the solitary azaleas beyond were gathered together by distance, and from Lowlight to the horizon seemed all one garden in bloom. And afterwards, all his years, whenever Rodriguez heard the name of Spain, spoken by loyal men, it was thus that he thought of it, as he saw it now.

And here he used to walk with Serafina when she tended flowers in the cool of the morning or went at evening to water favourite blooms. And Rodriguez would bring with him his mandolin, and sometimes he touched it lightly or even sang, as they rested on some carved seat at the garden's end, looking out towards shadowy shrubs on the shining hill, but mostly he heard her speak of the things she loved, of what moths flew to their garden, and which birds sang, and how the flowers grew. Serafina sat no longer in her balcony but, disguising idleness by other names, they loitered along those paths that the seashells narrowed; yet there was a grace in their loitering such as we have not in our dances now. And evening stealing in from the wild places, from darkening azaleas upon distant hills, still found them in the garden, found Rodriguez singing in idleness undisguised, or anxiously helping in some trivial task, tying up some tendril that had gone awry, helping some magnolia that the wind had wounded. Almost unnoticed by him the sunlight would disappear, and the coloured blaze of the sunset, and then the gloaming; till the colours of all the flowers queerly changed and they shone with that curious glow which they wear in the dusk. They returned then to the house, the garden behind them with its dim hushed air of a secret, before them the candlelight like a different land. And after the evening meal Alderon and Rodriguez would sit late together discussing the future of the world, Rodriguez holding that it was intended that the earth should be ruled by Spain, and Alderon fearing it would all go to the Moors.

Days passed thus.

And then one evening Rodriguez was in the garden with Serafina; the flowers, dim and pale and more mysterious than ever, poured out their scent towards the coming night, luring huge hawk-moths from the far dusk that was gathering about the garden, to hover before each bloom on myriad wingbeats too rapid for human eye: another inch and the fairies had peeped out from behind azaleas, yet both of these late loiterers felt fairies were surely there: it seemed to be Nature's own most secret hour, upon which man trespasses if he venture forth from his house: an owl from his hidden haunt flew nearer the garden and uttered a clear call once to remind Rodriguez of this: and Rodriguez did not heed, but walked in silence.

He had played his mandolin. It had uttered to the solemn hush of the understanding evening all it was able to tell; and after that cry, grown piteous with so many human longings, for it was an old mandolin, Rodriguez felt there was nothing left for his poor words to say. So he went dumb and mournful.

Serafina would have heard him had he spoken, for her thoughts vibrated yet with the voice of the mandolin, which had come to her hearing as an ambassador from Rodriguez, but he found no words to match with the mandolin's high mood. His eyes said, and his sighs told, what the mandolin had uttered; but his tongue was silent.

And then Serafina said, as he walked all heavy with silence past a curving slope of dimly glowing azaleas, "You like flowers, senor?"

"Senorita, I adore them," he replied.

"Indeed?" said Dona Serafina.

"Indeed I do," said Rodriguez.

"And yet," asked Dona Serafina, "was it not a somewhat withered or altogether faded flower that you carried, unless I fancied wrong, when you rode past our balcony?"

"It was indeed faded," said Rodriguez, "for the rose was some weeks old."

"One who loved flowers, I thought," said Serafina, "would perhaps care more for them fresh."

Half-dumb though Rodriguez was his shrewdness did not desert him. To have said that he had the rose from Serafina would have been to claim as though proven what was yet no more than a hope.

"Senorita," he said, "I found the flower on holy ground."

"I did not know," she said, "that you had travelled so far."

"I found it here," he said, "under your balcony."

"Perchance I let it fall," said she. "It was idle of me."

"I guard it still," he said, and drew forth that worn brown rose.

"It was idle of me," said Serafina.

But then in that scented garden among the dim lights of late evening the ghost of that rose introduced their spirits one to the other, so that the listening flowers heard Rodriguez telling the story of his heart, and, bending over the shell-bordered path, heard Serafina's answer; and all they seemed to do was but to watch the evening, with leaves uplifted in the hope of rain.

Film after film of dusk dropped down from where twilight had been, like an army of darkness slowly pitching their tents on ground that had been lost to the children of light. Out of the wild lands all the owls flew nearer: their long, clear cries and the huge hush between them warned all those lands that this was not man's hour. And neither Rodriguez nor Serafina heard them.

In pale blue sky where none had thought to see it one smiling star appeared. It was Venus watching lovers, as men of the crumbled centuries had besought her to do, when they named her so long ago, kneeling upon their hills with bended heads, and arms stretched out to her sweet eternal scrutiny. Beneath her wandering rays as they danced down to bless them Rodriguez and Serafina talked low in the sight of the goddess, and their voices swayed through the flowers with whispers and winds, not troubling the little wild creatures that steal out shy in the dusk, and Nature forgave them for being abroad in that hour; although, so near that a single azalea seemed to hide it, so near seemed to beckon and whisper old Nature's eldest secret.

When flowers glimmered and Venus smiled and all things else were dim, they turned on one of those little paths hand in hand homeward.

Dona Mirana glanced once at her daughter's eyes and said nothing. Don Alderon renewed his talk with Rodriguez, giving reasons for his apprehension of the conquest of the world by the Moors, which he had thought of since last night; and Rodriguez agreed with all that Don Alderon said, but understood little, being full of dreams that seemed to dance on the further, side of the candlelight to a strange, new, unheard tune that his heart was aware of. He gazed much at Serafina and said little.

He drank no wine that night with Don Alderon: what need had he of wine? On wonderful journeys that my pen cannot follow, for all the swiftness of the wing from which it came; on darting journeys out-speeding the lithe swallow or that great wanderer the white- fronted goose, his young thoughts raced by a myriad of golden evenings far down the future years. And what of the days he saw? Did he see them truly? Enough that he saw them in vision. Saw them as some lone shepherd on lifted downs sees once go by with music a galleon out of the East, with windy sails, and masts ablaze with pennants, and heroes in strange dress singing new songs; and the galleon goes nameless by till the singing dies away. What ship was it? Whither bound? Why there? Enough that he has seen it. Thus do we glimpse the glory of rare days as we swing round the sun; and youth is like some high headland from which to see.

On the next day he spoke with Dona Mirano. There was little to say but to observe the courtesies appropriate to this occasion, for Dona Mirana and her daughter had spoken long together already; and of one thing he could say little, and indeed was dumb when asked of it, and that was the question of his home. And then he said that he had a castle; and when Dona Mirana asked him where it was he said vaguely it was to the North. He trusted the word of the King of Shadow Valley and so he spoke of his castle as a man speaks the truth. And when she asked him of his castle again, whether on rock or river or in leafy lands, he began to describe how its ten towers stood, being builded of a rock that was slightly pink, and how they glowed across a hundred fields, especially at evening; and suddenly he ceased, perceiving all in a moment he was speaking unwittingly in the words of Don Alvidar and describing to Dona Mirana that rose-pink castle on Ebro. And Dona Mirana knew then that there was some mystery about Rodriguez' home.

She spoke kindly to Rodriguez, yet she neither gave her consent nor yet withheld it, and he knew there was no immediate hope in her words. Graceful as were his bows as he withdrew, he left with scarcely another word to say. All day his castle hung over him like a cloud, not nebulous and evanescent only, but brooding darkly, boding storms, such as the orange blossoms dread.

He walked again in the garden with Serafina, but Dona Mirana was never far, and the glamour of the former evening, lit by one star, was driven from the garden by his anxieties about that castle of which he could not speak. Serafina asked him of his home. He would not parry her question, and yet he could not tell her that all their future hung on the promise of a man in an old leathern jacket calling himself a king. So the mystery of his habitation deepened, spoiling the glamour of the evening. He spoke, instead, of the forest, hoping she might know something of that strange monarch to whom they dwelt so near; but she glanced uneasily towards Shadow Valley and told him that none in Lowlight went that way. Sorrow grew heavier round Rodriguez' heart at this: believing in the promise of a man whose eyes he trusted he had asked Serafina to marry him, and Serafina had said Yes; and now he found she knew nothing of such a man, which seemed somehow to Rodriguez to weaken his promise, and, worst of all, she feared the place where he lived. He welcomed the approach of Dona Mirana, and all three returned to the house. For the rest of that evening he spoke little; but he had formed his project.

When the two ladies retired Rodriguez, who had seemed tongue-tied for many hours, turned to Don Alderon. His mother had told Don Alderon nothing yet; for she was troubled by the mystery of Rodriguez' castle, and would give him time to make it clear if he could; for there was something about Rodriguez of which with many pages I have tried to acquaint my reader but which was clear when first she saw him to Dona Mirana. In fact she liked him at once, as I hope that perhaps by now my reader may. He turned to Don Alderon, who was surprised to see the vehemence with which his guest suddenly spoke after those hours of silence, and Rodriguez told him the story of his love and the story of both his castles, that which had vanished from the bank of the Ebro and that which was promised him by the King of Shadow Valley. And often Don Alderon interrupted.

"Oh, Rodriguez," he said, "you are welcome to our ancient, unfortunate house": and later he said, "I have met no man that had a prettier way with the sword."

But Rodriguez held on to the end, telling all he had to tell; and especially that he was landless and penniless but for that one promise; and as for the sword, he said, he was but as a child playing before the sword of Don Alderon. And this Don Alderon said was in no wise so, though there were a few cunning passes that he had learned, hoping that the day might come for him to do God a service thereby by slaying some of the Moors: and heartily he gave his consent and felicitation. But this Rodriguez would not have: "Come with me," he said, "to the forest to the place where I met this man, and if we find him not there we will go to the house in which his bowmen feast and there have news of him, and he shall show us the castle of his promise and, if it be such a castle as you approve, then your consent shall be given, but if not ..."

"Gladly indeed," said Don Alderon. "We will start tomorrow."

And Rodriguez took his words literally, though his host had meant no more than what we should call "one of these days," but Rodriguez was being consumed with a great impatience. And so they arranged it, and Don Alderon went to bed with a feeling, which is favourable to dreams, that on the next day they went upon an adventure; for neither he nor anyone in that village had entered Shadow Valley.

Once more next morning Rodriguez walked with Serafina, with something of the romance of the garden gone, for Dona Mirana walked there too; and romance is like one of those sudden, wonderful colours that flash for a moment out of a drop of dew; a passing shadow obscures them; and ask another to see it, and the colour is not the same: move but a yard and the ray of enchantment is gone. Dona Mirana saw the romance of that garden, but she saw it from thirty years away; it was all different what she saw, all changed from a certain day (for love was love in the old days): and to Rodriguez and Serafina it seemed that she could not see romance at all, and somehow that dimmed it. Almost their eyes seemed to search amongst the azaleas for the romance of that other evening.

And then Rodriguez told Serafina that he was riding away with her brother to see about the affairs of his castle, and that they would return in a few days. Scarcely a hint he gave that those affairs might not prosper, for he trusted the word of the King of Shadow Valley. His confidence had returned: and soon, with swords at side and cloaks floating brilliant on light winds of April, Rodriguez and Alderon rode away together.

Soon in the distance they saw Shadow Valley. And then Rodriguez bethought him of Morano and of the foul wrong he committed against Don Alderon with his frying-pan, and how he was there in the camp to which he was bringing his friend. And so he said: "That vile knave Morano still lives and insists on serving me."

"If he be near," said Don Alderon, "I pray you to disarm him of his frying-pan for the sake of my honour, which does not suffer me to be stricken with culinary weapons, but only with the sword, the lance, or even bolts of cannon or arquebuss ..." He was thinking of yet more weapons when Rodriguez put spurs to his horse. "He is near," he said; "I will ride on and disarm him."

So Rodriguez came cantering into the forest while Don Alderon ambled a mile or so behind him.

And there he found his old camp and saw Morano, sitting upon the ground by a small fire. Morano sprang up at once with joy in his eyes, his face wreathed with questions, which he did not put into words for he did not pry openly into his master's affairs.

"Morano," said Rodriguez, "give me your frying-pan."

"My frying-pan?" said Morano.

"Yes," said Rodriguez. And when he held in his hand that blackened, greasy utensil he told Morano, "That senor you met in Lowlight rides with me."

The cheerfulness faded out of Morano's face as light fades at sunset. "Master," he said, "he will surely slay me now."

"He will not slay you," said Rodriguez.

"Master," Morano said, "he hopes for my fat carcase as much as men hope for the unicorn, when they wear their bright green coats and hunt him with dogs in Spring." I know not what legend Morano stored in his mind, nor how much of it was true. "And when he finds me without my frying-pan he will surely slay me."

"That senor," said Rodriguez emphatically, "must not be hit with the frying-pan."

"That is a hard rule, master," said Morano.

And Rodriguez was indignant, when he heard that, that anyone should thus blaspheme against an obvious law of chivalry: while Morano's only thought was upon the injustice of giving up the sweets of life for the sake of a frying-pan. Thus they were at cross-purposes. And for some while they stood silent, while Rodriguez hung the reins of his horse over the broken branch of a tree. And then Don Alderon rode into the wood.

All then that was most pathetic in Morano's sense of injustice looked out of his eyes as he turned them upon his master. But Don Alderon scarcely glanced at all at Morano, even when he handed to him the reins of his horse as he walked on towards Rodriguez.

And there in that leafy place they rested all through the evening, for they had not started so early upon their journey as travellers should. Eight days had gone since Rodriguez had left that small camp to ride to Lowlight, and to the apex of his life towards which all his days had ascended; and in that time Morano had collected good store of wood and, in little ways unthought of by dwellers in cities, had made the place like such homes as wanderers find. Don Alderon was charmed with their roof of towering greenness, and with the choirs of those which inhabited it and which were now all coming home to sing. And at some moment in the twilight, neither Rodriguez nor Alderon noticed when, Morano repossessed himself of his frying-pan, unbidden by Rodriguez, but acting on a certain tacit permission that there seemed to be in the twilight or in the mood of the two young men as they sat by the fire. And soon he was cooking once more, at a fire of his own, with something of the air that you see upon a Field Marshal's face who has lost his baton and found it again. Have you ever noticed it, reader?

And when the meal was ready Morano served it in silence, moving unobtrusively in the gloom of the wood; for he knew that he was forgiven, yet not so openly that he wished to insist on his presence or even to imply his possession of the weapon that fried the bacon. So, like a dryad he moved from tree to tree, and like any fabulous creature was gone again. And the two young men supped well, and sat on and on, watching the sparks go up on innumerable journeys from the fire at which they sat, to be lost to sight in huge wastes of blackness and stars, lost to sight utterly, lost like the spirit of man to the gaze of our wonder when we try to follow its journey beyond the hearths that we know.

All the next day they rode on through the forest, till they came to the black circle of the old fire of their next camp. And here Rodriguez halted on account of the attraction that one of his old camps seems to have for a wanderer. It drew his feet towards it, this blackened circle, this hearth that for one night made one spot in the wilderness home. Don Alderon did not care whether they tarried or hurried; he loved his journey through this leafy land; the cool night-breeze slipping round the tree-trunks was new to him, and new was the comradeship of the abundant stars; the quest itself was a joy to him; with his fancy he built Rodriguez' mysterious castle no less magnificently than did Don Alvidar. Sometimes they talked of the castle, each of the young men picturing it as he saw it; but in the warmth of the camp-fire after Morano slept they talked of more than these chronicles can tell.

In the morning they pressed on as fast as the forest's low boughs would allow them. They passed somewhere near the great cottage in which the bowmen feasted; but they held on, as they had decided after discussion to do, for the last place in which Rodriguez had seen the King of Shadow Valley, which was the place of his promise. And before any dimness came even to the forest, or golden shafts down colonnades which were before all cathedrals, they found the old camp that they sought, which still had a clear flavour of magic for Morano on account of the moth-like coming and going of his three horses after he had tied them to that tree. And here they looked for the King of Shadow Valley; and then Rodriguez called him; and then all three of them called him, shouting "King of Shadow Valley" all together. No answer came: the woods were without echo: nothing stirred but fallen leaves. But before those miles of silence could depress them Rodriguez hit upon a simple plan, which was that he and Alderon should search all round, far from the track, while Morano stayed in the camp and shouted frequently, and they would not go out of hearing of his voice: for Shadow Valley had a reputation of being a bad forest for travellers to find their way there; indeed, few ever attempted to. So they did as he said, he and Alderon searching in different directions, while Morano remained in the camp, lifting a large and melancholy voice. And though rumour said it was hard to find the way when twenty yards from the track in Shadow Valley, it did not say it was hard to find the green bowmen: and Rodriguez, knowing that they guarded the forest as the shadows of trees guard the coolness, was assured he would meet with some of them even though he should miss their master. So he and Alderon searched till the forest darkness came and only birds on high branches still had light; and they never saw the King of Shadow Valley or any trace whatever of any man. And Alderon first returned to the encampment; but Rodriguez searched on into the night, searching and calling through the darkness, and feeling, as every minute went by and every faint call of Morano, that his castle was fading away, slipping past oak-tree and thorn-bush, to take its place among the unpitying stars. And when he returned at last from his useless search he found Morano standing by a good fire, and the sight of it a little cheered Rodriguez, and the sight of the firelight on Morano's face, and the homely comfort of the camp, for everything is comparative.

And over their supper Rodriguez and Alderon agreed that they had come to a part of the forest too remote from the home of the King of Shadow Valley, and decided to go the next day to the house of the green bowmen: and before he slept Rodriguez felt once more that all was well with his castle.

Yet when the next day came they searched again, for Rodriguez remembered how it was to this very place that the King of Shadow Valley had bidden him come in four weeks, and though this period was not yet accomplished, he felt, and Alderon fully agreed, they had waited long enough: so they searched all the morning, and then fulfilled their decision of overnight by riding for the great cottage Rodriguez knew. All the way they met no one. And Rodriguez' gaiety came back as they rode, for he and Don Alderon recognised more and more clearly that the bowmen's great cottage was the place they should have gone at first.

In early evening they were just at their journey's end; but barely had they left the track that they had ridden the day before, barely taken the smaller path that led after a few hundred yards to the cottage when they found themselves stopped by huge chains that hung from tree to tree. High into the trees went the chains above their heads where they sat their horses, and a chain ran every six inches down to the very ground: the road was well blocked.

Rodriguez and Alderon hastily consulted; then, leaving the horses with Morano, they followed the chains through dense forest to find a place where they could get the horses through. Finding the chains go on and on and on, and as evening was drawing in, the two friends divided, Alderon going back and

Rodriguez on, agreeing to meet again on the path where Morano was.

It was darkening when they met there, Rodriguez having found nothing but that iron barrier going on from trunk to trunk, and Alderon having found a great gateway of iron; but it was shut. Through the silent shadows stealing abroad at evening the three men crashed their way on foot, leading their horses, towards this gate; but their way was slow and difficult for no path at all led up to it. It was dark when they reached it and they saw the high gate in the night, a black barrier among the trees where no one would wish to come, and in forest that seemed to these three to be nearly impenetrable. And what astonished Rodriguez most of all was that the chains had not been across the path when he had feasted with the green bowmen.

They stood there gazing, all three, at the dark locked gate, and then they saw two shields that met in the midst of it, and Rodriguez mounted his horse and stretched up to feel what device there was on the beaten iron; and both the shields were blank.

There they camped as well as men can when darkness has fallen before they reach their camping-ground; and Morano lit a great fire before the gate, and the smooth blank shields touching shoulders there up above them shone on Rodriguez and Alderon in the firelight. For a while they wondered at that strange gate that stood there dividing the wilderness; and then sleep came.

As soon as they woke they called loudly, but no one guarded that gate, no step but theirs stirred in the forest. Then, leaving Morano in the camp with its great gate that led nowhere, the two young men climbed up by branches and chains, and were soon on the other side of the gate and pressing on through the silence of the forest to find the cottage in which Rodriguez had slept. And almost at once the green bowmen appeared, ten of them with their bows, in front of Rodriguez and Alderon. "Stop," said the ten green bowmen. When the bowmen said that, there was nothing else to do.

"What do you seek?" said the bowmen.

"The King of Shadow Valley," answered Rodriguez.

"He is not here," they said.

"Where is he?" asked Rodriguez.

"He is nowhere," said one, "when he does not wish to be seen."

"Then show me the castle that he promised me," said Rodriguez.

"We know nothing of any castle," said one of the bowmen, and they all shook their heads.

"No castle?" said Rodriguez.

"No," they said.

"Has the King of Shadow Valley no castle?" he asked, beginning now to despair.

"We know of none," they said. "He lives in the forest."

Before Rodriguez quite despaired he asked each one if they knew not of any castle of which their King was possessed; and each of them said that there was no castle in all Shadow Valley. The ten still stood in front of them with their bows: and Rodriguez turned away then indeed in despair, and walked slowly back to the camp, and Alderon walked behind him. In silence they reached their camp by the great gate that led nowhere, and there Rodriguez sat down on a log beside the dwindling fire, gazing at the grey ashes and thinking of his dead hopes. He had not the heart to speak to Alderon, and the silence was unbroken by Morano who, for all his loquacity, knew when his words were not welcome. Don Alderon tried to break that melancholy silence, saying that these ten bowmen did not know the whole world; but he could not cheer Rodriguez. For, sitting there in dejection on his log, thinking of all the assurance with which he had often spoken of his castle, there was one more thing to trouble him than Don Alderon knew. And this was that when the bowmen had appeared he had hung once more round his neck that golden badge that was worked for him by the King of Shadow Valley; and they must have seen it, and they had paid no heed to it whatever: its magic was wholly departed. And one thing troubled him that Rodriguez did not know, a very potent factor in human sorrow: he had left in the morning so eagerly that he had had no breakfast, and this he entirely forgot and knew not how much of his dejection came from this cause, thinking that the loss of his castle was of itself enough.

So with downcast head he sat empty and hopeless, and the little camp was silent.

In this mournful atmosphere while no one spoke, and no one seemed to watch, stood, when at last Rodriguez raised his head, with folded arms before the gate to nowhere, the King of Shadow Valley. His face was surly, as though the face of a ghost, called from important work among asteroids needing his care, by the trivial legerdemain of some foolish novice. Rodriguez, looking into those angry eyes, wholly forgot it was he that had a grievance. The silence continued. And then the King of Shadow Valley spoke.

"When have I broken my word?" he said.

Rodriguez did not know. The man was still looking at him, still standing there with folded arms before the great gate, confronting him, demanding some kind of answer: and Rodriguez had nothing to say.

"I came because you promised me the castle," he said at last.

"I did not bid you come here," the man with the folded arms answered.

"I went where you bade me," said Rodriguez, "and you were not there."

"In four weeks, I said," answered the King angrily.

And then Alderon spoke. "Have you any castle for my friend?" he said.

"No," said the King of Shadow Valley.

"You promised him one," said Don Alderon.

The King of Shadow Valley raised with his left hand a horn that hung below his elbow by a green cord round his body. He made no answer to Don

Alderon, but put the horn against his lips and blew. They watched him all three in silence, till the silence was broken by many men moving swiftly through covert, and the green bowmen appeared.

When seven or eight were there he turned and looked at them. "When have I broken my word?" he said to his men.

And they all answered him, "Never!"

More broke into sight through the bushes.

"Ask them" he said. And Rodriguez did not speak.

"Ask them," he said again, "when I have broken my word."

Still Rodriguez and Alderon said nothing. And the bowmen answered them. "He has never broken his word," every bowman said.

"You promised me a castle," said Rodriguez, seeing that man's fierce eyes upon him still.

"Then do as I bid you," answered the King of Shadow Valley; and he turned round and touched the lock of the gates with some key that he had. The gates moved open and the King went through.

Don Alderon ran forward after him, and caught up with him as he strode away, and spoke to him, and the King answered. Rodriguez did not hear what they said, and never afterwards knew. These words he heard only, from the King of Shadow Valley as he and Don Alderon parted: ".... and therefore, senor, it were better for some holy man to do his blessed work before we come." And the King of Shadow Valley passed into the deeps of the wood.

As the great gates were slowly swinging to, Don Alderon came back thoughtfully. The gates clanged, clicked, and were shut again. The King of Shadow Valley and all his bowmen were gone.

Don Alderon went to his horse, and Rodriguez and Morano did the same, drawn by the act of the only man of the three that seemed to have made up his mind. Don Alderon led his horse back toward the path, and Rodriguez followed with his. When they came to the path they mounted in silence; and presently Morano followed them, with his blankets rolled up in front of him on his horse and his frying-pan slung behind him.

"Which way?" said Rodriguez.

"Home," said Don Alderon.

"But I cannot go to your home," said Rodriguez.

"Come," said Don Alderon, as one whose plans were made. Rodriguez without a home, without plans, without hope, went with Don Alderon as thistledown goes with the warm wind. They rode through the forest till it grew all so dim that only a faint tinge of greenness lay on the dark leaves: above were patches of bluish sky like broken pieces of steel. And a star or two were out when they left the forest. And cantering on they came to Lowlight when the Milky Way appeared.

And there were Dona Mirana and Serafina in the hall to greet them as they entered the door.

"What news?" they asked.

But Rodriguez hung back; he had no news to give. It was Don Alderon that went forward, speaking cheerily to Serafina, and afterwards to his mother, with whom he spoke long and anxiously, pointing toward the forest sometimes, almost, as Rodriguez thought, in fear.

And a little later, when the ladies had retired, Don Alderon told Rodriguez over the wine, with which he had tried to cheer his forlorn companion, that it was arranged that he should marry Serafina. And when Rodriguez lamented that this was impossible he replied that the King of Shadow Valley wished it. And when Rodriguez heard this his astonishment equalled his happiness, for he marvelled that Don Alderon should not only believe that strange man's unsupported promise, but that he should even obey him as though he held him in awe.

And on the next day Rodriguez spoke with Dona Mirana as they walked in the glory of the garden. And Dona Mirana gave him her consent as Don Alderon had done: and when Rodriguez spoke humbly of postponement she glanced uneasily towards Shadow Valley, as though she too feared the strange man who ruled over the forest which she had never entered.

And so it was that Rodriguez walked with his lady, with the sweet Serafina in that garden again. And walking there they forgot the need of house or land, forgot Shadow Valley with its hopes and its doubts, and all the anxieties of the thoughts that we take for the morrow: and when evening came and the birds sang in azaleas, and the shadows grew solemn and long, and winds blew cool from the blazing bed of the

Sun, into the garden now all strange and still, they forgot our Earth and, beyond the mundane coasts, drifted on dreams of their own into aureate regions of twilight, to wander in lands wherein lovers walk briefly and only once.

The Twelfth Chronicle

THE BUILDING OF CASTLE RODRIGUEZ AND
THE ENDING OF THESE CHRONICLES

When the King of Shadow Valley met Rodriguez, for the first time in the forest, and gave him his promise and left him by his camp- fire, he went back some way towards the bowmen's cottage and blew his horn; and his hundred bowmen were about him almost at once. To these he gave their orders and they went back, whence they had come, into the forest's darkness. But he went to the bowmen's cottage and paced before it, a dark and lonely figure of the night; and wherever he paced the ground he marked it with small sticks. And next morning the hundred bowmen came with axes as soon as the earliest light had entered the forest, and each of them chose out one of the giant trees that stood before the cottage, and attacked it. All day they swung their axes against the forest's elders, of which nearly a hundred were fallen when evening came. And the stoutest of these, great trunks that were four feet through, were dragged by horses to the bowmen's cottage and laid by the little sticks that the King of Shadow Valley had put overnight in the ground. The bowmen's cottage and the kitchen that was in the wood behind it, and a few trees that still stood, were now all enclosed by four lines of fallen trees which made a large rectangle on the ground with a small square at each of its corners. And craftsmen came, and smoothed and hollowed the inner sides of the four rows of trees, working far into the night. So was the first day's work accomplished and so was built the first layer of the walls of Castle Rodriguez.

On the next day the bowmen again felled a hundred trees; the top of the first layer was cut flat by carpenters; at evening the second layer was hoisted up after their under sides had been flattened to fit the layer below them; quantities more were cast in to make the floor when they had been gradually smoothed and fitted: at the end of the second day a man could not see over the walls of Castle Rodriguez. And on the third day more craftsmen arrived, men from distant villages at the forest's edge, whence the King of Shadow Valley had summoned them; and they carved the walls as they grew. And a hundred trees fell that day, and the castle was another layer higher. And all the while a park was growing in the forest, as they felled the great trees; but the greatest trees of all the bowmen spared, oaks that had stood there for ages and ages of men; they left them to grip the earth for a while longer, for a few more human generations.

On the fourth day the two windows at the back of the bowmen's cottage began to darken, and that evening Castle Rodriguez was fifteen feet high. And still the hundred bowmen hewed at the forest, bringing sunlight bright on to grass that was shadowed by oaks for ages. And at the end of the fifth day they began to roof the lower rooms and make their second floor: and still the castle grew a layer a day, though the second storey they built with thinner trees that were only three feet through, which were more easily carried to their place by the pulleys. And now they began to heap up rocks in a mass of mortar against the wall on the outside, till a steep slope guarded the whole of the lower part of the castle against fire from any attacker if war should come that way, in any of the centuries that were yet to be: and the deep windows they guarded with bars of iron.

The shape of the castle showed itself clearly now, rising on each side of the bowmen's cottage and behind it, with a tower at each of its corners. To the left of the old cottage the main doorway opened to the great hall, in which a pile of a few huge oaks was being transformed into a massive stair. Three figures of strange men held up this ceiling with their heads and uplifted hands, when the castle was finished; but as yet the carvers had only begun their work, so that only here and there an eye peeped out, or a smile flickered, to give any expression to the curious faces of these fabulous creatures of the wood, which were slowly taking their shape out of three trees whose roots were still in the earth below the floor. In an upper storey one of these trees became a tall cupboard; and the shelves and the sides and the back and the top of it were all one piece of oak.

All the interior of the castle was of wood, hollowed into alcoves and polished, or carved into figures leaning out from the walls. So vast were the timbers that the walls, at a glance, seemed almost one piece of wood. And the centuries that were coming to Spain darkened the walls as they came, through autumnal shades until they were all black, as though they all mourned in secret for lost generations; but they have not yet crumbled.

The fireplaces they made with great square red tiles, which they also put in the chimneys amongst rude masses of mortar: and these great dark holes remained always mysterious to those that looked for mystery in the family that whiled away the ages in that castle. And by every fireplace two queer carved creatures stood upholding the mantlepiece, with mystery in their faces and curious limbs, uniting the hearth with fable and with tales told in the wood. Years after the men that carved them were all dust the shadows of these creatures would come out and dance in the room, on wintry nights when all the lamps were gone and flames stole out and flickered above the smouldering logs.

In the second storey one great saloon ran all the length of the castle. In it was a long table with eight legs that had carvings of roses rambling along its edges: the table and its legs were all of one piece with the floor. They would never have hollowed the great trunk in time had they not used fire. The second storey was barely complete on the day that Rodriguez and Don Alderon and Morano came to the chains that guarded the park. And the King of Shadow Valley would not permit his gift to be seen in anything less than its full magnificence, and had commanded that no man in the world might enter to see the work of his bowmen and craftsmen until it should frown at all comers a castle formidable as any in Spain.

And then they heaped up the mortar and rock to the top of the second storey, but above that they let the timbers show, except where they filled in plaster between the curving trunks: and the ages blackened the timber in amongst the white plaster; but not a storm that blew in all the years that came, nor the moss of so many Springs, ever rotted away those beams that the forest had given and on which the bowmen had laboured so long ago. But the castle weathered the ages and reached our days, worn, battered even, by its journey through the long and sometimes troubled years, but splendid with the traffic that it had with history in many gorgeous periods. Here Valdar the Excellent came once in his youth. And Charles the Magnificent stayed a night in this castle when on a pilgrimage to a holy place of the South.

It was here that Peter the Arrogant in his cups gave Africa, one Spring night, to his sister's son. What grandeurs this castle has seen! What chronicles could be writ of it! But not these chronicles, for they draw near their close, and they have yet to tell how the castle was built. Others shall tell what banners flew from all four of its towers, adding a splendour to the wind, and for what cause they flew. I have yet to tell of their building.

The second storey was roofed, and Castle Rodriguez still rose one layer day by day, with a hauling at pulleys and the work of a hundred men: and all the while the park swept farther into the forest.

And the trees that grew up through the building were worked by the craftsmen in every chamber into which they grew: and a great branch of the hugest of them made a little crooked stair in an upper storey. On the floors they laid down skins of beasts that the bowmen slew in the forest; and on the walls there hung all manner of leather, tooled and dyed as they had the art to do in that far-away period in Spain.

When the third storey was finished they roofed the castle over, laying upon the huge rafters red tiles that they made of clay. But the towers were not yet finished.

At this time the King of Shadow Valley sent a runner into Lowlight to shoot a blunt arrow with a message tied to it into Don Alderon's garden, near to the door, at evening.

And they went on building the towers above the height of the roof And near the top of them they made homes for archers, little turrets that leaned like swallows' nests out from each tower, high places where they could see and shoot and not be seen from below. And little narrow passages wound away behind perched battlements of stone, by which archers could slip from place to place, and shoot from here or from there and never be known. So were built in that distant age the towers of Castle Rodriguez.

And one day four weeks from the felling of the first oak, the period of his promise being accomplished, the King of Shadow Valley blew his horn. And standing by what had been the bowmen's cottage, now all shut in by sheer walls of Castle Rodriguez, he gathered his bowmen to him. And when they were all about him he gave them their orders. They were to go by stealth to the village of Lowlight, and were to be by daylight before the house of Don Alderon; and, whether wed or unwed, whether she fled or folk defended the house, to bring Dona Serafina of the Valley of Dawnlight to be the chatelaine of Castle Rodriguez.

For this purpose he bade them take with them a chariot that he thought magnificent, though the mighty timbers that gave grandeur to Castle Rodriguez had a cumbrous look in the heavy vehicle that was to the bowmen's eyes the triumphal car of the forest. So they took their bows and obeyed, leaving the craftsmen at their work in the castle, which was now quite roofed over, towers and all. They went through the forest by little paths that they knew, going swiftly and warily in the bowmen's way: and just before nightfall they were at the forest's edge, though they went no farther from it than its shadows go in the evening. And there they rested under the oak trees for the early part of the night except those whose art it was to gather news for their king; and three of those went into Lowlight and mixed with the villagers there.

When white mists moved over the fields near dawn and wavered ghostly about Lowlight, the green bowman moved with them. And just out of hearing of the village, behind wild shrubs that hid them, the bowmen that were coming from the forest met the three that had spent the night in taverns of Lowlight. And the three told the hundred of the great wedding that there was to be in the Church of the Renunciation that morning in Lowlight: and of the preparations that were made, and how holy men had come from far on mules, and had slept the night in the village, and the Bishop of Toledo himself would bless the bridegroom's sword. The bowmen therefore retired a little way and, moving through the mists, came forward to points whence they could watch the church, well concealed on the wild plain, which here and there gave up a field to man but was mostly the playground of wild creatures whose ways were the bowmen's ways. And here they waited.

This was the wedding of Rodriguez and Serafina, of which gossips often spoke at their doors in summer evenings, old women mumbling of fair weddings that each had seen; and they had been children when they saw this wedding; they were those that threw small handfuls of anemones on the path before the porch. They told the tale of it till they could tell no more. It is the account of the last two or three of them, old,

old women, that came at last to these chronicles, so that their tongues may wag as it were a little longer through these pages although they have been for so many centuries dead. And this is all that books are able to do.

First there was bell-ringing and many voices, and then the voices hushed, and there came the procession of eight divines of Murcia, whose vestments were strange to Lowlight. Then there came a priest from the South, near the border of Andalusia, who overnight had sanctified the ring. (It was he who had entertained Rodriguez when he first escaped from la Garda, and Rodriguez had sent for him now.) Each note of the bells came clear through the hush as they entered the church. And then with suitable attendants the bishop strode by and they saw quite close the blessed cope of Toledo. And the bridegroom followed him in, wearing his sword, and Don Alderon went with him. And then the voices rose again in the street: the bells rang on: they all saw Dona Mirana. The little bunches of bright anemones grew sticky in their hands: the bells seemed louder: cheering rose in the street and came all down it nearer. Then Dona Serafina walked past them with all her maids: and that is what the gossips chiefly remembered, telling how she smiled at them, and praising her dress, through those distant summer evenings. Then there was music in the church. And afterwards the forest-people had come. And the people screamed, for none knew what they would do. But they bowed so low to the bride and bridegroom, and showed their great hunting bows so willingly to all who wished to see, that the people lost their alarm and only feared lest the Bishop of Toledo should blast the merry bowmen with one of his curses.

And presently the bride and bridegroom entered the chariot, and the people cheered; and there were farewells and the casting of flowers; and the bishop blessed three of their bows; and a fat man sat beside the driver with folded arms, wearing bright on his face a look of foolish contentment; and the bowmen and bride and bridegroom all went away to the forest.

Four huge white horses drew that bridal chariot, the bowmen ran beside it, and soon it was lost to sight of the girls that watched it from Lowlight; but their memories held it close till their eyes could no longer see to knit and they could only sit by their porches in fine weather and talk of the days that were.

So came Rodriguez and his bride to the forest; he silent, perplexed, wondering always to what home and what future he brought her; she knowing less than he and trusting more. And on the untended road that the bowmen shared with stags and with rare, very venturous travellers, the wheels of the woodland chariot sank so deep in the sandy earth that the escort of bowmen needed seldom to run any more; and he who sat by the driver climbed down and walked silent for once, perhaps awed by the occasion, though he was none other than Morano. Serafina was delighted with the forest, but between Rodriguez and its beautiful grandeur his anxieties crowded thickly. He leaned over once from the chariot and asked one of the bowmen again about that castle; but the bowman only bowed and answered with a proverb of Spain, not easily carried so far from its own soil to thrive in our language, but signifying that the morrow showeth all things. He was silent then, for he knew that there was no way to a direct answer through those proverbs, and after a while perhaps there came to him some of Serafma's trustfulness. By evening they came to a wide avenue leading to great gates.

Rodriguez did not know the avenue, he knew no paths so wide in Shadow Valley; but he knew those gates. They were the gates of iron that led nowhere. But now an avenue went from them upon the other side, and opened widely into a park dotted with clumps of trees. And the two great iron shields, they too had changed with the changes that had bewitched the forest, for their surfaces that had glowed so unmistakably blank, side by side in the firelight, not many nights before, blazoned now the armorial bearings of Rodriguez upon the one and those of the house of Dawnlight upon the other. Through the opened gates they entered the young park that seemed to wonder at its own ancient trees, where wild deer drifted away from them like shadows through the evening: for the bowmen had driven in deer for miles through the forest. They passed a pool where water-lilies lay in languid beauty for hundreds of summers, but as yet no flower peeped into the water, for the pond was all hallowed newly.

A clump of trees stood right ahead of their way; they passed round it; and Castle Rodriguez came all at once into view. Serafina gasped joyously. Rodriguez saw its towers, its turrets for archers, its guarded windows deep in the mass of stone, its solemn row of battlements, but he did not believe what he saw. He did not believe that here at last was his castle, that here was his dream fulfilled and his journey done. He expected to wake suddenly in the cold in some lonely camp, he expected the Ebro to unfold its coils in the North and to come and sweep it away. It was but another strayed hope, he thought, taking the form of dream. But Castle Rodriguez still stood frowning there, and none of its towers vanished, or changed as things change in dreams; but the servants of the King of Shadow Valley opened the great door, and Serafina and Rodriguez entered, and all the hundred bowmen disappeared.

Here we will leave them, and let these Chronicles end. For whoever would tell more of Castle Rodriguez must wield one of those ponderous pens that hangs on the study wall in the house of historians. Great days in the story of Spain shone on those iron- barred windows, and things were said in its banqueting chamber and planned in its inner rooms that sometimes turned that story this way or that, as rocks turn a young river. And as a traveller meets a mighty river at one of its bends, and passes on his path, while the river sweeps on to its estuary and the sea, so I leave the triumphs and troubles of that story which I touched for one moment by the door of Castle Rodriguez.

My concern is but with Rodriguez and Serafina and to tell that they lived here in happiness; and to tell that the humble Morano found his happiness too. For he became the magnificent steward of Castle Rodriguez, the majordomo, and upon august occasions he wore as much red plush as he had ever seen in his dreams, when he saw this very event, sleeping by dying camp-fires. And he slept not upon straw but upon good heaps of wolf-skins. But pining a little in the second year of his somewhat lonely splendour, he married one of the maidens of the forest, the child of a bowman that hunted boars with their king. And all the green bowmen came and built him a house by the gates of the park, whence he walked solemnly on proper occasions to wait upon his master. Morano, good, faithful man, come forward for but a moment out of the Golden Age and bow across all those centuries to the reader: say one farewell to him in your Spanish tongue, though the sound of it be no louder than the sound of shadows moving, and so back to the dim splendour of the past, for the Senor or Senora shall hear your name no more.

For years Rodriguez lived a chieftain of the forest, owning the overlordship of the King of Shadow Valley, whom he and Serafina would entertain with all the magnificence of which their castle was capable on such occasions as he appeared before the iron gates. They seldom saw him. Sometimes they heard his horn as he went by. They heard his bow-men follow. And all would pass and perhaps they would see none. But upon occasions he came. He came to the christening of the eldest son of Rodri-guez and Serafina, for whom he was godfather. He came again to see the boy shoot for the first time with a bow. And later he came to give little presents, small treasures of the forest, to Rodriguez' daugh-ters; who treated him always, not as sole lord of that forest that travellers dreaded, but as a friend of their very own that they had found for themselves. He had his favourites among them and none quite knew which they were.

And one day he came in his old age to give Rodri-guez a message. And he spoke long and tenderly of the forest as though all its glades were sacred.

And soon after that day he died, and was buried with the mourning of all his men in the deeps of Shadow Valley, where only Rodriguez and the bow-men knew. And Rodriguez became, as the old king had commanded, the ruler of Shadow Valley and all its faithful men. With them he hunted and defended the forest, holding all its ways to be sacred, as the old king had taught. It is told how Rodriguez ruled the forest well.

And later he made a treaty with the Spanish King acknowledging him sole Lord of Spain, including Shadow Valley, saving that certain right should per-tain to the foresters and should be theirs for ever. And these rights are written on parchment and sealed with the seal of Spain; and none may harm the forest without the bowmen's leave.

Rodriguez was made Duke of Shadow Valley and a Magnifico of the first degree; though little he went with other hidalgos to Court, but lived with his family in Shadow Valley, travelling seldom beyond the splendour of the forest farther than Lowlight.

Thus he saw the glory of autumn turning the woods to fairyland: and when the stags were roaring and winter coming on he would take a boar-spear down from the wall and go hunting through the forest, whose twigs were black and slender and still against the bright menace of winter. Spring found him viewing the fields that his men had sown, along the forest's edge, and finding in the chaunt of the myriad birds a stirring of memories, a beckoning towards past days. In summer he would see his boys and girls at play, running through shafts of sunlight that made leaves and grass like pale emeralds. He gave his days to the forest and the four seasons. Thus he dwelt amidst splendours such as History has never seen in any visit of hers to the courts of men.

Of him and Serafina it has been written and sung that they lived happily ever after; and though they are now so many centuries dead, may they have in the memories of such of my readers as will let them linger there, that afterglow of life that remembrance gives, which is all that there is on earth for those that walked it once and that walk the paths of their old haunts no more.

www.ingramcontent.com/pod-product-compliance
Lightning Source LLC
Chambersburg PA
CBHW060544180626
46817CB00002B/722